Don't Read This Book If You're Stupid

Also by Tibor Fischer

The Collector Collector

The Thought Gang

Under the Frog

Tibor Fischer

Don't Read This Book If You're Stupid

stories

Picador USA
A Metropolitan Book
Henry Holt and Company
New York

www.picadorusa.com

Picador® is a U.S. registered trademark and is used by Henry Holt and Company under license from Pan Books Limited.

For information on Picador USA Reading Group Guides, as well as ordering, please contact the Trade Marketing department at St. Martin's Press.
Phone: 1-800-221-7945 extension 763
Fax: 212-677-7456
E-mail: trademarketing@stmartins.com

ISBN 0-312-27852-7

First published in the United Kingdom in 2000
under the same title by Secker and Warburg.

First Picador USA Edition: November 2001

10 9 8 7 6 5 4 3 2 1

For the Martel/Ballou Gang

Contents

We Ate the Chef

As he crossed Cambridge Circus, Jim wished he'd become a banker.

Visions of a paid holiday now assailed him with a ferocity greater than any physical lust. Spectral beaches swooped down from Shaftesbury Avenue. The notion of being paid to do nothing, even if it was simply spending time at home watching the walls, made him almost swoon.

Of course he had the consolation of being his own boss, a condition so overrated he had no idea why anyone paid any respect to it; it was perhaps the most overrated concept in the annals of thinking. Being your own boss boiled down to choosing which arse you hoped to lick next or which pile of shit you shoveled next; that was it.

The other aspect of banking that was most appealing was getting a salary, something that happened to bankers apparently. Jim had the most important qualifications to be a banker: he had several suits and a willingness to do anything for money. He had the suits, he had the ties, he had no pleasure left in life, no preferences about his comportment, but he had no salary. Having your own company was the best thing in the world if it was successful, but there was the converse . . .

Once (although he had never discussed it with anyone), a long time ago, he had tried to be a banker. Three banks had given him an interview, two British and one Japanese. Big, big fuckers, whose names made people in finance shift uncomfortably. Jim had taken the interviews seriously because he'd already beaten off hundreds of people to get the interview, and because he had always had a keen appreciation of money.

He'd made an effort, but now with the wisdom of additional decades, Jim recognized he could have tried harder. He hadn't gotten right down on the floor and crawled and bawled that this job was far more important than life, death, the universe, and anything yet to be discovered. Having been through the process of interviewing prospective employees, he now understood that whatever the wording of the questions, however solemn the atmosphere, the chief pleasure lay in getting the interviewee to grovel, to debase himself or herself, to stand on one leg, roll over, bark. *I'm boring, I'm insignificant, we both know you only want this job for the money, but if you want it, what are you going to do for me? Are you going to jiggle your tits? Are you going to show me how desperate you are?*

Naturally, apart from his failure to grovel, they might well have sensed he thought they were arseholes, because he had. Unfortunately, his foresight had been blocked by a get-everything-you-want-quick scheme: managing a rock 'n' roll band in Exeter. Why he had been asked to manage them would always remain a mystery; though Jim strongly suspected it was linked to his ability to read and write, ownership of a suit, and because they were positive he would never try to cheat them, since they knew where his parents lived and because every one of the nine-member band was capable of beating him senseless.

4

Fifty Frenzied Fingers (okay, not that funny) had been, oddly enough, very good; that was why he had agreed to manage them (apart from his inability to play an instrument making management the only way he could sign up for truly global debauchery). They couldn't play very well, their ten-song set included only two songs they had written (and they were by far the weakest), but there was an exciting and genuinely dangerous quality about them, especially the lead guitarist, Benny, whom everyone within a hundred miles of Exeter was terrified of. A good time for Benny was going to a club where no one knew him and while not exactly picking a fight with a gang of half a dozen or more, doing nothing to unpick one. Jim had made the mistake once of accompanying Benny to a club in Plymouth; he'd had to lock himself in the toilet while Benny took on a dance-floor load of the Devonport Gun Crew. After what had felt like a week, there had been a little tap on the door. "Jim? It's me, Benny. We can go now."

Fifty Frenzied Fingers had played thirteen gigs; getting all nine of them together each time had reduced him to incoherent rage and exhaustion. The last gig, he had arranged for a top music journalist to come down. The journalist had arrived in Exeter but had eventually missed the gig, as he had been hospitalized by Gary, the saxophonist, during the journalist's pre-gig let's-all-be-mates session. Jim might have expected Benny or Vince (oozing evil—it was rumored, and Jim believed it, that the landlords of Exeter had a contract out on him because he had trashed so many of their properties and ripped them off in several innovative ways) to put the boot in; or frankly any of the others, but not Gary, who was a vegetarian because, as he explained whether you wanted to hear it or not, he couldn't bear animal suffering. Gary was also blind. Jim had rescued the journalist as Vince had been urging Gary, "Kick to the left now, mate."

They had played the gig, and then the police had steamed in to arrest everyone except Vince, who, as always, managed to dodge retribution. It could have easily been the start of an excessive, energetic, moneymaking wildness; but it hadn't been. The journalist never wrote a word about them—nor did anyone else. Jim had seen Benny being bundled into his own police van. Every time he went back to Exeter, he asked about Benny, but no one had any news. Benny had been his own gang. On the other hand, Benny's younger brother, who couldn't tune a guitar and who had never so much as parked on a yellow line, was now a respected producer and owned large buildings in Docklands.

Then Jim had got a job with Mr. Ice, not through any talent or any initiative on his part, but because he had been at the right golf club. Jim loathed golf, but he had been working behind the bar and, perhaps because he had no idea he was being interviewed, got on very well with Mr. Ice, who had astonished him by offering him a job.

There were so many lies. So much nonsense. So much rubbish—this rubbish talked about gangsters, for instance. What did, according to general belief, gangsters do? They ran drugs, prostitution, committed armed robbery. Of those businesses, Jim had had brief glimpses.

The consultant anesthetist who had lived above Jim in Ealing (when he had been house-sitting) used to invest his money buying flats in the West End and filling them with tarts from Israel and Japan (supplied by fellow anesthetists); the anesthetist regarded it as a stimulating cross between an investment and a hobby. He'd drive out to the airport to pick up the girls, worry about the decor of the flats, and would always be running around buying extra potted plants. Jim was offered half-price.

Drugs: the best dealer he had ever had, in the days when he indulged (youth, some disposable income), was a retired brigadier (Falklands veteran) with a handlebar mustache who lived in Tunbridge Wells, but who came up to town and made deliveries with a precision that could have been studied at Sandhurst. Admittedly, most of the others Jim had come across were no-hopers who could never make it as far as stacking supermarket shelves, or single mothers with snotty brats who were good for their customers because they were always at home (and because if nabbed could wave their children for clemency).

Armed robbery: he knew Herbie, the bartender at Blacks, who had done four years for knocking off a security van (collared because he had left his wallet behind). Herbie was one of the friendliest types he knew, who fainted at the sight of blood, who had only survived in prison because he had ironed all the hard-men's shirts, and now earned most of his money on the side by making soft toys for Blacks' clientele (fake antique teddy bears his specialty), having picked up sewing skills inside; he liked to relax by translating Spanish poetry (apparently very badly).

No, the real gangsters, the real criminals, the true scumbuckets didn't bother with crime; crime was for the incompetent, the knotted-up, the stupid, the bored, counterfeit thugs, the day-trippers. There was no real money in it, and sooner or later you went to jail. Genuine gangsters went into sports management or the music business.

He had worked with Mr. Ice looking after snooker players and boxers so he had seen it. He had done it for six years, and it had been a job with a lot to recommend it. Travel, dream money, boozing with celebrities.

But he had left. This is what happens when things are good; you can't see past the good things.

At first, he had been full of it; intoxicated with being his own boss and relieved because some aspects of working for Ice had

unnerved him. Not that anything unpleasant had ever happened. The mere fact he had worked for Ice meant everyone
assumed he was hard, and there was a great deal of courtesy in
boxing circles because everyone was aware the consequences of
a bust-up would be grave. Compare the anesthetist's rundown
on Israel: "Everyone has a gun. Everyone. So there's less crime.
You break into someone's home. You get shot dead. You rob a
bank. You get shot dead. You play music too loud. You get shot
dead. You go round firing off your gun for no good reason. You
get shot dead." Folk in sports management were very polite, but
he'd always had the fear that one morning Ice would turn up
with a couple of dead promoters for him to bury.

Finally, his work, although entertaining, had been very
minor. Light correspondence, wearing a suit. Bag-carrying.
Taxi-calling. Drink-buying. Laughing at jokes. And there wasn't
much satisfaction. One morning, at four, he had been woken up
by a call. Getting to the phone, he had stumbled in the dark,
cracking his head open on a door frame. The call was from one
of their contenders, staying in a hotel in Las Vegas.

"Jim, man, I got a real problem . . ."

His stomach clenched. Rape? Murder? Drugs? Broken limb?
Gambling clean-out? Assault?

". . . there's no plug in my bathtub."

Even half-asleep, half-stunned, his blood plopping onto the
carpet, Jim balanced things up, the distance between London
and Las Vegas, the knowledge that the boxer wouldn't be back
for a few days, Ice's well-known affection for him, the boxer's
promising but not star status (only a bantamweight who lived
with his mother). There were two responses gleaming in the
night: Eat your own shit, you moron. Or: Darius, just talk to
reception and they'll sort you out. He had gone the route of the
plug provider but had never really forgiven himself.

But then he had left. And for a while he hadn't regretted leaving. Garrido, the salesman who had computerized Ice's office, told him about the Web. Garrido was the only honest computer salesman in Britain and the only one who could explain things, probably because he knew what he was selling. This was when mention of the Web would provoke: what? Working for Ice (small, terrible glasses, haircut twenty years out of place, bargain suit, third-generation East End villain living in Chislehurst) hadn't taught him anything apart from which clubs boxers liked to frequent.

What he would have liked to have learned from Ice was how to run a business. Suddenly, after you have set up your business, Jim found the satisfaction of independence was crushed like a puppy going under the wheels of a juggernaut; the government, the council, the utility companies, your customers, your employees, your cleaners, your neighbors, the postal system, manufacturers of answering machines, public transport, traffic lights, the whole planet queues up to give you a kicking when you have a company; he had never felt truly alone until he had started Ultimate Truth Ltd. (named after a style of karate he had studied for two weeks).

Jim had begun to wonder if he was just stupid. There were so many lies. Mistruths. Was he the only one to have believed them? Were these lies just conventions, there for people to recognize, like street names, but that no one had to take seriously? Cambridge Circus, for instance, had nothing to do with Cambridge or the circus. An overbustled shithole was what it was. As disappointing as the adage that hard work is rewarded. Uh-uh. It isn't.

Or take the great lie about London being a city. It wasn't a city; it was a war. Fine people weren't dispatched on the pavement and their bodies dumped in the gutters. Some discretion was maintained. The pillaging and the slaughtering were usually behind doors, but no less relentless for being secluded. This had only recently sunk in. The truth was horrible. The truth tasted awful. Perhaps as in one of those bad thrillers, when you found out you would be silenced, or perhaps in the non-imagined world, when you really understood what was going on, you silenced yourself.

Jim expended a great deal of energy trying to wish himself back into the past, so he could have the chance to get back to his younger self, so he could slap himself around the face and say: crawl, get the job, take the money, and do what you want on Sunday afternoons. His obsession with a paid holiday, simply being able to go away, not for two weeks, not a week, but even a weekend when you could completely switch off, do nothing, was starting to frighten him. The only way he could stop thinking about having a paid holiday was fantasizing about sick leave; being ill and staying at home in bed for two days (getting paid for it, while other people at your place of work were forced to cover for you, even if they didn't do it particularly well) was paradise itself. Jim could see that being an employee was a wondrous thing and how he envied humble, lowly employees who could walk out of their offices and not have to think about work until the following day. The joys of employeedom overpowered him.

The adventurers who thought they lived dangerously by biking through civil wars, skydiving, mountaineering, bungee-jumping, freebasing finally didn't know real risk. There was nothing more dangerous than having your own company. You jumped out of an airplane, you were merely wagering your life; you ran a company, no matter how small, even a corner shop, you were risking your soul.

As he walked past the St. Martin's Theatre, a skinny, small sixteen-year-old (accompanied by another skinny, small sixteen-year-old and an extremely ugly sixteen-year-old girl) bumped into him with more force than you'd expect from a skinny, small sixteen-year-old. The sixteeners each had a can of Tennent's. None of them were paying attention because they came from Sutton Whatsit and were mildly drunk.

This was about the only thing that made living in the poisonous hubbub of London occasionally worthwhile: that you could look down spectacularly on provincials who lived in places where the most exciting news was a special offer at the supermarket.

Jim was sick of tourists; you couldn't go anywhere without hitting a smog of fourteen-year-old Italians, adamant they were having a major revelation because they were standing on a bit of concrete just north of that great trough of fickle sewage called the Thames.

The weed hadn't pushed into him deliberately, which made it worse. He hadn't even noticed Jim glowering. A frail and five-foot-fourer shoving into someone who was six foot one and (despite running his own company) fifteen stone was wrong; there was something primevally amiss about it. Jim eyed the pimply face of the weed, and he could suddenly understand why slavery had been such a big hit; he had known dogs with more depth and intelligence.

The desire to punch the weed destructively in the face, to teach him a lesson in the significance of larger people, was almost irresistible. To his horror, Jim realized that the only reason he didn't thump him was because he was going to see a client and blood wouldn't look good on his suit. Something odious was going on in his heart. He really needed a holiday.

He arrived at the address and trudged up four flights of steep steps; inevitably any prospective client wasn't going to have a plush first-floor office or be in a building with a lift. It was a new company that consisted of a designer, a goatee beard, and a school leaver.

But the designer and the goatee beard weren't there.

"We've been trying to phone you," said the secretary with surprisingly genuine concern. The designer's mother had been taken ill half an hour ago, and he'd had to rush away. Jim's mobile phone had been off, because he hadn't bought a new battery for it because he couldn't afford it; he couldn't afford the mobile phone either, but you couldn't not have one. Infuriatingly, it was the most reasonable of excuses. It was a pity; he almost wished it was the usual case of having forgotten the appointment or enjoying lunch too much, so he could get angry, aggrieved, and write off this possible income.

Instead he'd have to come back another time to hear one of the hundred and one reasons why they wouldn't need him to set up a Web site for them. Here I am, he brooded, in the right place at the right time, and I still can't get it right.

Rejoining Old Compton Street, Jim was nearly knocked into the gutter by a large messenger striding out of an off-license. The messenger was too big to consider hitting, so Jim made do with giving him a dirty look. On his massive back, embroidered into his leather jacket, was an image of a scrupulously rendered skeleton riding a chopper; it was a strapping skeleton, with fine pecs, mighty arms, striking cheekbones, and good posture. Wearing a bandanna and ostentatious jewelry, a scythe strapped to its back, the skeleton was grinning and opening up the throttle above the legend, *"Death Rides a Harley."*

This was a lie. A month before, Jim had been lumbered with taking an elderly neighbor's dog to the vet's for the last jab. Worried at first that his total lack of concern for the mangy cocker spaniel might cause offense, Jim had been indignant about the blasé way the vet carried out the task. One moment Oslo was an irritating, deaf, and smelly dog, the next merely a furball; all character gone. Erased. The vet made no attempt to soothe Jim's feelings, issued no hollow formula. He probably took more care over making a cup of tea.

Death wouldn't be cocky. Wouldn't be a dandy. Wouldn't be sexy. Wouldn't be impressive at all. Death would be like the vet. Boring. Bored. Bored with people's posturings, bored with people. Bald. Fat. Badly dressed. With nothing to say. No bedside manner. No prospects. No money. The enemy of character. Death would be the last to be picked for football. Death would have a peanut-sized dick. Death would be the figure opposite you in the dole office. Death would be the small dustman who keeps quiet. Death would take the bus, and not make any interesting remarks in the queue.

Jim strolled back to the office. Betty was there, even though he had nothing to do. Betty would always be adoring his computer, prodding code. Betty didn't even ask him how it went with the client; he was engrossed in some shoot-'em-up game, not playing it but stripping the 3-D engine for code and redesigning it.

When they had first met, Betty (who had turned up as part of a load of computers from a bankrupt computer shop), with uncharacteristic, unrepeated, and insane frankness, had revealed his nickname at school and how much he had hated it; you think you have for a while, but finally you never escape school. Jim took every opportunity to use it, because there was no point in denying it was fun torturing others.

There were only the two of them left in the office now. Betty should have been employed by a government somewhere encrypting or decrypting things. Nearly all their work was off-the-shelf software, which Jim, if he could have been bothered to read the manuals closely, could have used. Having Betty working there was like owning a grocery and having Einstein mopping the floor.

So why was Betty there? There were some things Jim couldn't do. He couldn't ride a unicycle; he couldn't juggle machetes; he couldn't speak Portuguese. With a huge investment of time he stood a chance of making some progress in any one of these fields. Betty couldn't deal with people. Betty could never learn how to deal with people. He couldn't phone anyone, for instance. If he were trapped in a building on fire, the fire brigade wouldn't hear about it from Betty. He could, by gritting his teeth, bring himself to answer the phone very occasionally (although it would tire him out for the rest of the day), but he couldn't phone anyone, any more than he was capable of doing a triple back flip.

With the trade they generated, Betty could have made a modest living if he had worked at home. So could Jim if he had operated from his flat. But they were bound together in a bizarre impoverishment pact. Betty had been woefully underpaid from the beginning; after a while Jim had uneasily cut his salary from two hundred to one hundred a week, citing (honestly) ludicrously bad luck with clients and assuring him that it was an exceptional, emergency, and temporary measure. When he had finally cut Betty's salary down to fifty, he had quite looked forward to it, hoping that Betty would storm off and that he could pack it all in. Betty hadn't been paid a penny for two months now, but the nominal salary loitered there, nominally making him boss. Nominally reducing the salary to thirty pounds had crossed Jim's mind, but he concluded it would reflect badly on him, moving the situation from the rousingly exploitative to the pathetic.

"I see," said Betty quietly into the phone. Betty had a habit of speaking very quietly during his phone calls and covering his mouth with his hand, imagining that Jim, in an office bereft of activity, sitting five feet away, wouldn't be able to hear him.

For a long time, there had been a secretary, Vera. It had taken Jim a while to work out why he had liked her so much: Vera was a home for bad luck. For two hours every morning before work, she would go to the gym; the fat laughed. She was burgled or mugged or had her car stolen at least once a month. Washing machines ate up her clothes. The married men she had awful affairs with treated her like dirt. She was always having rows with her flatmates and spent her leisure time getting new abodes and retrieving her mail from previous ones. She regularly left her shopping on buses.

But Vera's bracing qualities had only been fully appreciated when he had hired Rebecca. Rebecca was beautiful, and the possibility of entanglement with a beautiful woman (something that had eluded him for years) had been at the forefront of his hiring her.

But Rebecca had a flaw; she was happy. One evening when Jim had gone into a bar and had spotted Rebecca laughing with her friends, he had decided to fire her. Lack of business would have required her dismissal anyway, but he couldn't deceive himself as to what the trigger was: she had had the temerity to enjoy herself. He realized that for five years, pretty much the time he had been in business, he hadn't been happy. He hadn't had cancer, he hadn't been in anguished misery every minute of the day, but he had either been working, or worrying about work, or indulging in unsatisfactory pursuits in his private life. He woke up in the morning washed up, and there was no improvement during the day. Not so much as five minutes of oomph. His vengeance on Rebecca had appalled him, but it had been like watching on the television another poorly filmed atrocity in some country you wouldn't be able to find on the map; barely a pang before you go to the fridge.

"I see," said Betty.

Jim glimpsed Serafina going in gaudily next door and gave her a smile. Why a personal trainer had to have an office, he couldn't fathom. Hers was a tiny office, but you would have thought Serafina could have run everything by mobile. The office was, he supposed, an appendage of success, like her sports car. She only turned up twice a week, for half an hour or an hour if that. As usual, she wore the loudest colors possible, parrot green and yellow today, a tiny amount of Lycra that was so stretched you were sorry for it, although her beauty and physical perfection were such, she could have worn a tent and still had more attention than any woman wanted; you could stare and stare at her and still not believe her body; it was her job—a stainless form of prostitution.

Even two or three years ago, he would have tried it on. Clearly, she was too beautiful and too thriving to understand him (Serafina spoke Success), but he would have tried. He was losing his fight; a ghastly stagnation was taking place inside. He detected a smell, a dishrag odor that tracked him everywhere. No matter how often he washed, the reek was there; he changed clothes, scrubbed, was brave with the aftershave, but it was as if he were splashing on the scent of finished; his body was taking up decomposition without the incentive of a grave.

No, the real treat now would be to have a good picture of Serafina naked, so he could take it home for lengthy imaginings. Easier, for everyone. No one would get hurt. When he had been at school, what he had looked forward to most of all—although obviously he had never admitted it—was a wife he could die for and a wife who would die for him. Now, the choosing of restaurants (and their expense), agreeing on a film they both wanted to see, concentrating on saying the right thing or at least not saying the wrong thing, these exertions had become too onerous for him. It was incredible the remarks that had cost him girlfriends ("Labour will win," "you have great legs," "I love you"); basically there was nothing you could say that was safe, but you tried to filter out the relationship-wrecking declarations.

It was going to be over soon. The anger was largely gone; it was more that state of acceptance that terminally ill people purportedly reach when they realize that raging's not doing any good. Bankruptcy would be a relief, a balm, because he could give up. He could probably get a job somewhere, and while he wouldn't get rich, it would be a mindless living.

"I see," said Betty putting down the phone.

"There's a . . . well . . . I shouldn't be long." Betty put on his jacket and left Jim in the huge twenty-by-twenty-two-by-ten-foot mouth that only ate cash. Betty was off to defuck something. He had friends who worked for the big players, who would phone up from time to time. When they got really stuck, when their highly paid codeheads were stumped by some career-ending impasse and their clients weren't looking too closely, they'd smuggle Betty in to sort it out. Naturally, he wasn't paid. He loved doing it, as long as it was a serious problem. Simple problems (computer not plugged in) made him angry; a disaster that would require him to work five days and nights nonstop, he'd come back glowing.

When Jim had started, there had been three Web companies in London. First of all, the problem had been explaining the Web. The noes had come in three shapes: the I-don't-quite-understand-this shape. Then the this-is-very-exciting-and-you're-absolutely-right-but-we-have-to-wait-for-the-dust-to-settle-but-we'll-get-back-to-you shape. And finally the but-we-already-have-a-Web-site shape.

And suddenly there were dozens of competitors, plus now the big companies had their own softhow and small companies bought their Web sites from the corner shop. He'd been in a gold rush and ended up with an unamusing lump of coal. Pioneers don't make it, he realized; they finish up penniless in bars seeking listeners, or die of cold, their bones to be trampled by fur-encased freebooters.

Jim went over to Betty's desktop computer. It was Betty's own. Jim couldn't have afforded it. It was the most powerful desktop you could buy this month, with the most feared chip.

Betty, however, knew next to nothing about hardware. Jim didn't grasp much either, but he knew enough to unscrew the computer and take out the motherboard. He put it under his right foot and scrunched gently. Then he returned the motherboard to the computer.

That'll keep him busy while I'm away, Jim thought. This trip to France wasn't a holiday. It was his last chance.

———

The rain came down viciously, as if it were trying to get at Jim. As he looked out the cabin window at Nice airport blackened by the storm, he strove to talk himself into a state of calm.

Yes, it was unfair. He had flown all the way to the South of France in August from London (where the sun had been shining for the first time in four months) to encounter rain, having spent money he didn't have on the holiday. He hadn't had a holiday in eight years. He had worked it out on the flight. It had been eight years since he had paid money and gone somewhere to enjoy himself. He hadn't worked every day of those eight years, but near enough.

Since landing, he had been wrestling with a powerful urge to burst into tears and scream: "I've spent eight years without a holiday. I live in a sun-free city. All I ask is five days in the sunshine, and that is why I have flown to the South of France, a region famous for the abundance of its sunshine, especially in the middle of August, a month famous for its insufferable heat. I don't want culture. I don't want entertainment. I don't dream of women. All I ask is five days of sunshine."

When Jim had sat in the travel agent's aghast at the price of the ticket (he had left it too late to get an economy seat), he had been unable to make up his mind about how long he wanted to stay.

A long weekend, four days, was very tempting, but then that meant only two days unwinding since the time of the flights precluded any sunning arriving or departing. And if he was going down there, he might as well spend some time there. He liked the idea of two weeks (who wouldn't?), but that was impossible. The office would have been rented out to someone by then; even his creditors would have forgotten him by then. A week really wasn't much longer than five days, but it sounded so much longer; five days was in effect a working week, but it didn't sound like it. Five days sounded like only a few days; it had the same resonance as two or three days, although you were getting the extra. And the truth was he was uneasy even going away for five days, because there might be that phone call, the fat cat call handing him a big deal. Granted, there were very few calls at all, and if someone was interested, waiting a few days shouldn't be a problem, because even when he did manage to sell his services it was a dragged-out process (involving months of negotiation and repetition), but he couldn't shake the fear that if he weren't there to say, "I'll be round next week," the deal would go down the drain.

Jim knew this dread stemmed from that one occasion during the period when he had relished being his own boss and he had treated himself to a long lunch and twenty minutes sunning himself in Soho Square. He had returned to the office to find that the French Embassy had left a message at 12:15 (three minutes after he had left), and when he phoned back at 3:37 (he had noted the time), the job had already gone. He had been gutted about it, because he fancied hanging around the French Embassy as French women really did it for him, even ones that weren't attractive, and because, worst of all, he had later discovered the job had gone to Cresswell. It was fear of missing that lifesaving, fortune-making phone call that had been the paramount factor in his not taking a holiday for eight years (along with not having any money).

The travel agent had stared at him. She was evidently an easygoing woman, but impatience was seeping through. He was stuck. He couldn't make up his mind. He couldn't make a decision. Many couples got married with less deliberation than he was taking. He was so defeated he couldn't make a decision about five days or a week; it was a cramp of the thoughtways. It was as if she were asking him to multiply 123,768 by 341,977 in his head.

Jim had cast around for something else to talk about to disguise his paralysis. It was pathetic; this was what it had come to, sitting in a travel agent's unable to choose, and unable to get up and leave, all in all, unable. He had the belief this was the most important decision he would never make and he couldn't make it, but if he left now he would never go on holiday and he would just crumble. All he could think of was how he always made the wrong decision. He rummaged internally for signs, for clues, for desires within himself.

"Do you follow the football?" he asked the travel agent.

"Five days is a good break," said the agent. You couldn't blame her; selling one ticket to Nice was hardly the highlight of her day. Three other people were waiting impatiently for service, inevitably wanting to take their extended families to Melbourne. Maybe this happened regularly, burnouts sitting vacantly in front of her. To his astonishment, his credit card cleared, which showed how little diligence credit card companies paid to spending limits. Gratitude toward the travel agent suffused him, and he considered buying her a bunch of flowers, but that would have been admitting that he was a goner, and besides which he didn't have the money for that, if he wanted lunch. Perhaps this was the most valuable help he'd ever have in his life; perhaps this was the clutchable hand that would prevent him from drowning in himself.

As he shuffled his way off the plane, Jim repeated to himself that the rain wasn't a problem. It was after five, he wouldn't have been able to get to a beach today anyway, and since it never rained here in August, present rain increased the odds of no rain tomorrow when he could be at the beach for as long as his skin would permit.

By the baggage carousel, he saw it was definitely Charles Kidd. He had spotted someone Kidd-like at the other end of the departure lounge at Heathrow, but he hadn't been sure and he had been too tired to get up to see. Kidd was a lawyer who had done some contracts for Ice, and Jim had last seen him years ago getting into a taxi with two women he was going to bed with; the women hadn't been beautiful, but they hadn't been ugly either. He had talked to one of them earlier at the party, a half-Burmese physiotherapist with company clearly on her mind, but Jim had been concentrating on a better-looking American student who was doing a doctorate in conflict resolution who had been very friendly, and too late he had realized she was very friendly to anyone who would listen to her and not in the slightest bit interested in having anything to do with him.

Kidd was at the other end of the baggage carousel, which still had no baggage. Jim decided not to go and say hello. He was totally exhausted. He had no beef with Kidd, indeed he quite liked him, but he didn't have anything he needed to say to him, and if he did go over and have a chat, he'd get asked the question "How's business?" and he'd have to say, "Fine." It was the lying that was the hardest part. To people in the business, you couldn't let out the least whiff of distress, and to friends it was improper to say, "Unless there's a miracle, I'm going to be booking a noose for next week."

The baggage continued not coming. After ten minutes, Jim was struggling so hard to keep his eyes open he sauntered over to Kidd, who was remarkably pleased to see him:

"What are you doing here?"

"Staying with a friend for a few days."

"I'm visiting a friend who's got a massive place over at Saint-Tropez. It's got its own pool; it's obscenely large, high walls; you don't have to set foot outside. I don't have to tell you the beaches are pretty grim this time of year. You must come over."

Suddenly, everyone was inviting him to stay with them in the south of France. It was tantalizing. Hugo's place was outside Nice somewhere, and he had no doubt it would be dowdy and rustic compared with Kidd's offer. Kidd didn't have to sell the place; Jim was certain it would be palatial, full of beautiful rich Frenchwomen, naked and gagging for it. It really would. You start off thinking that life is exciting and glamorous; then after a while you decide that it isn't; then you realize that it is, but not for you. Guest list only. You only got to peep through the key-hole, Jim reflected.

In fact, that was probably his only route to a decent life: an advantageous marriage. The old-rich-wife stunt. Kidd's father owned a couple of streets in London, one of his brothers was an MP, the other had a string of nightclubs across Europe, and despite all that Kidd was extremely likable. Jim was severely receptive to Kidd, and inclined to forget Hugo, who was rather wearing at times; but he knew Hugo would be waiting for him outside, and much as he wanted to be, he wasn't much good at being a shit.

Kidd's bag was the second off the plane. Jim wished him a happy holiday and then had to wait half an hour for his bag to turn up, at the point when he thought he was going to have to do some form-filling.

Hugo was waiting for him outside, in shorts despite the torrential weather.

"Where the hell have you been?"

"I had to satisfy one of the stewardesses," Jim replied. For a second he could see Hugo taking him seriously. That he had for twenty minutes, peculiarly incompetently, managed a rock 'n' roll outfit had left Hugo with an indelible image of him as a wild animal; those who had never had any dealing with the business couldn't help thinking of it as round-the-clock debauchery, whereas Jim had carried out the whole operation from his mother's kitchen, the only payment he had received during the whole enterprise had been a death threat, and if asked always chose to describe the trade as exciting as waiting in line at the post office.

Hugo had been at school with him. They hadn't been particularly close, but they had walked home the same way every day. Jim had two salient memories of Hugo from school. Hugo being beaten up a lot because he was German (nothing short of being black could have been worse); although Hugo did invite punishment by openly supporting Germany during international football matches; he also had a cock like a marrow, which might have provoked further beatings. Hugo was an arresting example of heredity not working; his father lectured in literature at university, and his mother was a violin teacher. Hugo had probably read five non-textbook books in his life (under duress), and even at the age of twelve Jim remembered wishing he didn't have to be seen in public with Hugo because of the shitty records he was carrying.

Jim hadn't seen him much after school, though he had learned of his progress as his mother met Hugo's mother in supermarkets from time to time. Then, a month ago, he had bumped into Hugo in an Italian restaurant in Charlotte Street. Hugo explained he had a Russian girlfriend, was renting a place for a few weeks in Châteauneuf outside of Nice, and why didn't he come and stay? The warmth of Hugo's greeting and the generosity of the gesture had touched Jim, but he'd said no. Then he'd reconsidered and thought he might as well go. He undoubtedly needed a holiday, and he was too miserable and old to go on his own anywhere.

Jim was also touched by Hugo coming to the airport to pick him up, until he remembered that while Hugo wouldn't lend you a fiver, he'd quite happily drive you from London to Inverness; he'd drive to the bathroom if he could.

They ran zaggily across the car park, in the rain, sidestepping the vast puddles. Jim cared little for cars, but he knew an expensive, brand-new BMW when he saw one. Seeing it was like sighting an alternative universe. He had never told Hugo that he had applied for a job at the same bank Hugo had started at. It was one of those humiliations you could have laughed about with a close mate; but Jim had always fancied himself as cleverer than Hugo, and it had hurt, because Hugo had made it (although Hugo's father had written the application letter for him) and because there was nothing worse than prostituting yourself and then discovering that no one was buying.

This car could have been his; the rented villa could have been his; he could have been in the driving seat picking up some impecunious acquaintance from London.

Despite the persistence of the rain, even the French road signs elated him. They were more elegant, more sophisticated than British ones. It was wonderful to be out of London, on holiday. Jim had remembered Châteauneuf as a suburb of Nice, a short bus ride. It soon became clear after they had been driving at high speed for twenty minutes, that the Châteauneuf where Hugo had hired a villa was a different one, and that outside Nice was a very elastic term. As they rocketed farther and farther away from the coast, Jim pined with growing bitterness for Kidd and his pad in Saint-Tropez full of aristocratic beauties.

"Katerina's going to cook something, and then we can all go to a club in Cannes," said Hugo, giving him a supposedly playful punch on his right thigh, an especially knuckly, exceedingly painful punch that deadened the whole leg.

Jim shuddered at the idea of clubbing and resolved to wait five minutes until Hugo thought he had forgotten about the punch and there wasn't a bend and then to stick a good one on him. Jim hadn't been to a club for years. He hadn't had a desire to go to one for years; from the age of sixteen to twenty-four he had lived in clubs, but the prospect of paying to be deafened and crushed by teenagers fighting to get served at the bar made him almost break out in a sweat. He hadn't had any sleep for three days, having slaved for a last-minute proposal for a record company. You spend weeks with nothing to do but cleaning your nails, and the moment you book a holiday someone wants you to tender for a multimillion-pound site. After forty-eight hours without sleep, he had had another urgent demand for service.

It was a call from a television company, from the inappropriately but unforgettably named Mr. Heaven. Jim remembered Mr. Heaven very well; one of the salient features of big companies was that the individuals responsible for Web work were always those who were too useless to do anything important. They were the bumblers who should have been fired but weren't, either because they were related to someone at the top or because there was sympathy for their families. In spite of the clawish reputation of the business world, Jim had never witnessed anyone fired for incompetence or general infirmity; sackings only occurred when the loot dried up, and then it didn't matter how on the ball you were. And naturally, the nonentities like Heaven were the ones keenest on having their khybers extensively licked.

Jim had worked flat out for a week producing a package for Heaven, not just for the hope of money but because the possibilities had genuinely excited him. Perhaps Heaven hadn't liked it. Perhaps he hadn't understood it. Perhaps he had found it too expensive. Perhaps he had had a better offer. Perhaps he hadn't received the stuff. Jim had never found out because he hadn't been able to talk to Heaven or get any sort of answer or anything even approaching information from the secretaries in his office; getting the brush-off from Heaven was annoying, but it was even more painful when it came from airheads whose greatest achievement in life was the application of makeup. After a summer of phoning at different times of the day, Jim had given up.

But eighteen months after Jim had got tired of tackling his office, Heaven phoned. "There are a few things I'd like to discuss in your proposal," Heaven said. Jim had been quite astonished by Heaven's reappearance; this was why he wasn't getting anywhere, he simply couldn't put himself in other people's shoes. Why wait a year and a half before replying to someone? Presumably, Heaven's regular stable of salesmen seeking favor, toadies, and other assorted ego blowers was out of action; but even so, he couldn't seriously expect to phone up after a *year and a half* and get some groveling?

"Really?" Jim had replied.

"Could you come up for a chat tomorrow?" Jim had only had one meeting with Heaven. At his office in Newcastle. At nine in the morning. Jim had started from home at four-thirty, spent a small fortune on railfare, but had been excited by the significance of the meeting; when you got face-to-face, it was close to check time. The meeting with Heaven had lasted four minutes: Jim unable to think of anything but how the secretaries must spend their whole days taking the piss out of Heaven, Heaven occupying three minutes and forty-seconds of the meeting extolling the charms of Newcastle, and then asking for a proposal, the sort of request that telephones or the Royal Mail had been designed to communicate.

"I'm too busy," Jim had said. The funny thing was it was true; he had a plane to catch in twenty-four hours. He hadn't slept for two days; he had another day's work to go before he could rush to the airport. He watched the receiver shaking in his hand.

His business was sinking so fast he didn't have any time for business. Of course, Heaven was a hard-core time-waster. Jim was as sure as he could be of anything that Heaven only wanted someone to turn up as confirmation of his own power; that was why he wasn't going to suggest a meeting when he got back. What if he were wrong? What if this unlikely-looking proposition was his salvation, a repellent opening to wealth and triumph? what if Heaven, the arch company teaser, was finally offering a contract?

"We can always take our business somewhere else," Heaven chided. Jim noted with distaste Heaven's tone had changed from old mate to thug without a break.

"No, what you're doing is taking your fucking around somewhere else."

★

"I was thinking of having an early night," Jim replied.

"You miserable bastard," said Hugo. That settled it; he had made a mistake; he should have generated wild enthusiasm about going to the club and then faked food poisoning after the meal. He was so tired he was almost hallucinating; he had thought Kidd a figment at first.

Since Jim had indicated he didn't want to go, Hugo would do everything to drag him there. Hugo loved this sort of small-scale sadism. Plus, he should have guessed that Hugo was in the full throes of much-younger-girlfriend syndrome; he wanted to show he was still up to boogalooing the night away. A pair of in-line skates rested prominently on the backseat, another declaration of vigor and hipness.

"How old is Katerina?"

"Twenty-two," admitted Hugo with a trace of embarrassment. A fourteen-year difference was outside the cradle-snatching range, when the divide is thirty-six/twenty-two, but not by much.

"So how did you meet her?"

"You remember my friend Gavin?"

"No."

"Of course you do."

"No, I don't."

"Gavin. Gavin. You met him at one of my parties."

"Oh, yes, I remember now." Jim didn't, but Hugo was getting exercised about it.

"So what does he look like?"

"What's that got to do with anything?"

"If you remember him, what does he look like?"

"I don't know. Human being–like . . ."

"What color is his hair?"

"Dark hair."

"Try again."

"Blond hair?"

"Does he wear glasses?"

"I don't remember him wearing glasses when I met him."

"You don't remember him at all. Why did you say you remembered him?"

"Because I didn't want to get into an argument about it."

"Well, he ended up in St. Petersburg running supermarkets. So he got a Russian girlfriend, got married. I went out there for the wedding and met Katerina; she's a friend of Gavin's wife. And it went from there."

"But she's living with you in London?"

"At the moment. The trouble I had getting her a visa. I had to hire a fucking lawyer. I had to write to my MP. It took months. And I had to pay for her to do a course at Christie's; do you have any idea how much one of those courses costs? They're convinced that any single Russian girl wanting to come to Britain is on the game. And as for the French . . . I thought we were going to have to cancel the holiday. She only got the visa the day before, the bastards."

He had heard from Ian that Hugo's girlfriend was the most beautiful woman he had ever seen. She would have to be pretty remarkable to get Hugo to cough up that much cash.

"What does she do?"

"Nothing really. You know, nearly everyone's unemployed in Russia now."

Jim couldn't believe they were still driving. Where was this place? They must be halfway to Paris by now. Should he give Hugo a thump?

"She's got a friend with her, Alzbeta," Hugo continued. "She's quite grumpy because she hasn't fancied any of the men who've been staying so far. You'd be doing us all a favor if you gave her a good seeing-to."

If Hugo was suggesting it, it had to be a no-no.

"The situation with the sleeping arrangements is . . . pretty complicated at the moment," Hugo said. Jim tensed,

29

remembering Hugo's invitation in the restaurant: "There's all this space going begging."

"And if you got on with Alzbeta, it would also simplify the sleeping arrangements. I remember you're a pretty slow worker, though, so we'll have to sort something out for this evening; we've got four bedrooms, which would have been enough, but a friend of Ralph's turned up unexpectedly a couple of days ago. So Katerina and I are in one, Ralph's in the other, Alzbeta's in the third; I wanted to give you that one, but she spent the whole of last week sleeping on the sofa, while Udo was here, so she's earned her turn. So until you've smoothed your way into Alzbeta's room, you have a choice of the sofa or sharing with Derek; that's Ralph's friend. At least for two nights, and then Marcus and Jane'll be coming and we'll have to think again."

Jim badly wanted to strangle Hugo. This was why, as if he needed reminding, he hadn't stayed in close touch with Hugo; he was an arsehole or, as they said in the city, a prize lombard. Why couldn't Hugo have admitted that he'd overdone it on the hospitality front? He'd be in Saint-Tropez by now, enjoying the lifestyle he had so distantly glimpsed for so long.

When he had been in his teens, Jim had slept on floors, doorways, in beds overloaded with strangers, railway stations, even in a barn. No problem. Something happened after thirty: you needed your own space; you needed minimal comfort. Never mind Saint-Tropez; even a fleabag hotel in Nice would have been better. A long peaceful sleep, late rising, and so to the beach and the company of the most serene breasts. Instead here he was halfway to Paris about to have his sleep damaged by the snoring of some wanky financier.

His rage dozed off. He would have remonstrated with Hugo, but it would have only added to Hugo's pleasure. And he was too tired to keep up being angry; he was so sleepy, if Hugo had thrown him into a ditch and told him to spend the night there, he wouldn't have mounted a protest.

"So how's business?" asked Hugo.

"Fine," said Jim.

★

Hugo reversed the car into the driveway with the care of a man who loves his paintwork more than his mother, and who loves showing how masterfully he reverses.

There was a freedom in exhaustion, Jim acknowledged as he went inside; he didn't care whether he looked presentable or whether he made a favorable impression on the girls. Katerina and Alzbeta were seated at the kitchen table, with the relaxed air of women who had supper subjugated. They were poring over a copy of the *Sun,* open at the sports pages. Jim had no doubt that in exchange for their stay in the South of France, they were doing all the housework and cooking, Hugo not being burdened with any shame or notions of fairness.

Katerina wasn't the most beautiful woman Jim had ever seen, but *beautiful* would always be among the words used to describe her. Blonde, she wore a light dress that gave her tan plenty of room.

"Jim, we have heard so much about you," she said with a laugh, a light accent, and a slight, polite flirt. "We have heard so much about you" was one of those lines you got a couple of times a year, but Jim had never managed to come up with a snappy retort and he wasn't about to start now. He liked Katerina instantly as he realized he'd forgotten to return Hugo's punch. Alzbeta was freckly; her brown hair tied back, she wore a bulky T-shirt and baggy shorts. She looked like the quiet sort who would take love very seriously. He took a liking to her too, but no.

"We have important question for you: who is Mock-meanman?" asked Katerina.

"Markmonmang," said Alzbeta.

"No, Meekmarr-mormon," Katerina read from the paper.

"You mean MacManaman," said Jim, looking over her shoulder.

"Yes. There is everything here. When he born, what does he in bed, what clothes he like. But it doesn't say who he is."

"He's a footballer," said Jim. Katerina's and Alzbeta's faces lit up, they had a laughing exchange in Russian, and Jim felt as if he had cracked cold fusion. "He's a very good footballer. Plays for Liverpool," he added to show he really knew what he was talking about.

"Russian footballers best in the world," said Alzbeta.

Hugo came in. "So . . . any news of supper?" He obviously wanted to demand his food but was a little inhibited by Jim.

Katerina pointed at a large simmering pan. "Soup is ready; but we are reading newspaper. Ten minutes." She and Alzbeta resumed their excursion through the sports pages.

"Where's Ralph?"

"Ralph and Derek out; in car." Katerina said this as if she were very happy about it.

Hugo led Jim through the villa. It was either new or exceedingly redecorated; there were two large leather sofas for him to choose from, spotlessly clean apart from English newspapers lying in sections here and there, jewel cases for Russian CDs, and several stuffed ashtrays. They walked out into the garden.

It was a chunk of paradise. A huge garden, walled, but the flowers, trees, and bushes were so numerous and expansive that they would have cut the property off from the road and the rest of the village on their own. There was a swimming pool, which Jim was disappointed to find a little small for swimming in, one of these birdbath jobs put in so the brochure could say there was a pool; but it served its purpose in encouraging the removal of clothes, and it was certainly large enough to have sex in, really the main justification behind swimming pools. Jim was distantly aware that he'd quite like to see Katerina wearing less, surely an inevitability in this setup, though he was also aware that what he desperately wanted was a small enclosed space with a mattress where he could lock himself away for twelve hours; then he'd be ready to tackle the universe again.

Far away, on the horizon, there was something vaguely industrial, but you had to strain your eyes.

Hugo got him a beer. "They're temperamental, those Russians." Hugo got from Katerina's making him wait ten minutes for his soup, to his eldest uncle machine-gunning Russians soldiers on the Eastern Front during the Second World War. "They just kept on coming and coming; their whole strategy was to find German guns and run at them. My uncle only stopped when his barrel melted."

Jim wondered why Katerina was with Hugo. Why Hugo was with her was not in question; Katerina was ravishing, clever, and no doubt went like a dynamited whippet. To be fair to Hugo, he could be entertaining when he put his mind to it, he was tall, and for a thirty-six-year-old moneyman he was in reasonable shape and carried a real warhead. He would drive you anywhere you wanted. Was Hugo going to settle down? Do the repro stuff?

Hugo had never had a girlfriend who had penetrated his life; some women had lasted a year or so, but Jim had never been aware of Hugo having a mad, out-of-control, brought-to-his-knees love. One evening in their last year at school after Jim had taken a girlfriend to the expensive fish restaurant in Exeter, he had met Hugo outside. He had been going out with Sophie for two months by then. The next day Hugo had asked him: "But I though you'd already slept with her." "Yeah." "Then why are you taking her out for an expensive meal?"

Not that having insane passion had done Jim any good. That had ended badly, as he had the feeling insane passion usually did. He had tried to be a responsible adult, but Hugo was the one with the proper job, the villa, the car, the displayable Russian girlfriend.

Katerina and Alzbeta laid the table in a practiced way. The mushroom soup was served from a china tureen; it was good, but Jim could have made that. Next came, appropriately enough, Russian salad, and it was spectacularly delicious. Hugo stuffed himself noisily without offering any compliments on the cooking. Jim praised the salad and helped himself to another serving, while Alzbeta inspected him:

"You don't look like computerman," she said.

"How should a computerman look?"

"Like Derek." She laughed and cleared away the dishes speedily before he could grab something to carry out. Her observation was surely meant as a compliment, but perhaps she had unearthed some deep truth; maybe his avoidance of success had something to do with this. What did he look like? He should ask. Maybe Alzbeta could give him career advice.

They heard the door dooring. A short figure with black, rickety glasses stepped in. Hugo introduced him as Ralph. For someone who played with billions, the spectacles were laughable; it was what you'd expect the twelve-year-old son of a single mother with no income and no taste to be wearing. Close up, Jim noticed one of the arms was lightly taped.

"Where've you been?" Hugo asked.

"Oh . . . you know, driving around," replied Ralph. Ralph had the unmistakable mien of a man who has spent another day of his precious annual holiday, the twenty-eight holy days he doesn't have to work his bollocks off, without getting laid. Jim recognized the tactic from his teenage years: pile into a car and drive around in the hope that women would suddenly materialize in the backseat.

"Alzbeta? Are you going to sleep with me?" asked Ralph.

"No." She disappeared back into the kitchen. It was always the short ones who were worst; because getting a girl taller than them into bed wasn't about rumpy-pumpy, it was about showing they weren't short. Ralph lit a cigarette and took a deep puff.

"Hugo says you're a Webhead; you can have a good chat with Derek about that. He's into that too." Jim nodded as if nothing could give him greater pleasure. He was sure he was going to pass out. There was a silence as they observed Alzbeta bring back the soup and salad. Jim would have paid anything for the right to go to sleep. With a few herculean drags, Ralph ashed his cigarette.

"Alzbeta, Derek and I have already eaten. We paid a visit to Ronald McDonald's."

"Then why I bring food?" asked Alzbeta.

"No idea," said Ralph.

The door went again. A figure stooped out from the darkness, tall, rakelike, white, and tentatively British, warily looking around as if there might be foreigners about to get too close: the British ponce abroad.

"Jim, this is Derek," announced Ralph.

Jim knew it was Derek. Of all the Dereks in the world, with an involvement with the Web, it had to be this Derek. Derek Cresswell. The man he hated the most. He hated Derek so much, he was rather embarrassed about it, because it was a hatred that twisted him, a hatred so strong it was poisoning him. He had used his last reserves of energy, spent a day travel-ing to the South of France, spent hundreds of pounds he didn't have to share a room with a man he believed he could kill with enormous pleasure.

Why he hated Derek so furiously wasn't that easy to explain. There were a number of glaring reasons: Derek ran a very suc-cessful Web company. Derek's success was largely due to his having pilfered contracts that Jim had sweated blood over. Derek had almost single-handedly driven him to penury. And Derek wasn't even any good; again and again Jim heard from clients that had gone with Derek that the site didn't do what it was supposed to, that it crashed with the persistence of a blindfolded one-armed driver crossing the Alps. If Derek had been competent, his victories might have been a little more tolerable.

Then in addition to Derek the biz wiz, there was Derek the man. As the midgets were the pushiest, so those who were sky-scrapers (Derek had to be six-four) never fitted in; they were apologetic, overgrown plants flopping everywhere. And there was something in names; Jim had always disliked Dereks. Amandas, for example, he'd always liked (he'd slept with three), but he'd always disliked (intensely) the Dereks he'd come across.

The only consolation was that Derek wasn't happy to see him either; he didn't hate Jim the way Jim hated Derek (that wasn't possible), but his discomfort showed.

Jim was so drained, if there had been a suicide suite in the villa, he would have excused himself and popped some bottles of pills. Then he considered phoning for a taxi, simply fleeing, but rejected that. He wasn't going to be the one to back out.

The figuring out was all too much.

"How's business, Jim?" asked Derek.

"Fine."

"You two know each other?" asked Hugo. Even he had noticed something was going on. Derek meandered over to a sofa, slumped down, and started picking at a newspaper. Ralph and Hugo registered some surprise that he and Derek had nothing more to say to each other, but they said nothing.

Alzbeta came in again to pick up the remains of supper.

"Alzbeta," said Ralph, lighting another cigarette, "I was reading an article about a Russian cargo plane crashing and killing everyone on board; it reminded me of what you were saying about Russian pilots, that they were the best in the world."

Alzbeta didn't respond; she disappeared with the plates. She wasn't pretending to ignore Ralph; his existence didn't reach her.

"Well, why don't we all have a drink?" said Ralph, heading for what was the largest bottle of whiskey Jim had ever seen.

Hugo saw Katerina going upstairs. "I'm just going to have a shower," he said. "A long one. Let's aim to set off at nine."

Derek put down the paper and with a "right" padded off.

"Do you want a whiskey, Jim?" Ralph inquired.

"No, thanks." Booze would finish him off. What he needed was a bucket of strong coffee. Ralph went over to the phone and started dialing.

Jim struggled with the anvil-like weight of injustice, which refused to leave his being. One of the few benefits of getting older was you cared less what others thought. He was untroubled about being accused of being a miserable bastard or a party pooper, although this indifference to room temperature was the first step to beating off in the park in front of young girls. To go upstairs and switch off would be the greatest happiness, but the expectation of waking up in the same room as Derek, hearing his breathing, inhaling his skin, being presented with his arse, was unbearable.

The sofas radiated comfort, but bedding down on one of them—that would be giving ground. Jim wished he could consult some meter so he could gauge who, he or Derek, would be the more appalled by sharing. He was prepared to endure hell, as long as Derek was suffering hell and a bit.

Ralph was now cooing into the receiver. "Suzy, why don't you come down for a few days? The place is incredible. Here," he said, directing the receiver at Jim. "Tell Suzy this place is incredible."

"Suzy, this place is incredible," Jim obliged.

"That was Jim, the most trustworthy man I know."

So Ralph was at that stage of the holiday where you're so desperate you try importing pleasure from your address book. He could visualize Ralph before he set off debating whether he should invite Suzy and deciding not to, charmed by adventure, the lure of the unknown, banking on a late, foreign delivery of that package of rectifying happiness. Jim watched Ralph yawn as Suzy was doubtless explaining she had to wash her hair or defrost the fridge. What the fuck was Ralph yawning about? How long had he been up for? Ten hours? Twenty hours? Real men didn't even consider yawning until they'd clocked up forty-eight hours.

What he had to do, Jim resolved, was go out to the club and pull (despite this only ever happening once before in his life) in order to get a bed. It made him chuckle as he knew his married, offspringed friends were convinced he was rutting around the clock, and here he was plotting to get a woman into bed merely for the bed. Whichever way you played it, it was hard; he had seen his friends (even those with the successful marriages) crawling on all fours and making bestial noises under their responsibilities.

At the age of eight, stopping to take a pee after a school swimming class, Jim had missed the coach and found himself unimaginable distances from home, cold, with no money or any idea of what to do. He had dealt with the problem by bursting into tears. That sensation of abandonment and hopelessness was revisiting him more and more often. You created your own torches for yourself for a few years to push back the darkness, and you believed the terrors were gone, but they had just withdrawn, waiting to return when you were weaker.

London wasn't an expensive city; it was a ten-handed pickpocket, going through your every item of clothing as well as checking under your tongue and in your rectum for any valuables. You could just stand on a corner; your money would evaporate, and no one cared if you cried.

He sensed that soon he would give up, and that frightened him; he knew once you donned the truly black sunglasses of despair, you'd never see sunlight again. He had to start hoping again, though he couldn't help remarking to himself, that had done fuck-all good so far in his thirty-six years.

A rapid bumping started to emanate from the ceiling.

"Hugo," commented Ralph. "Katerina could complain about all sorts of things when it comes to Hugo. Philistine. Lombard. The sensitivity of a bulldozer. But it's three times every day."

Ralph yawned, "I'm going to spruce up." Compassion prodded Jim to say to Ralph: don't bother; a splash of aftershave isn't going to change anything.

His eyelids were sliding together of their own accord, although he was afraid he was too tired to fall asleep. A sickness was swelling in his stomach. The furniture started to flit about. Jim wanted to cry, he felt so sorry for himself. Left alone in the lounge, he decided to put on some music; that was what you were supposed to do on holiday. He had two tapes with him.

Jim bought only bootlegs now. Having been in the music business, however fleetingly, he had a snobbery about stuff you could buy in any high street. The quality of most bootlegs was outrageously bad, but you consoled yourself with the reflection that Joe Mall wouldn't own it.

But after a while, Jim began to savor the rubbishy texture, especially on the live recordings. Most official live albums weren't live; they were studio remakes, and usually the only relationship they had to the concert was the photo on the sleeve. What he liked about the bootlegs was there was nowhere to hide; what you hear is what there was. He had also discovered that he had developed a very specialized taste: in the last year, he had an overwhelming fondness for last concerts.

Many of them were available officially, but they weren't the same; it was the bootleg made with the mike stuffed in the bootlegger's bra that told the truth. And they always knew it was the end. Sometimes it was meant to be the end, some-times it wasn't, but they always knew. Jim came to understand he was seeking something from them; he was searching for advice on crashing into the wall. Even when it came to groups whom he hated, their last musical moments were endlessly fascinating.

That was why you wanted your heroes to live fast, so fast they had to burn up. Dying in a plane crash or car accident was no good; that could happen to anyone. They had to perish through excess, so that when you pretended to be them, you could have the full packet, because true-life adventure was something to be avoided. The penalties were too stiff.

It was one of the most terrible lessons, but your parents were right (assuming you had parents with a willingness to parent) when they said get a proper job, save your money, buy a house, get a pension; all the nagging was spot-on. It was always the handful of successful adventurers who got the scrutiny, and no attention was paid to the hordes of unwashed crazies in pubs or on park benches slurping up their dole, the fifty-five-year-old security guards, the sixty-year-old private teachers of French verbs; the throng of bores who had missed the boredom; the boredom of nondesperation.

★

Taking a cold shower in the downstairs bathroom shocked Jim into a closer alliance with reality, but the yearning to sag into a coffin and wait for the undertakers remained. On top of which the way his mind treated on an equal basis the notion of going into the kitchen and getting a glass of water with the notion of going into the kitchen and getting a carving knife to fillet Derek was perturbing. Drink water. Stab Derek. Drink water. Stab Derek. He could hardly tell the difference.

When Alzbeta came down, Jim wouldn't have recognized her if he hadn't known it had to be her. (Katerina was the blonde one.) He conceded this was the whole purpose of the cosmetic and fashion industries and why they had been so gainfully in business for thousands of years, wars and messiahs no obstacle.

The transformation was formidable; Jim was stumped where to ogle first, her cleavage, her search-and-destroy lipstick, her hair that had been medusa'd into all sorts of strange curls that probably had names (but that he didn't know), high heels, a black silk jacket, trousers that owned tightness; the stunner's sidekick had become unattainable club royalty. In every language the message was: worship here.

He wished he'd smartened himself up a bit more and that his face wasn't an assembly of bruised potatoes.

Hugo edged his car out of the driveway centimeter by centimeter. Jim was anxious whether Alzbeta would get into Hugo's car with him and Katerina, or get into the other one with Ralph and Derek. She got in the right car.

Hugo drove fast and, on emaciated roads full of machismo-mad Latins, thus recklessly. It was rather juvenile fun, driving fast in the South of France with loud music and two young and beautiful Russian women in the back, but it was fun, and Jim pronounced himself, to his surprise, to be in a state of enjoyment. Was all fun juvenile?

He didn't mind really if Hugo were to crash the car; better to go like this—looking stylish—than alone in his flat. Lately he had fears of being one of those half-skeleton messes that is discovered weeks after no one has seen you—this followed an incident with an excruciating cramp: as he had lain on the floor, unable to move, getting to know the carpet better than he wanted to, he had brooded about how if it had been something nastier, that would have been it. Betty would have taken a week to have noticed his absence and then a few more days to locate a responsible adult he could discuss the problem with.

The girls chatted in Russian.

"No Russian," said Hugo, clearly worried that they might be conspiring behind his back or amusing themselves with a lengthy discussion of his disgusting habits—an odd mixture of arrogance and insecurity. If you were loaded, well-hung, and doing it three times a day, what could your girlfriend have to complain about? Apart from not being able to talk with her friend in Russian.

"Why not?" asked Alzbeta.

"No Russian."

"Okay, we speak Ukrainian," and they carried on in what sounded suspiciously like Russian.

The thrill of teasing death wore off, and Jim started to lose snatches of time, a few seconds, a minute, it was hard to say; sleep was pecking at him as they drove on. He cheered himself with the thought that Derek couldn't be doing that well in his private life either, or he wouldn't be here on his own.

Behind them Ralph was keeping up with Hugo's furious cornering and acceleration, although he must have been flogging the Fiat rental car to bits. It was like being seventeen again, going out, birds in the back, racing your mates for all you're worth; except twenty years on, it was depressing to be still in the same routine, fatter, balder, and weaker.

They stopped off at a petrol station. Jim offered to get out and help translate—he knew Hugo didn't speak any French—but Hugo reckoned he could manage. He watched Hugo fill up the tank and speculated how much Hugo was worth now. He had to be more than a millionaire. His flat in Docklands was worth at least half a million, and while his job wasn't one of the obscenely paid jobs that incenses left-wing playwrights, Hugo had to be pulling in a fat salary every year, if not six figures, only a fiver or so short. He didn't spend anything on himself; he had lavish lunches or suppers at the bank's expense and then would come home and eat beans on toast or some fruit; he bought all his clothes on sale. Hugo hardly ever went out, because his huge wedge required a twelve-hour day, not to mention a lot of shuffling of papers on the weekends. More important, he had been salting away his savings in tax-free loopholes for years. Hugo had strongly advised him to buy Brazilian telecom shares as if it were the greatest secret ever told. A car and a holiday were his only indulgences.

A warmth of perfume surrounded him. Alzbeta had leaned forward.

"Jim, you have met Russian girls before?"

"No." He hadn't.

"How you like Russians girls?"

"Uh, so far, so good." What wit. He'd been glibber when he was seventeen.

More Russian or Ukrainian discussion took place. Giggles.

"Russian girls best in world."

Jim watched Hugo bully the cashier, using that old technique of speaking English louder and louder when you met someone who didn't speak it. Hugo was probably demanding his free tumbler. He had to admire Hugo. Get the job. Get the money. Get the gorgeous girlfriend. Get the tumbler. It was the small things that gave you away. Jim wouldn't have bothered trying to get someone who didn't understand what he was saying to hand over a tumbler. That was why the bailiffs had probably cleared the scant furniture out of his office that afternoon. He pictured Betty sitting on the floor, unable to figure out why his computer wasn't responding.

They drove into Cannes. He had always hated Cannes; it was the snottiest place on the Côte, but it was still the Côte. At the age of twenty-one, Jim had lived in Nice with a beautiful girl with whom he was insanely in love; for four months he had explored happiness. That had been that. It was gone.

For four months, he had been . . . a hero in everything, a champion in opening jammed windows, starting recalcitrant cars, nibbling buttocks. Now he woke up every morning, as he had done for the last two years, trying to think of a good reason not to kill himself.

As they inched along the Croisette, the sight of the cafés engendered a profound nostalgia in Jim; there was nothing to compare to a French café. French clubs, on the other hand, were crap and expensive. The one they were approaching looked determined, though, with laser beams on its roof cutting through the air with disregard for low-flying aircraft.

The club had its own car park. Jim got out and sank in the mud. Hugo strode on, since he had to fork out for the girls. As he walked up, Jim saw the bullet-headed bouncer (complete with earpiece) shaking his head at Hugo (apparently there was a law that even with five black belts and five languages they wouldn't give you the job unless you were chunky and shaven headed). They had been rumbled as too old and too uncool to be admitted.

"You're not going to believe this," Hugo reported. "The rain got into the club and flooded it. They won't be open till later."

"When?"

"They don't know." Of course, there was no door policy in France. They did that picking and choosing thing in Britain and America. What they did in France was rush you in if you could afford the insolent prices.

It was just like being seventeen again. It wasn't worth getting in the cars because apparently the car park got really full and Hugo didn't want to lose his place. They opted for aimless wandering.

Incredibly, they had to look hard for a café; in this stretch of Cannes everything was closed. But that was what you did on holiday; either you did nothing, or you spent your time finding food or drink, interspersed with rutting. Or if you were pretentious or cultural, you squeezed in a museum. Finally, they reached a huge open-air place that still had the lights on and a waiter in attendance.

In this café with some thirty tables, they were the only customers. The waiter steadfastly refused to budge from his little hut, where he was evidently chatting on the phone with his girlfriend. It wasn't that late, they were grateful for somewhere to sit, and they were on holiday, so by definition, they weren't in a rush, but after several minutes, his refusal to come over, when there was no way he could miss them, began to grate.

Hugo waved. Ralph whistled. Hugo shouted. Derek clapped. Even Alzbeta put two fingers in her mouth and let out a protracted whistle. The waiter was quite impressive; he genuinely didn't give a shit.

Jim was curious to see who was going to be the most infuriated by the gabbling waiter. Normally, he'd be irritated. Jim worked hard and unprofessionalism inflamed him, but he was so whacked and so insolvent that he couldn't get worked up about the waiter or any of the current genocides only a few hours' flying time away. What he wanted to do was to go to bed with Alzbeta, not because he desired her, he doubted he was up to the act, but because he wanted somewhere cosy and fragrant to sleep and because he suspected claiming Alzbeta would smite Derek.

He was tempted, very strongly tempted, to sneak off and find a hotel and go to bed. But he knew however justifiable his desertion would be, it would be judged as terminally antisocial. Plus it would be hard to find a hotel with empty rooms at this time of the year. Followed by the especially hard to crack problem of how to pay. He had forty quid on him, which around here wouldn't be enough for a large coffee, and his credit card was about to go up in flames any second.

The same hurdle presented itself with Alzbeta; he had been hoping to get her in the club, buy her a few drinks, quick slow dance, off home. The difficulty was home was a fifty-minute drive away, and, assuming they could find a taxi driver willing to go that far, he would barely have the fare, knowing what chiseling fuckers taxi drivers were. Jim doubted if the others would want to leave; once Hugo had paid the admission, he would want to stay till chucking-out time to get his money's worth, and naturally Ralph and Derek were the Men Who Wanted to Get Laid and wouldn't leave until they had propositioned every female on the dance floor. Of course, if Derek got lucky, that would solve the bed nightmare, though it wouldn't solve his predicament of not being able to hit the sack for hours.

He looked at Alzbeta. He supposed he should issue some compliments or something. It was traditional and might come in useful. In fact he should have said something when she came downstairs, but he had been so amazed by her elegance that he hadn't been able to compliment her.

"You look very . . . beautiful." A dull, but safe endearment that rarely failed, and it was a word that Alzbeta surely understood.

"Here is nothing new," she replied.

"All right," said Ralph, getting up, "I'm going in. What do you want to drink? I can't believe we've been here ten minutes and we haven't even ordered."

"I'll have four coffees," said Jim.

Ralph staggered over to the waiter, who didn't pause in his conversation, even with Ralph blowing cigarette smoke at him.

"I have an IQ of 165, I earn two hundred thousand pounds a year, I am a British subject, and it is your privilege, I repeat, your privilege to serve me."

The waiter wrote down the order without stopping his flow.

Derek, Jim noticed, was leaking misery, which immediately made him feel much better. Was it just fucked holiday blues, or was there something serious? Illness? Business crisis?

Jim was glad he had ordered four coffees. It took the drinks forty-five minutes to arrive. Presumably the waiter had something else going on inside the kitchen, a poker game, another assignation.

"Où sont les hard drugs, garçon?" asked Ralph. "Where's the *e* in the EU? Les persian rugs? Nous avons besoin de . . . scoring. We want to be alles-super-gut, compris?" The waiter forced a small grin and left. He had processed much more offensive holiday makers.

The coffee was cold. Jim and everyone else noticed that Ralph had ordered himself three extraordinarily large glasses of spirits.

"I got some numbers for dealers in Nice before I came, but you know what, there's no reply on any of the numbers," Ralph fulminated. "I think the buggers must all be on holiday."

Katerina and Alzbeta were comparing hair products, apparently, since both were fingering one of Alzbeta's locks. Jim wished he was in the club, where at least the music would bump him up. "And the bugger hasn't brought me Armagnac; this is Cognac. I don't know why some people do what they do. But it's astonishing how you can get away without doing anything. I met this guy once in a bar in Tokyo who turned out to be a photographer. And all he did was photograph naked Japanese women. So I toddled off to one of his exhibitions, and it was all very classy, you know, lovely lighting; it was stuff you were meant to hang on the wall, rather than use to indulge in the abominable sin of onan. They were quite well-composed pictures; pictures of naked Japanese women on their own, pictures of two Japanese women naked together, pictures of three Japanese women together, even one picture of six Japanese women naked together. Some with big breasts, some with small breasts. Nothing filthy, just standing there. You get the idea; Japanese women, clothes off. And he made a good living out of it. I mean anyone can do that. I know there might be a certain skill in keeping the dust off your lens, but that's it. What I do doesn't take any skill, but at least it looks as if it does."

They walked back to the club while Ralph complained about how he had gone to the police station to ask if there were any dangerous areas with drug dealers and so on in Nice it wouldn't be safe for tourists to visit. "'No, Monsieur,' they said there are no problems with drugs here. I could barely resist saying well I have a problem: I can't get any. I even tried the simple trick of going to the nearest black man, but he tried to sell me some carving."

Hugo went to check on his car and came back fuming. "Some bastard's stolen my aerial. The radio, you expect that. What's the logic of stealing the aerial?"

The club was now open. There were Lamborghinis, Ferraris, Porsches nestled together outside. The Côte still had no objection to ostentation. Hugo went first and paid for Katerina and Alzbeta. Jim tapped him for some francs, saying he hadn't had a chance to change any pounds. Inside, the club was rapidly filling up. One girl, who couldn't have been more than seventeen and might have been as young as thirteen, was the most beautiful girl Jim had ever seen. That was the wonder of the Côte; it attracted impossibly attractive women. Jim was aware that she would never have anything to do with him. Not that he was too old for the girl. For her, twenty-five was too old. He wasn't too old; he simply didn't exist. He was invisible, in another dimension.

The inside was becomingly noisy, but there was an outdoor section, which offered the possibility of conversation. The seats were still wet from the rain. Jim was buffeted by wilting sensations; he cursed himself for not having had the gumption to go off to a hotel. He was no longer capable of anything. He sat feeling the damp uniting with the trousers, as the waitress ignored them and kept the greatest possible distance, while Hugo whinged about his aerial and Ralph continued his repertoire:

"I was at a party in New York with Madonna, so I said to her, forget the beefcake, love, try some British flab. For a second, just for a second, she was mulling it over; you're humped by bronzed gym instructors continually, some white wobbly stuff can be a relief. Are you going to bed with me, Alzbeta?"

"No, Ralph."

Ralph went off to demand some drinks. Jim was at the end; invisible weights were pressing on him from several directions, and even sitting became too demanding. Some music from his youth came on, and, praying that some activity would wake him up, he asked Alzbeta to dance and was astonished when she shook her head. What was going on? She had been wafting perfume at him, and even if she wasn't interested, she could have partnered him out of courtesy.

Hugo was totally deformed about the aerial and perhaps fearful that some further indignity might be inflicted on his car. That was highly seventeen: devaluing other people's cars. No end of fun, coins along the side, potatoes up the exhaust pipe, sugar in the tank, battery acid, drop-kicking off the wing-mirrors, chewing gum in the locks, jumping up and down on the roof.

"I'm going to go in an hour," Hugo seethed. "You can stay. Ralph and Derek'll give you a lift back."

Pitifully, it was the best news Jim had heard all year. Even if it promised only a few hours on a sofa.

Ralph returned with a tray of drinks, two bottles, one vodka, the other whiskey, and four beers. "I didn't want to go to the bar every fifteen minutes." Jim dreaded to think what the booze must have cost. Would Ralph need a Web site? he wondered. Hugo had explained what Ralph's hedge fund did, but he hadn't understood. And if he needed Webbing, Derek would have provided it already.

"Right," said Ralph. "Why don't we have a drinking game?"

Hugo demurred. Katerina and Alzbeta claimed they wouldn't understand. Derek indicated he was willing.

"Sorry," said Jim. "I'm really not up to it. Tomorrow night if you want."

"You miserable bastards. It's no good with two. Still, you have to know your limits," reflected Ralph. "But the trouble is, I don't see how you can know your limits, until you go past them so you have that . . . I've gone past my limits feeling; you know very definitely when you've gone past them. But then it's often too late to get back to the limits. I had a friend in Frankfurt, who worked late every day, but who, before he went to bed, would drink a whole bottle of whiskey. In the morning he'd be fine. Then one night he drank a bottle of whiskey and a quick snifter from a second bottle. He died."

"So who are you working for at the moment?" asked Derek. It was the question Jim had been dreading. It was difficult: if he lied it would be easy to be caught out; on the other hand, if he pretended it was confidential, it would sound either very unconvincing or pretentious.

"You can't always see where the line is. There isn't an announcement: you're reaching the limits," continued Ralph loudly, changing seats and slumping between Jim and Derek. "No flashing lights. I had another friend, a photographer, a war photographer, did Afghanistan, did the Gulf, Rwanda, and never got a scratch. Well, he got a black eye once when he came back from, what was that place in Yugoslavia, had a lot of fighting?"

"Could be anywhere in Yugoslavia."

"Yes. Anyway, he came back with this incredible shiner, and I said, what happened? Someone trying to censor you? No, some bloke got blown up half a mile down the road by a shell, and his arm, on a solo mission, came and punched him in the face. That didn't bother him at all. So one day he's in Rwanda, in a village where everyone's been killed, he does the moldering corpses, blood-splattered walls, he's got more than he needs, there's a limited market for atrocity, and he's about to leave, when he notices a ditch outside the village, and he thinks, I'll just stroll over there. He was quite emphatic about hits; he didn't need to go and look; it was just habit, to go a bit farther. And that's when it happened." Ralph took a long drag on his cigarette and let the smoke curl out.

"What?" Jim furnished the cue.

"He saw something that was too much. It was just too much. And he was never able to see any point in life again. That was, what, seven years ago. He hasn't got over it. Gave up journalism. He takes photographs of churches and listed buildings; doesn't want to work with people anymore."

Jim waited for Ralph to say what it was. You had to find out. Ralph was now concentrating on a young lady dancing on a table.

"So what did he see?"

"I'm not going to tell you."

"Why not?"

"Because you might find life pointless too if I tell you."

"It can't be that bad."

"That's what I said. I kept on pestering him until he told me, and I can tell you I wish he hadn't."

"Then why did you tell us about it?" asked Jim.

"I haven't told you what he saw. Maybe it wouldn't bother you that much, but maybe it would. Have another drink."

The girls didn't like the vodka. Alzbeta went off to the loo and was gone, even by the standards of female visits to the toilets, a fantastically long time.

"Let's go," said Hugo.

"What about Alzbeta?"

"Derek's going to stay. Ralph's coming back with us; he's not in a fit state to walk home."

As they were going out, they spotted Alzbeta in a corner jabbering away with a group of five men. Since her English wasn't that good, she had to be speaking Russian. No doubt about their nationality, Jim thought, and no doubt about their profession either; they were gangsters, or New Russians, as Katerina had referred to the mobsters.

Another public misconception was that gangsters were like the Krays, thuggish-looking hardmen. However, real gangsters don't spend more than thirty years inside. Real gangsters don't even end up in court. The Krays were morons who got their pictures in newspapers and served more time than child murderers. The real gangsters were the ones earning money and living well while the Krays were inside. Gangsters didn't look dangerous; that was rubbish—bouncers, prizefighters, rottweilers, sharks have to look dangerous; if you look dangerous, that puts people on their guard. Real gangsters were like the best spies were supposed to be: invisible, unmemorable. The real gangster would wait until no one was looking, walk up behind you, bash your brains in with an ice pick while thinking about where he was going to eat lunch. The real gangsters looked like this lot: heartless, dead.

It was raining heavily, so Hugo went off to collect the car while they waited. From the foyer Jim could see Derek hanging around Alzbeta, like a ridiculously overmagnified mosquito. Derek was obviously far stupider than he had guessed. Women were always hard to read with certainty, but there was no way she was sleeping with Derek. Also from the looks Derek was getting from the Russians, if this were Russia he'd already be brown bread. Booze, lust, or an insane notion of sticking up for himself had got the upper hand. Something bad was about to happen, and Jim didn't want to be around when it did. Seventeen. Seventeen. The fights never just exploded; there was always that smell that came first, fistite.

Hugo drove back so fast, Jim should have been terrified, but he couldn't remember how to do that. When he got into the villa, he decided to go for the I-was-so-tired-I-crashed-on-the-sofa routine; he couldn't stomach sleeping in the same room as Derek.

He put his head down on the sofa and . . .

★

He became aware of the light on the ceiling enjoying itself. He was sleepy, but a good sleepy. Then he saw that his T-shirt was covered with a long strand of saliva. Drooling was an interesting new development in his body's campaign to humiliate him. As he moved, and intense pain burst in his neck, a pain informing him that the sofa wasn't so good to sleep on after all, that his neck was severely racked and would be tormenting him for at least the duration of the holiday. So stop moving. Effortlessly, he reacquainted himself with his dreams . . .

. . . an unknowable time later, Hugo playfully kicked him in the stomach.

"Come on, you're on holiday, you should be out and about enjoying yourself."

Hugo had the bounce of a well-shagged man who had spent the night in a sumptuous bed: "I'm going to get some croissants for breakfast." Jim rolled over to chase some more sleep, but the pain in his neck was uncommonly awakening . . .

Then Hugo was shaking him.

"Have you seen Derek or Alzbeta?"

"No?"

"The other car isn't here."

Hugo dashed upstairs.

"Derek isn't in his room."

"Perhaps they're on their way back."

"It's twelve, for Christ's sake. That place closes at four."

"Perhaps Derek got drunk, and they decided to stay in a hotel."

"Look, I know you think I'm tight, but I've got nothing on Derek. You'd have to pay him to get him to buy you a drink. He won't be in a hotel."

Jim tried to work it out while Hugo went to share his panic with Ralph. Ralph came down, still drunk, in a pair of boxer shorts that he must have owned for at least fifteen years.

"No use getting flustered. Whatever's happened has happened," said Ralph, lighting a cigarette; Ralph was incomprehensibly white and hairless for an adult male on holiday in the South of France, and had the remarkable achievement of one body that was both skinny and fat (matchstick limbs meet beer gut). He was right, though, whether they were at it on a beach or recumbent on a morgue slab, there was nothing they could do about it.

It was knotty. If Derek were seriously injured or dead, Jim didn't mind at all. He couldn't be cock-a-hoop about it, but he wouldn't be in the slightest saddened about Derek being dead. Another sign of aging; if he'd been ten years younger, he'd have felt guilty about his lack of concern. Of course, the absence of elation was due largely to Derek's demise now not being much help to him. Derek getting annulled five years ago, three years ago, possibly even two years would have been a real buck-up, but now every git in London had a Web company.

The other impediment to full-scale celebration was Alzbeta; the satisfaction of Derek's demise would be outweighed by anything happening to her. Middle-aged men, who needs 'em? But Alzbeta, how old was she? Twenty-two? You should at least have the chance to be fully disillusioned.

Ralph poured himself a hearty eau-de-vie.

"Derek and Alzbeta both have our phone number here," Hugo said. "Why haven't they phoned if they decided to do something else?"

"Perhaps they didn't want to disturb us," said Ralph. It was plausible, but Jim couldn't help thinking of the narrow, winding roads and metals converging at high speed.

"Jim, you should phone the police," said Hugo. And say what? We seem to have lost a tourist? He could imagine the warmth with which the French police would greet that. Hugo wasn't fooling him, or maybe Hugo wasn't even trying to fool him. Hugo's alarm was not of someone concerned for fellow human beings; it was the flapping of a holiday maker faced with awkward phone calls and bureaucracy, paperwork, a fellatrix too grieving for her friend.

Ralph was scouting for fluff in his navel. Derek was, reputedly, his friend. Was he just cool or a cunt? Or were those two things the same anyway? Jim wondered. Why was it impossible for him to enjoy himself? Outside the sun was blasting away; why couldn't he go for a swim in peace? Christ, what a bunch they were.

"Has anyone checked Alzbeta's room?" Jim asked. Hugo and Ralph glanced at each other in a haven't-you-done-that? way.

Jim walked up. It was one of those moments you don't want to experience. There was always the possibility that Derek and Alzbeta were in there. The car might have broken down or been stolen, Derek might have had too much to drink. They might have come back by taxi. He couldn't imagine Alzbeta going to bed with him, but nothing was certain. If they were in there together, it would be one of the most mortifying moments of his life. If they weren't in there, then it would also be rather unpleasant because it would raise the probability of something nasty having occurred.

He knocked. Silence. He knocked again, loudly. He opened the door, and he saw Alzbeta asleep on top of the bedcover, wearing only black underwear, her skin wonderfully tanned; if the scene had been posed, she couldn't have been more alluring. Was he simply desperate, or was she that irresistible? A strong urge came over him to just mount up. Soaring, he went downstairs.

"Alzbeta's having a lie-in," he said. He was off the hook; if Derek had gone into the worm-food trade, it wasn't his problem. "Time for a swim," he said.

Hugo, confident that Derek's disappearance wouldn't upset Katerina, reached for the yellow pages to look for BMW dealers, sensing that Jim would refuse to phone around for a new aerial for him. Jim took off his trousers and walked to the pool. It had grown, packed with light and dazzling blue; the sunshine was already tightening his skin. The pool was still too small to risk a dive, however, so he lowered himself in.

It was bliss. It was better than anything else, being rich, unlimited sex. The water was cool, but just right; the light frolicked around him; all he could hear was the movements of the water under his arms or slapping against the side of the pool. He could smell the scent from the flowers. Why didn't the whole world come and live here? It was a great conundrum. London was unbearable enough, but when you thought about Hull, Aberdeen, Gothenburg, Bremen, Rotterdam, why the hell did people live there when they could be here, sunshine, the best food and drink known to man, the most beautiful women in the world, and enough foreigners so you wouldn't have to talk to the French too much.

The ten-minute splashing (it took him three strokes to get from one end of the pool to the other) made it all worthwhile. He hadn't had peace like this for years. That was it, really; when you were young you wanted pleasure, but then you discovered the delights of peace, although he could still handle some pleasure.

Back inside, Hugo was still on the phone loudly asking for an aerial.

"We were just discussing regrets, Jim," said Ralph, lighting another cigarette. "Do you think it's best to live your life without any regrets?"

"How the hell do you do that?"

"By doing everything you want, without fear or regard for the consequences. I was thinking, though, that it would be good to have one regret, so you know what it's like. It would be a terrible thing not to have a regret, like being the most successful football player of all time, and never having been on a losing side once."

"I've got a lot more than one. It's too late to have just one."

"A-E-R-I-A-L," enunciated Hugo. "For a radio. Ray-Dee-Oooh. B. M. W."

Derek ambled in; he looked rough, and, more intriguingly, his face was purplish. His white trousers had a dry but uriney stain on them.

"Where the fuck is she?"

The three of them were silenced.

"WHERE THE FUCK IS THAT BITCH?" Derek wasn't angry; he had completely snapped. There were tears in his eyes. Derek loped off upstairs.

Again, years ago, Jim would have had to get involved. He heard Derek shrieking some more, then Alzbeta shrieking back, then Katerina backing up Alzbeta's shrieking, Ralph and Hugo trying to reason them down. He was curious, but he was going to have a shower in the downstairs bathroom. The shrieking went on for a while; then there was a selection of door-slamming. When he came out of the shower, he was feeling awful (he was still, he guessed, a week's sleep short) but able to deal with the day's outrages. Hugo was sitting having a cigarette.

"Thanks for helping," said Hugo.

"I thought everyone knew what to shout."

Hugo grimaced with his cigarette. Jim softened toward Hugo. He was tight. He was arrogant. He was a philistine. He had lots of money. He was thoughtless. But he wasn't rotten. He would sleep with your girlfriend, but only if she really wanted to and he'd make some effort to keep it from you. And he had invited him to stay.

"God, now Alzbeta's upset, and Katerina's upset about Alzbeta's getting upset." Yes, the blowing wouldn't be as extravagant as of yore.

"What happened?" Jim asked, thinking he could give Hugo the pleasure of telling a good story.

Derek and Alzbeta leave the club. Just outside, Alzbeta decides she needs the loo and goes back in, telling Derek she'll meet him at the car. Derek strolls toward the car park, where he encounters the five New Russians, who persuade him to climb into the trunk of their car. They drive off, Derek predictably enjoying scenarios such as being driven to a secluded spot up in the hills and beaten to death.

But they have no such sinister intentions; they drive home but leave Derek in the trunk where after several hours, despite valiant attempts at retention, he has to piss. Later on when the Russians, having slept soundly, want to reclaim their trunk for the use of their cooler, they are outraged by Derek's behavior;

they make him shampoo their trunk for an hour before letting him go, and slam the trunk on three of his fingers, breaking them. Derek, inevitably, held Alzbeta responsible for this.

Alzbeta had come out of the club, gone to the car, waited ten minutes. Then it started raining again. She waits another twenty minutes in the rain. Finally she accepts a lift from an Italian, who happily spends fifty minutes driving her home, despite his living a hundred and sixty kilometers in the other direction.

In addition, Derek had now locked himself in his room, and Alzbeta and Katerina had locked themselves in Alzbeta's room.

"I'm amazed they're both alive," said Jim. He knew if there was one place on Earth he wouldn't hitchhike or accept lifts from strangers, it was the south of France; he remembered reading about hitchhikers being murdered with monotonous regularity on the Côte.

"I guess you have to be careful whom you go on holiday with," Jim said. "Do you want me to phone someone about your aerial?"

"Which beach should we go to?" asked Ralph, reappearing.

Hugo slapped his head in disbelief.

"Hugo, the girls'll have calmed down in an hour. Derek needs some sleep."

The doorbell rang. Ralph, unusually helpful, went to answer it.

"Yes, I thought it was for me." He had a little jiffy envelope. Three envelopes and a lot of masking tape later, he revealed a sachet of creamish powder. He went and got a mirror and a razor and started chopping the powder up and arranging it into lines.

"Gentlemen, it is our duty to fortify ourselves and then to provide comfort and cheer for the womenfolk in the form of a trip to the beach."

"How the hell did you get that?" asked Hugo.

"There are some cultural differences between banking in Great Britain and France." Sniff. "When you phone up a bank in Britain and ask them to send you round some cocaine because you put billions of pounds of business their way, they will say fuck off. When you phone up a bank in France, they send you the stuff by courier from Paris, even if they take two days to do it, the lazy shits"—Ralph took another line up his nose—"and it's a stingy amount, and the stuff is rubbish. I'd offer you some, but it's just not good enough," he said, eliminating the last lines.

"Aren't you worried about becoming a cokehead?" Hugo inquired.

"No danger of that. The secret is to keep moving around. Be a moving target. A bit of sensi here, a snort of gianluca there, some vintage French wines, then some Scotch, a chase of the dragon, a tab of acid, some mushrooms, that way you don't end up being dependent on anything."

"So which bank sent that?" asked Hugo, incredulous.

"Client confidentiality. Have you seen that bottle of Scotch?"

★

Ralph was right. The girls emerged forty minutes later, with their beach gear. The choosing of a beach was a lengthy process. Some were too rocky. Some had poor restaurants. Some had been visited too often. Some would be too crowded. Jim suspected they'd never get out.

"Let's go to Antibes," Hugo said finally. They took both cars, since Hugo wanted to stop off to buy an aerial.

Derek was still sulking in his room. Never mind seventeen; the regression had now reached the age of six. I might want to lock myself in my room, Jim pondered, but I'd be too ashamed to do it. Derek would be going back to a snazzy pad in Little Venice and a thriving business; Jim was going back to some tired suits, dirty underwear, several crumbling paperbacks, a massive bootleg collection. Derek would be greeted by a dozen obsequious employees all trying to outdo themselves in generating more revenue; if Jim were lucky, there would be one anorak waiting for him, who had trouble saying "good morning" to people he had worked with for years. It was depressing unless you forgot about it.

Jim firmly offered to drive. The girls went with Hugo. Ralph had a cigarette in one hand and a bottle of mescal in the other; he was wearing a black string vest of the sort much favored by bodybuilders or backing dancers with no taste, and an LA raiders baseball cap. The tattoo that Jim had been trying to decipher (the handicap was the small diameter of Ralph's bicep) read, "Once you understand I'm God, everything'll be fine," with a death's-head holding a dagger between its teeth in the center.

"The tattoo?" he asked.

"I didn't want it at all. San Francisco. Bet. Ten thousand dollars. I've offered the same guy that I'd cut it off with a knife, but he won't go higher than twenty thousand. For that level of self-mutilation, a hundred thousand's the minimum."

Ralph had another pull on the mescal. "Aren't you supposed to get hallucinations with this stuff? I'm totally wrecked, but my vision's normal."

Jim had been having hallucinations. He realized that last night had been the first time that he hadn't had one for a long while. He'd been regularly waking up in the middle of the night, and seeing in the blackness of his bedroom a blacker silhouette standing at the foot of his bed. His hallucination, in the end, was embarrassingly dull, but it had been frightening at first. The figure had no features, but it was male and seemed to be about to speak. But the presence just stood there, swaying ever so slightly, glowering at him darkly. Jim had learned that shouting fuck got rid of it, so all in all, it was rather soft as hallucinations went.

Ralph's mobile trilled. He listened intently.

"Do you know the most expensive hotel in Saint-Tropez?"

Jim admitted he didn't.

"My backer's flying in. Owns Colorado. But he's Mr. Portfolio himself. A packaging plant in Malaysia. Pizza place in Tehran. A couple of hotels in the Seychelles. Small hospital in Austria. And then he has me stuffing money into all sorts of unusual financial orifices. Anyway, he gets very upset if he discovers he's not staying in the most expensive hotel; he doesn't mind if it's a pigsty, as long as it's the priciest. God, I hate the rich."

When they reached Antibes, the traffic slowed to a crawl. The coastal road was narrow and packed with showy cars. Jim watched a canine threesome on the roadside, a pair of red setters at it, with a collie licking at the peripheries.

"How do you know Derek?" he asked Ralph.

"Through our flying club. I don't know him that well. He's an odd character, Derek. He once bet me a thousand quid that I couldn't land a plane after drinking three bottles of Johnny Walker."

"That's an odd bet."

"Yes; it got very complicated because Derek wouldn't take my word for it that I'd drunk the three bottles. On the other hand, he didn't really want to come up with me to check that I was drinking the bottles, and he didn't want me drinking around the clubhouse, because someone officious might have found out about the bet. So finally, someone else agreed to go up with me, verify the consumption, then parachute out while I landed the plane."

"So how did you get on?"

"I cheated. For a thousand quid I'm not going to bother. For ten thousand I'd have drunk all three bottles. I had the booze watered down, so I only drank a bottle's worth of Scotch."

When they got to the beaches, they spent fifteen minutes finding a place to park, and had to walk for five minutes to get to the beach, which seemed a failure of sorts, but at least they had managed to get some shade for the car.

The beach, a private one, was so full Jim would have left instantly if they hadn't agreed to meet Hugo and the girls there. One false step and you'd be treading on some nymphet's breast. He and Ralph threaded their way through the bodies in a hesitant and unbelonging manner. You always wanted to arrive in a cool way on the beach, because the chief activity was watching, but he knew he was too white to impress anyone there and, besides, Ralph was a great walking tube of chic repellent.

Some spaces were available in front of a pair of arresting Italian buttocks, exceptional even surrounded by the exceptional; they looked more like geometric designs, a landmark rather than part of a body. The proud owner was lying so close to Jim that he could see the very fine blonde hairs on her legs that you normally only notice while kissing a woman's thigh in good light, and he could smell her suntan lotion. She had two small children, who only gave further testimony to the indestructibility of her beauty. Fatigue precluded any desire, but he did consider shaking her hand in congratulation.

Ralph took up residence under a parasol (extra charge). Jim didn't see the point of soldiering through a crowded beach if you weren't going to get some rays, but he didn't care. He was virtually bankrupt, nothing was going right, he had a dodgy left hip (he thought the doctor had been joking when he had suggested a hip replacement), but the sun was shining, and he didn't care, he honestly didn't. The sun carried drowsiness; he wanted some more sleep but was afraid of burning up or doing something distasteful like snoring or drooling amid such magnificence.

Ralph opened up his mobile. "Chad? Really? I'm enjoying myself so much I'll need a holiday to recover. You've heard all about Russian women? I promise you some Polaroids. Okay, a hundred million but no more."

So it was done like that, Jim observed.

"You could do all your business from here," Ralph remarked, extinguishing his mobile. "Set up a laptop in the restaurant there, stuff yourself, go for a swim, rub suntan lotion on pert breasts, sell a little, buy a little. The only reason you couldn't do it would be because all those cunts stuck back in London would be so jealous they'd stab you in the back. One mistake . . ."

"How did you get into the business? Did you study economics?"

"No. I did history of art. I did a Ph.D. on eyelines in Madonna and Child portraits, and the bizarre thing is I'm still interested. Do you want to phone anyone?"

Jim debated it. There was the very very unlikely possibility of good news, and a strong likelihood of no news, which, in effect, would be bad news. The Italian woman slipped a finger into her thong to give her cat a good and loud scratch. If there was bad news, the moping would be extreme. On the other hand, there was something appealing about phoning the office with sand in your toes. He decided to risk it.

The phone rang and rang. He imagined Betty agonizing whether to pick up or not. He hoped the answering machine was on at least.

"Yes?" It was Betty. His greeting was sodden with gray. Londoned. Jim could hear the rain.

"It's Jim." He let that information work in. "How are things?" There was a silence as he realized it was too complicated a question.

"Any news?"

There was a pause as Betty thought not about the news, but how he would phrase his answer.

"No." Betty didn't sound that tense; hadn't he trod hard enough on the motherboard?

"Everything okay?"

Some breathing. "Yes."

"All right, Betty. You're not abusing your position while I'm away, are you?"

Keyboard being tapped. "I wouldn't do that."

He had to ask. "And no news about the proposal?"

"No. It's here. The courier couldn't find the address."

Jim handed the phone back to Ralph. He got up and walked groggily to the toilets. He locked himself into a cubicle and cried as quietly as he could for ten minutes. It was better to let it out.

Ralph was still hiding under the parasol when he returned. "How do you know Hugo? Do you do business with him?" Jim asked to pass the time.

"Christ, no. We met on a skiing holiday a couple of years ago. You were at school with him?"

"Yeah."

Jim studied the prodigiously fat woman opposite him, who had flesh breaking out in every direction (fortunately she wore a commodious swimsuit), and her husband, who looked like a hundred-year-old stick insect. No matter how hard he tried, he couldn't not think about them having sex. She was the worst grade of British tourist, boiled-lobster tint, loud, speaking a handful of French words so badly it made him cringe, and cheap. She was chiding the waiter over the price of Coca-Cola. Yes, it was expensive, so if you don't want to spend money, don't order it. Waiters are rarely responsible for the pricing arrangements. Inconceivably, the couple had three angelic children.

Jim was desperate to order some water, and his sympathy for the waiter guaranteed that he walked right past him without noticing his raised hand or hearing his entreaty.

A revival of pain in his neck reminded him he had to think of a solution to the Derek problem. If he'd been smart, of course, he wouldn't have a Derek problem. He'd have taken Kidd's address in Saint-Tropez; in an emergency like this, he'd have no shame about turning up on the doorstep. What about Derek? With a bit of luck, he'd have huffed himself home. But that would be too convenient. That was an invariable law of party-going; the most unpulling would be the last to leave. The hopeless would never look at their watches at eleven o'clock and say, "Well, everyone here has noticed my total unsuitability for any sort of intimacy, so I'm off home," no, they'd be there till three, four, five, six in the morning until the last cigarette had been stubbed out. And maybe they were right; strange things happened at the end.

It was a pity Derek had survived the boot; it was a pity it hadn't been airtight, or that it hadn't just polished him off. You read these stories about passengers dying of thrombosis on long-haul flights through insufficient legroom. It was disappointing that being cooped up in such a restricted space hadn't done him more damage.

Hugo hovered into view, with Katerina and Alzbeta. "I got an aerial. Do you know how much it cost?"

"Would I win anything if I successfully predict that we'll find out shortly?" asked Ralph.

Jim watched Alzbeta and Katerina break out the towels. Indubitably, women were much more skillful at going to the beach: meticulous, military-like preparation. He gazed out at the blue waves as if he wasn't waiting for Alzbeta and Katerina to take their clothes off. Regrettably, it wasn't a nudist beach, but he'd settle for their breasts. You could spend your whole life looking at breasts, but there'd always be curiosity for one more pair. Katerina took off her top, quite leisurely, exposing a tanned bust, but then put on a bikini top. Alzbeta had her bikini already on under her dress. He had a theory that blondes had better breasts than brunettes, but he was unsure how he could prove this, and even if he succeeded in doing so, what good it would do him.

"I'll get some drinks," said Ralph.

"And get some watermelon," said Hugo. "What's the French for *watermelon*, Jim?"

He was on trial. His French was not as good as it was, it was seized up, but as soon as Hugo asked, he knew the word wasn't drifting slowly to his tongue; no patience could lure it out. Jim knew some preposterous things in French. *Guinea fowl. Knurl. Pumice.* He knew vocabulary in French that didn't exist in English: The name for a stone trough that collects the olive oil in a press. A woman who stirs up water to help crayfish catchers catch crayfish. There were words you knew but wouldn't come. There were words you thought you knew but didn't; but this was a word he knew he didn't know. In all his time in France, in all his discussions and reading, he realized the subject of watermelon had never come up once; it had never appeared on the menu in all the restaurants he had eaten in. Melon, yes, melon was easy, but watermelon . . .

"Can't think of it." The girls looked disappointed. Here on the beach, when he had greatly needed a triumph, operating in his area of expertise, his manhood had taken a knock.

"I'll try *melon d'eau*," said Ralph.

"Isn't it something like *pastèque*?" asked Hugo. Jim immediately suspected him of organizing a linguistic ambush. Ralph went off to the bar, and the girls sauntered down to the water to paddle.

"So are you marrying Katerina?" Jim probed.

"Are you marrying Alzbeta?" Hugo fired back.

He thought it would be a sensitive subject. He hadn't met many of Hugo's girlfriends because most of them had never lasted more than a few months. Was Hugo just invulnerable to the Great Burn, or had it taken place so rapidly that Jim had missed the evidence of it? It was like being seventeen, except they weren't and there was a funny shirking smell that went along with having no serious ties at their age. It wasn't merely about having someone to hand you the chamber pot when you were bedridden and seventy. It was the difference between seeing a film with someone and then reliving it afterward in pleasant conversation, and seeing it with six women sitting in for twenty minutes each: you had company, but you couldn't really discuss the film with any of them.

If Katerina was what she seemed, how could Hugo do better? True, one thing Katerina was not was rich, or even solvent. Not much of a reason not to carry on. She was far and away the most likable of Hugo's girlfriends. For her, Hugo wasn't a bad deal; you could have friends to go to concerts with. And there was always combat anyway; no matter how well you got on, the fireworks would come, disputes over shelf space, shoe polish, throwing out ghastly knickknacks given by the in-laws. Maybe that was the definition of love: someone you couldn't stay angry with for long.

Jim's reverie lighted on Alzbeta's legs as she waded; through his torpor he recognized a familiar stirring. No more thinking, he told himself, let lust do the work. Thinking had brought him to bankruptcy, and occupancy of a shoebox with strange mold on the walls in an unfashionable part of London. Banish thought; let the beast feast.

The girls saw Ralph approaching with the drinks and headed back to their spot. Alzbeta sat down. "Excuse my infinity," she said.

Ralph was having unfeigned difficulty with the tray, which carried two bottles of champagne and a bottle of vodka, each in a cooler, and two beers and three large bottles of mineral water. The cost of the tray, at beach prices, made Jim shudder.

"Why don't we have a drinking game?" said Ralph.

"It's not fair on the girls having to do it in English," said Hugo, with an element of panic in his voice. He was doubtless terrified of being asked to contribute to this purchase.

"Well, we can have a drinking game."

"No, I'm not in the mood. They're so stupid. I am ripple-tipple number six, and none of my dipples are fipples?"

"Point taken. I've got a better idea. Let's each tell a story, and the best storyteller doesn't have to pay his share of the booze."

Hugo examined the labels on the champagne.

"Have you gone mad? Anyway, it's still unfair on Katerina and Alzbeta."

"Katerina and Alzbeta can be the judges. Let's each tell a story on the theme of . . . transgression. Yes, transgression's always good."

"I'm game," said Jim. Even if there was no competition, he'd have to pay; he had literally nothing to lose.

"Tell story, Hugo," Alzbeta urged.

"Yes, Hugo, tell us a story," said Ralph, firing off the champagne cork, which landed between the breasts of an olive-skinned model dozing under a paperback, who fortunately didn't wake up.

"Don't even think about it," Hugo admonished Ralph as he moved off to retrieve the cork. "I can't make up stories."

"Tell us something true."

Hugo rubbed his stubble thoughtfully.

"Oh God. Let me just say before I start, Katerina, Alzbeta, remember who drives you everywhere and who pays for everything.

"You're not going to believe this. I had a drinks party a few months ago, and then the day after I get a call from one of the guests, some guy I hardly know. 'Look, I enjoyed visiting your flat,' he goes, 'I noticed you had a large guest bedroom, and I have some friends staying with me this week, so I was wondering whether the girlfriend and I could come and stay with you for a week or so.' I explained sadly I had some refugees staying with me for a while. The fucker was just so cheap he wouldn't get a hotel for his guests."

"Is that it?" asked Ralph.

"Yeah. It's funny."

"I think you're disqualified and you should pay the whole bill. Do you know what the words *story* and *transgressive* mean?"

"So what's your story?"

Ralph lit a cigarette and poured himself a quadruple vodka. "I have a friend, also a colleague, who had a very unusual hobby. He was keen on defecating in places of worship."

"What?" said Katerina.

"Sorry. He liked to shit in churches."

"Why?"

"Here's the interesting bit. He was a bit overmetaphysical. He was extremely worried about whether God existed or not."

"I don't see the connection," said Hugo.

"That was why he did it. He couldn't see any evidence for the existence of God, so he chose to desecrate places of worship in the hope that something terrible would happen to him, to prove that God existed. I mean, he was radical about it; this wasn't just

71

having a sneaky dump in the nearest Methodist Hall. He went to enormous lengths to wind God up. The Vatican, St. Paul's, the Golden Temple at Amritsar, scenic Buddhist temples in Japan all got his calling card. He even started working his way through American cults to sort of complete the set."

"Wasn't he ever caught?"

"Once in a Quaker ceremony. They just thought he was ill."

"Good guess," Hugo interjected.

"Though the irony is that in a sense it's not transgressive because I doubt if you study any major religion you'll find an injunction against doing that."

"So did anything terrible happen to him?"

"No." Ralph took another drink. "You know, he committed suicide; but he made it clear that the reason he was doing it was because after years of this hobby nothing terrible had happened to him. He'd had promotion after promotion."

"Is sick," said Alzbeta.

"Yes," said Ralph, "and grim. I shouldn't have chosen that one, however transgressive."

"Yes, my story was funny, wouldn't you say so, Katerina?" said Hugo, pouring her another glass of champagne.

"It's Jim's story, now," said Katerina.

"Well," he said, pretending to ponder, "there once was this young man, a great hit with the ladies, who fell hopelessly in love with a woman from New Zealand; unfortunately her father became very ill, and so she had to go home to look after him. The young man quickly realized that he couldn't live without her, so he decided to go out to New Zealand; but he didn't have any money. He had already borrowed too much money from his family and friends, so he couldn't do that again, and since his only employment had been playing bongos, he didn't try for a bank loan. And he wanted the money fast.

"So first of all, he bought a lottery ticket. He didn't win anything, and he began to understand why people had so much trouble winning the lottery. Then he had the idea of a robbery. He had a friend who had a replica pistol and another who had a car. He borrowed both and drove off to the sticks to find a liquor store. No cameras, no one who knows him (he believes he has a reputation for bongo playing). He parks the car out of sight. He has a very distinctive Zapata mustache, but he doesn't mask himself, because no one knows him and he'll be out of the country soon.

"He gets the assistant to empty the till and begins to understand why small, countryside liquor stores aren't often robbed. Then he scoots out to his car. Tries to start the car, but it dies. He doesn't panic; he tries again and again. He knows something about engines, so he looks under the hood. Tries again. By now some minutes have elapsed, and it occurs to him that the assistant might well have phoned the police. Looking down the street, he sees that the assistant has left the shop and is smoking a cigarette watching him. He reviews his situation: with a Zapata mustache and orange combat trousers, he won't get far on foot, and in any case his friend could be traced through the car. So he has another idea.

"He goes back to the assistant and says: 'Look, I was only joking. Here's your thirty quid back, and let's say not more about it, all right?'"

"'I did five years for armed robbery,' says the assistant.

"'Look, I'd love to chat, but I really need to go and see a sick relative. The money's all there, see, you can count it. Let me buy you a drink or something. There's a great choice here, isn't there?'

"'I did five years for armed robbery,' says the assistant.

"'Look, it's not a real gun, it's a replica; nothing to worry about,' he says.

"'I had a replica. I did five years for armed robbery.'

"'I was wondering, can we settle this without the police?'

"'All right,' says the former armed robber, unzipping his fly, 'down you go.'

"And this is the best part: after the settlement, when the novice armed robber wanted to phone for a breakdown service, he discovered the phone had been disconnected due to nonpayment."

Hugo had to explain the punchline to Katerina and Alzbeta, who giggled.

"That's too good to be true," Hugo commented with annoyance. "This whole idea is stupid anyway."

"Yes," said Ralph, "and it's not the sort of story you'd go around telling about yourself."

"Did I say which participant told me that?" said Jim, grateful for Herbie's favorite anecdote.

"Jim's story best," said Katerina.

"Seems we'll have to pay the bill, Hugo."

A stupor of dejection overwhelmed Hugo. Jim surveyed the beach. Was there anyone here really happy? The too-young-to-be-married, the unmarried, the hoping-to-be-married, the married, the no-longer married, the remarried? There was a lot of chatter and bouts of enjoyment; but was anyone happy? The beach, if you paid enough attention, was an amalgam of frictions and sighs; everyone here was working, working desperately hard to be happy. Doped by the sun, the holiday makers were trying to forget bills, betrayals, bereavements, illnesses, and a variety of pocket despairs. He admired their heroism; the families, the singles, the hawkers, the waiters: they were all battling. He wanted them to succeed. If agents of the all-powerful were to come up to him, press a gun in his ear, and say, "Jim, if we shoot you now, it will guarantee happiness for everyone here," he would readily trade in his life to have the others flourish, because it would be that treasure he had been searching for all his life: something worthwhile. To be the gloom broom.

"Hang on, I've got a better story," Hugo suddenly re-animated.

"No you haven't, Hugo. Your stories are crap."

"No, I should have thought of this earlier. I had a colleague who liked to go on naturist holidays. Right before a big presentation, he went on holiday to Cap d' Agde in one of these nude villages. He was there for two weeks; he drank a lot, and there was an eat-all-you-want deal so he pigged out. And he thought about traveling back the evening before his presentation, but he said to himself: I've been working like a dog all year. I'll travel back tomorrow; there's a dawn flight, and even if it's delayed I'll get back in time for the afternoon presentation. You know how it is when you have to travel a lot for work, you don't want to get to the airport any earlier than you need to; so he had the taxi waiting outside, he packs his bag, goes to put on his suit, but he can't get into his trousers; we're not talking about them being tight or hard to do up. He can't even get a leg in. He also has a kinky habit of not wearing underwear, because it makes him feel like a dangerous revolutionary at meetings. He's been in the buff all the holiday, and he doesn't even have any swimming trunks. So it's five-thirty in the morning, and he's got nothing to wear on his nether regions. Looks at the taxi driver who's half his size, so no hope of offering to buy his trousers. He hammers on a few doors of fat people he got to know, and offers a thousand quid for a pair of trousers. No go. All too small. Asks taxi driver if he knows any really fat people; they drive around to a cousin of the taxi driver's wife, who does, to his relief, have a pair of trousers the right size. Off they shoot to the airport, where there's been an accident and traffic's solid. He leaves his bag and runs the last mile to the airport, in time to see his plane take off. Never mind, there's another flight three hours later, but it's fully booked. All the flights that morning are fully booked. He offers people staggering sums of money, but they're all going to visit relatives on their deathbeds. He has to take a taxi to Paris, where he gets a flight, and arrives two hours after the presentation, and is fired."

"You obviously don't know what *transgressive* means," Ralph said.

"He missed the presentation."

"He didn't miss it deliberately; he wanted to be there, Hugo. Alzbeta," cooed Ralph, "I just want you to know I am still fully available, body and soul, threesomes, bondage, whippings, not a problem."

"Here is nothing new," said Alzbeta.

Alzbeta got up and went to the water; she lay down on a jetty, in what was almost a magazine pose, toying with her tresses. Jim waited a minute and then advanced to lay some chat on her. He needed a bed. They appreciated the waves in silence for a few minutes.

"Why did you talk to those men last night?" he asked.

"I not talk to them. They talk to me."

"How did they know you were Russian?"

"I am Russian girl. I look like Russian girl. I say to Derek, these are bad men. I say, these are bad men. One goes. Derek sits in chair. He returns; he tell Derek go. Derek say not."

A small boy and his small friend ran incessantly up and down the jetty, spraying them with water from their limbs and hair, and then splashing them when they bombed into the water, bumping into Jim, in addition, nearly every jump. Their lack of awareness was astonishing. For the pleasure of punching the boy in the face, Jim realized he would trade fun with Alzbeta; he'd only need to do it once, and he consoled himself with the knowledge it was only because you couldn't do it that it was so appealing. A couple of times he said, "Careful!" to the boy, who didn't even hear him.

"No self-awareness," he said.

"What?" said Alzbeta.

"Self-awareness. He doesn't understand what's going on around him . . . doesn't know what he's doing."

They chatted for a while, discussing Russian films. ("Russian films best in the world. But you must see them with me. I explain for you," said Alzbeta.) Jim expressed his admiration for Alzbeta's legs. Feeling he had delivered the right amount of praise, he went off to the loo. There was a shower, and he wanted to freshen up, but the diver was no longer diving; now he was in the shower. Jim waited. He looked at his watch. The diver had been in there for at least eight minutes, fiddling with every bit of his body, even giving the inside of his eyelids a rinse; he had to be the cleanest ten-year-old in France. Two others were waiting behind Jim. The boy then started rinsing out his trunks in the same lethargic but methodical style with which he had washed. A tectonic rage was surfacing in Jim, and he beat a retreat. He still had too much London in him; the boy was annoying but not that annoying.

He got back to find Alzbeta using Ralph's mobile and blowing kisses into it.

"Alzbeta's just been phoning her boyfriend," said Hugo. Ralph drained the last drops of the champagne. The girls had had one glass each, Hugo a couple; the rest had disappeared into the sands of Ralph's thirst. Ralph now seized the vodka bottle between his feet and, lying on his back, attempted to pour a shot into his mouth, with scant success. "Nothing like a little yoga."

It was embarrassing, but Jim was pleased that Hugo was showing signs of being really put out.

"It's amazing what people will tell you after a few drinks," said Ralph, speaking in the very deep, slow, portentous voice of advanced drunkenness. "Another good drinking game is asking people to tell you their deepest darkest secret, because it's astonishing how many people will. Well, Americans mostly."

"What is your darkest secret, Ralph?" asked Katerina.

"My dark secret is that I don't have one. It's very dull; everyone should have some disgrace in their past."

"Wait. Wait. I've got it," said Hugo, "I've got a great story. I can't believe I'd forgotten this."

"For God's sake, Hugo, I'll pay the tab," said Ralph.

"No. This is great. You're going to love this. Friend of mine goes to a club, and he's on the dance floor, and these Swedish girls come up and start dancing next to him; so he has the classic problem: are these Swedish girls dancing next to him, or are they just dancing?"

"How does he know they're Swedish? Did they have their passports stapled on their breasts?" inquired Ralph.

"Because he got talking to them."

"But he couldn't have known when they danced up; the classic problem is surely two blondes dancing up next to you."

"Look, the Swedes aren't important."

"Then why did you mention them?"

"So he finds out that the women weren't particularly interested in him, but of course, like every man, he has to buy them lots of expensive drinks. Then he has a few more to drown his disappointment. He's staggering out of the club, legless, when this huge Merc pulls up; it's some cowboy cab driver, hunting for customers. He thinks his luck is in and he hops in, and the guy starts driving him home at about a hundred miles an hour. Anyway, he's almost out cold, but it does occur to him that it's odd that a

Saturday night cowboy should be driving such a brand-new top-of-the-line model, as there are only about ten of them in the whole country; he knows because he's just bought one. He has a chat with the driver, and they both agree that it's a terrific car. Then he notices that the driver has chosen the same sound system for his car. He also thinks it's interesting that the driver is reading *War and Peace*, marked at about the same page he's got to. Finally, he notices that the car is in fact his, left outside a friend's house the previous night because he'd been legless again.

"What should he do? My friend isn't very large, he can hardly stand up, and the driver's burly, criminal-looking, and very aggressive. At the speed they're going at, he knows they'll be home in a minute or two. He remembers his mobile, but on further reflection, he realizes that if the police appear, there'd be a chase, with him in the back, and probably a crash, or if the driver lost the police, something unpleasant for him.

"He gets home, gives the guy a tenner, because the driver says he hasn't got any change.

"'You look tired,' he says. 'It must be miserable working Saturday night. Why don't you come in for a drink?' He thinks if he lures him into the house, he can call the police and have him carted away, car safe.

"'What's this about?' asks the driver. 'Do you want to fuck my arse?'

"'Of course not . . .'

"'Forget it then.' And that was the last he ever saw of his car."

"Car happy in Russia," says Katerina.

"You wouldn't have let him get away with it, would you, Hugo?" remarked Ralph.

"I'd have strangled him. Mind you, my friend wasn't too upset; he said at least he'd had a chance to say good-bye to the car. That's a good story, isn't it, girls?"

"I said I'd pay, Hugo."

"But that was the best story, right, girls?"

"I've got . . . one better," said Ralph. "I've got the ultimate . . . going on holiday with your mates crashing full-speed . . . head-on with full-on transgression . . . and no seat belts in a fucked-up style." Jim wondered if they should put Ralph in the recovery position.

"A friend of mine who shall have to remain nameless for reasons that will become obvious . . ."

"We want the name," said Katerina.

"All right. Fuck him. Anton. Anton hires a yacht to go island-hopping in the Aegean one summer. He has a girlfriend, and another couple want to come. But the yacht has three state-rooms. Anton asks around, but he can't find another couple. All he can get is someone else whom, the truth be told, he doesn't like much, but Anton being a bit of a Hugo . . ."

Hugo shook his head at the injustice.

"Anton wants a third contributor, and so they set sail. And for two days all is well. Then the third day out, they all have a little drinkie . . . and Anton and his chum decided to debag the late-comer, whom I'll call . . . Ginger; they all think it's hilarious . . . and as he's now paid for his share of the holiday, they don't mind his protests one little bit."

Ralph lit a cigarette.

"Ginger's a redhead and has been out of the sun most of the time and has this great white arse. . . . So they think it would be funny to tie him to the deck, leave him in the sun for an hour or two, and let his arse burn to a cinder. . . . They do that then. . . . Then tired by their exertions and the excessive mirth, they go down below for a little siesta and a bit of how's your father, despite Ginger's impassioned cries. Some hours later, Anton goes into the galley for a drink, where his ship-mate is also having a . . . postcoital beverage. 'How's Ginger?'

asks Anton. 'I don't know, I thought you untied him.' 'I thought you untied him.' 'He's gone quiet, so he must be all right.' They go up on deck and find that Ginger's not only quiet . . . he's dead."

"You can't die from sunburn," insisted Hugo.

"That's what they kept on saying . . . 'He can't be dead!' as they soused him with water and pounded his chest. But you know . . . the flies were already buzzing around."

"Let's do to Derek," said Alzbeta.

"They were all shocked, the girls especially. . . . After the blame had been passed round and round like port, they had the problem of what to do next. Ginger had, as you can imagine, struggled hard to get free . . . so beaucoup lacerations even the dimmest of coroners would have noticed; otherwise culpability could have gone to . . . booze and sun. They fear retribution. Their nice lives in the mincer. Well, after . . . heated debate, forgive the pun . . ."

"What is pun?" asked Alzbeta.

". . . the body goes overboard at night, and then next morning, there's a visit to a police post, where . . . surprise surprise, they are unexcited by another boozy tourist going missing. The body's found a couple of weeks later . . . when the sea's washed away the truth.

"Anton told me how . . . *amusing* . . . that was the word he used, it was at the memorial service that the priest went on about how at least the deceased had passed on in good company . . . and how the mother thanked him . . . for staying on for another week to help with the search."

"He told you it was amusing. Why the hell would anyone say that?" asked Hugo.

"Because it was amusing for him. Everything depends on . . . the sort of person you are."

"So nothing happened to them?"

"One of the girls committed suicide. Anton became vice president of . . . a bank."

"Which bank?" asked Hugo.

"The bank will have to remain nameless."

"Why?"

"Because you can't keep your mouth shut."

"Then why did you tell us about it?"

"I don't know, really . . . to warn you have to be very careful who you go on holiday with. I mean . . . we almost lost poor Derek."

"But why did he tell you?" asked Jim.

"Let's put it this way . . . Anton . . . enjoyed it . . . he enjoyed that taste of the . . . forbidden. If he'd lost his job and . . . done some bird, he would have blubbered like a five-year-old, but he got away with it and so he . . . discovered he was invincible."

"A lot of your friends commit suicide," said Hugo.

"No. I have a very large circle . . . of acquaintances, Hugo. Many people do. You know, I think I might have to phone a French banker."

"I fancy some food," said Hugo.

Jim hadn't been hungry; the sun and his weariness had stubbed out his appetite. But it was forty minutes before they got a menu, and although all of them apart from Hugo ordered salad, it was another half an hour before the food was served, though not Hugo's mussels. They discussed Russia's collapse.

"I don't know why people talk about economies collapsing. Economies don't collapse; they never do," said Ralph. "Economies may make citizens extremely miserable; the old, the poor, the weak may starve or freeze to death, everyone else might have to fight like animals over bones, some bankers and businessmen might jump out of windows, but the mess moves on."

"In Russia you can be with girl for all night for five hundred dollars," said Alzbeta.

"Five hundred dollars?" said Hugo. "That's not that cheap. That's almost the same price as London. I mean, I'm told that's the price."

"It depends," reflected Ralph. "What exactly all night is . . . midnight till six, or nine til nine. And perhaps the Russian girls throw in some of the really perverted stuff . . . like kissing."

Just then Hugo's mussels arrived. "Thank God," he said, shoveling a forkful of mussels into his mouth. Joy left his face. "Cold." He peered around for the waitress, who had swiftly vanished. "You're fussing over nothing," said Jim, trying one. The mussel wasn't even lukewarm; it was as if the plate had been in a fridge.

Ten minutes later, Hugo managed to catch the waitress, who looked at him as if he was asking the most unreasonable thing ever asked, while he explained about the mussels being cold. She carried them away as if she were obliged to porter them to the top of Everest without oxygen.

"This Bandol's being watered down, or they swopped the label. This stuff is just too disgusting to be Bandol," said Ralph, food suddenly having renewed his discrimination. His pager went, and he had to field another call from someone called Cedric.

"You make money?" asked Alzbeta.

"You make it . . . you lose it. No one really knows anything. The best deal I ever made was after a long lunch; the battery in my mobile had gone dead. I got back to discover shit city; I was so wrecked, I had to crawl to the phone. I was on the verge of losing everything, so I gambled, without thinking, without research, without consultation. Biggest earner I ever had. Professionals don't know everything; they hardly know anything. It's like poker or any form of gambling, if you know the odds and you're sensible, you can make a living, and when you're dealing with enormous sums of money, the living can be good, but no one knows anything."

"Speak for yourself," said Hugo. "I don't get it right, I'm out. I almost stuck a million into Barings. If I'd done that, I would have been out on my ear."

"Yes, I remember you telling me that you didn't want to give them any business because one of them had tried it on with your girlfriend. No," said Ralph, "if there's anyone who *knows* anything about the market, then he's not working in the city; he's not working anywhere; he's out in the wide blue yonder on a yacht with a year's supply of supermodels."

The mussels reappeared. Hugo tried one and then let out a sigh. "Dry." Ralph leaned over and plucked one. He immediately spat the bivalve out; it cruised sedately through a German family at the next table. "That's not dry; it's inedible."

"Manners," said Katerina.

"Sorry," said Ralph, "I went to a terrible school. When I tell you that half my classmates there shagged Princess Diana, it'll give you some idea of what a dump it was."

Several minutes later, Hugo managed to flag down the waitress again.

"The mussels are dry," he said. He was going for the pained, rather than the incandescent, complaint. It was mildly tragic, being on the beach, on holiday, hungry, and paying a lot of money for . . . a lunch you couldn't eat. The waitress glared at the mussels resentfully.

"Crise de moules," shouted Ralph, waving his arms helpfully to illustrate the gravity of the situation. "Les moules sont inedibles. Fucked. What's the French for *Maastricht*? The moules sont totalement Maastricht." Then he made gagging noises with his hands around his throat and fell off his chair.

Jim explained in French, twice, that the mussels were dry. But the waitress stood blankly. Jim was sorry for both Hugo and the waitress. They seemed to be in a situation that couldn't be resolved satisfactorily. Everyone looked at the mussels that condemned them both to misery. The waitress walked off. Hugo was proposing that they walk off without paying, when a man whose smugness indicated he was the boss came over. In smooth English he asked, "What's the problem?"

"Vous êtes rip-off artistes of the first kidney," said Ralph. "On me rip. Translate, Jim."

Jim explained in French that, regrettably, the mussels were dry.

"But we've changed them," said the boss in English.

Jim explained in French that the first lot of mussels had been cold; this lot was dry.

"They're dry," said Ralph, popping another mollusk into his mouth and spitting it a remarkable distance for one so indisputably unathletic. "See?" Jim decided that if anyone was going to hit Ralph, he wouldn't attempt to protect him. He was Hugo's contact.

"I see," Englished the boss. "So you would like us to change them for you?"

Jim said in French that would be very nice.

"Okay," said the owner, giving them one last look as if he were confirming something.

"Do you have any Bulgarian red?" Ralph shouted after him. Another twenty minutes went by, and the mussels reappeared. The steam was highly visible.

"Well?" asked Jim.

"Too hot," said Hugo, putting down his fork.

"I'm going to go for a drink," said Ralph. "Do you want to come, Jim?"

"Why not?" A walk might wake him up.

"Don't rush," said Hugo. "I haven't even asked for the bill yet."

They strolled off the beach, up to the road. Ralph's consumption was inhuman, Jim reflected, and he couldn't understand why dedicated drinkers liked to go to different bars. If you wanted to get paralytic, why bother with intermissions and wandering around?

There was no bar in sight.

"Let's go this way," said Ralph. "Alzbeta doesn't have a boyfriend, you know. She was talking to her son."

Son. That made sense. That toughness. He should have guessed. All mothers had that killer glint.

"Do you know anything about the father?"

"Some deadbeat. Usual story. Left her in the lurch."

After a few minutes, around the bend, they spotted a café. But as they approached, from behind the counter, the proprietor clocked them through the glass frontage and was standing in the doorway before they reached it, supported by the cook, who was conspicuously holding a carving knife.

"We know you. You will go away." The English was quite good.

Ralph was perplexed.

"Couldn't I come in and behave disgracefully before you bar me?"

"We know you."

"No, you don't. I've never been here before."

"We know you. You are ignorant and evil."

"Hey, you can accuse me of all sorts of things: skiing badly, of being overly fond of conceptual art, smoking too much. But you can't accuse me of being ignorant; I earn two hundred thousand a year, and I've shagged lots of famous actresses."

"Go."

"Liz Hurley—doggy style," said Ralph, making the motions. "I'm not joking."

"Go."

Jim took Ralph's arm. The cook, he could see, was itching to do it. They meandered back to the beach.

★

The police were arresting Derek when they arrived back at the villa. He had gone out to do some shopping and had lost his key. Not knowing when they were getting back and grumpy, he had broken a window to get in and then had been locked in battle with the burglar alarm that he had conscientiously primed before setting out and which didn't want to accept the disarm code. Derek's French wasn't any good.

Jim wouldn't have shared a room with Derek, but now he was really frightened about being in the house with him. His hatred of Derek had concealed from him that Derek was profoundly unpleasant and as twisted as the strands of a rope. Sniper-in-the-clocktower strength. Disappearing-twelve-year-old-girl level. A rage was leaning out of Derek that wasn't the whole-some anger of a healthy person; it was deeply unsettling. He could see the others had the same disquiet and distaste. Compassion only stretches so far. As Derek's official contact with the outside world, Ralph made some forays into conversation but acted relieved or at least unconcerned when Derek just sulked. The booming membership of Derek's hater club was something Jim wanted to revel in, but he was too exhausted. Gloating was a long way beyond him.

The girls went into the kitchen to get supper under way. It was an arrangement he couldn't argue with. In the hallway Jim saw

Alzbeta's polka-dot bikini top hung up over his leather jacket on the coat stand. The two articles of clothing lay comfortably next to teach other in a show of intimacy. Was it an omen?

He didn't know what to do; well, he did. The pain in his neck was so great he could hardly turn his head—the sofa was nothing but an ingeniously disguised instrument of torture. As he bumped into an armchair for the second time (he no longer had the capability of navigating a room successfully), he chanted to himself: you must seduce Alzbeta.

His investigative eulogy of Alzbeta's legs hadn't produced any identifiable encouragement from her. His praise had been sincere; she did probably have the best legs on the beach; bizarrely, although his record with women was something to avoid questioning about, the wild girls liked him. The women who looked vicissitude in the eye, the women who could crack walnuts with their pussies, the women who hitched alone in the South of France—they saw something in him. He wished he knew what it was. He had often come close to asking that question but hadn't, worried that asking it would reveal that he didn't know what it was he supposedly had, and that the reason he didn't know what it was he had was because he didn't—in fact—have it.

What he truly cared about was a long sleep in a large, comfortable, freshly sheeted bed, but he wasn't going to get that.

"Why don't we have a drinking game?" asked Ralph, who, astonishingly, was close to sober.

"Because we aren't alcoholics, Ralph," snapped Hugo, emptying the ashtrays.

Jim could tell Hugo was thinking about his office; only another five days and he'd be back in the saddle, pushing figures around, skipping lunch through overwork or enduring three-coursers with dreary Japanese suits, who, given a fortnight's preparation, couldn't succeed in concocting something amusing to say, trudging home having just enough energy to wash and climb into bed, doing your week's shopping on the weekend. Jim would be back there first, however, without the Japanese probably, certainly without the money, definitely with the grimness.

Money, in the end, was the great opiate, a provider at least of insulation. Jim imagined Hugo retired, eating in good restaurants, grouchy at poor service, with good doctors at hand, checking the interest rates on his savings each morning, hunting around for bargains in the wine racks, dabbling very modestly in cultured investments, art or antiques so he'd have something to talk about at parties. If he were still alive in thirty years, Jim knew he'd be hunched in some bookie's trying to rustle up some good luck, reading newspapers in public libraries to save cash and stay warm. There was such blackness ahead, he opted for the childish, ostrichy trick of pretending it wasn't there.

Why didn't they have an orgy in the swimming pool? That might make everything seem worthwhile.

As his contribution to the proceedings, Jim carried the knives and forks out to the table set up in the garden and made sure there was the correct number of chairs. Derek had wordlessly started cooking in the kitchen, ostensibly to annoy the girls. Katerina, Alzbeta, and he danced around each other with undisguised ill-humor, as he boiled some eggs and created some sort of curry sauce. They then watched Derek unfold a picnic table a short distance from them and install his own cutlery selection and napkin before sitting down to eat, his back to them, gazing languidly at the flora before him as if he were completely alone.

They started with fresh prawns with mayonnaise from a tube and then had succulent calves' livers with slivers of crisp bacon and a bewitching rocket salad, while Derek munched away at his breakaway table.

It was good to see that no one regretted Derek's defection in the least, and it was also good to see that Alzbeta was knocking back beer after beer; while every man wants to wrest a woman from her clothing by the application of his charm, nevertheless Jim couldn't but approve of the intercession of that old ally in matchmaking; the beers couldn't be making him any uglier. Made brash by the sublimity of the evening and the delicious food, Jim was entertaining himself choosing which position he would choose to make love to Alzbeta because he forecast that he would barely have the push for one round, when he swallowed a morsel of bacon. For one instant he detected the flake of bacon in his throat balanced between its natural course and an unnatural one.

To encourage compliance, he could have swallowed some water, but he waited to let the bacon settle, and it came down the wrong side. He tried to breathe, but he couldn't. He was definitely choking.

He saw Ralph, resoused, the girls laughing. He now had the knowledge that the best thing that could happen to him was to be ridiculous: that he would raucously cough up masticated bacon into Alzbeta's face or flail around imbecilically. And the worst was death. Fear gate-crashed unhelpfully.

The others were all accelerating away. He was so blocked he couldn't even make proper choking sounds. Alzbeta noticed his distress: "Jim, are you good?" He shook his head and got up to make a dash for survival. He was not making feeble wheezing sounds, but air was only on the way out; nothing was coming in. Hugo was thinking, Jim could tell, so that's what someone choking to death looks like.

Darkness was impinging on his vision, and their voices were too distant for words to reach him.

He was vaguely aware of a pair of arms coming around him and a sudden jolt as he was lifted up, as if he were back in the school playground. The morsel of bacon returned innocuously into Jim's mouth, unimportant mush no longer the blocker of his future, and he breathed in air, with an appreciation he had rarely experienced before.

He was also aware of Derek returning to his table and continuing to eat his curried eggs.

In addition to being tired, failed, and desperate, he had now attained contemptibility; he gasped a little more and wiped away tears. He was unable to look at the girls for some time and resigned himself to a night on the sofa. Although the bacon was a mishap that could happen to the most experienced of mercenaries or bare-knuckle fighters, he was bombarded by shame, and a blanket of unmasculinity was draped over his shoulders.

He drank his beer quietly, while the girls chatted in Russian and Hugo and Ralph discussed the markets, all of them doing overtime to make him feel unself-conscious. As Jim rebuilt his aplomb, he realized the fracas in his windpipe didn't count; the absurdity of it all suddenly came home to him: they were all going to die anyway. Hugo, Ralph, him, Katerina, Alzbeta, Alzbeta's son; no one was going to get away. The hitman had already been hired; camouflaged as a disregarded red light, faulty wiring, caramelized animal fat. The fact that he wanted to be desirable and he had just been burped like an oversized infant by the man he most hated didn't matter. Having the notion that your life was worthy of attention was an easy mistake to make. Was this enlightenment he was undergoing or a taste of insanity? Suddenly, he knew that he was going to sleep with Alzbeta, regardless of how much hunkiness he was giving off or failing to give off or how much beer she had guzzled, because it didn't matter to him anymore if he didn't. Personality and all its luggage had been left behind.

He noticed that Ralph was monitoring Alzbeta's consumption of beer with the eye of the incorrigible male, pondering that conjunction of the early morning and heavy drinking. Alzbeta put the empty bottles on the ground next to her, insisting it was bad luck to keep them on the table.

Ralph didn't have a hope. She's going to sleep with me, Jim reasoned, not only on account of my indifference but because I'm bigger than her. Ralph was a good two inches shorter than Alzbeta; women had little tolerance for men they could look down on; the women had to be very lonely, or the short men very famous when it came to big women–short men unions.

Women were better than men. They were flustered by small difficulties, like runs in stockings, heavy suitcases, or Irish drunks on public transport, and Jim had been called in to lay down the law to mice or spiders on several occasions; but with the big uglinesses they were laudably calm; when it came to misery, pain, slow death, they were the unflinching troopers.

Ralph, Hugo, and Katerina disappeared back into the kitchen with the dirty plates, where they instigated an argument about how a blender worked. Derek had strolled off to the bottom of the garden, drawn by the thickening darkness. Alzbeta swigged another bottle of beer. She gave him the invitation.

"In England, women must make first move?"

"Not always," he said, reaching out and kneading her right earlobe. That touch was enough to spin him. He wasn't so dislocated from all this after all.

He stroked her hair. You could just lose yourself in the preliminaries.

"Shall we go upstairs?"

Hugo stared at them as they went up, with a Christ-that-was-quick gape on his face. He obviously believed Jim's adroitness had fixed it.

Jim took a moment to admire the bed; it was wonderful. Wide-open sheets. A mattress gagging for it. Why were they doing this? What did she want? A passage to England? A father for her child? Easing of loneliness? A one-nighter? His speculations vanished as she took off her top. She switched off the light.

"Do you have self-everness, Jim?" she asked.

He kissed her; her tongue was small and flickering. Not exciting.

Alzbeta raised her legs so he could peel off her underwear; there was always something about the last piece of clothing; both invigorating and anticlimactic. After that last textile surrender, it was all so familiar: the tussling and the pounding, and sooner or later, the fuming and the crying. His attitude appalled him. Why did he have this rain cloud in his skull?

"Bite me," Alzbeta said. He did. "Bite me harder," she demanded. So he did. Her eyes lost their pupils. "Harder!" He did reluctantly, fearing he was drawing blood. This did nothing for him; he could have been gnawing an armchair.

The window was open; a wire mesh had been fitted to keep out insects. Directly below the room he could hear Hugo talking with Katerina: "They just went upstairs."

He couldn't postpone the act any longer. He guided her on to all fours and slapped away with a rhythm that could have been mistaken for passion. The century he lived in had pandered this match, millions had died to get the history right to provide this smooth woman under him. He struggled to be grateful and overpowered. For a few minutes more he pushed; then he discovered he didn't want to do this anymore, couldn't do it anymore.

He liked Alzbeta, but he didn't love her and he knew he never would; he was afraid he would never love anyone again. He slid off her like a raindrop, wondering how vexed she would be.

The truth was awful; that's why you had religion, romantic novels, football. You never saw the truth displayed anywhere:

you're alone, and you always will be no matter what you do. Why didn't you see that on billboards? Because if you knew that, you knew there was no benefit in telling anyone. Keep your mouth shut.

Jim wanted to hide in sleep. Alzbeta had other plans.

"This is more better."

A curtain of hair descended to his loins. Her mouth captured his cock, and she really went to work. Perhaps, he hoped, she's just being polite; but Alzbeta carried on pistonlike, rousing his suspicions. This wasn't right. Women didn't do this. You wanted them to, but they didn't. Not this ruthlessly. Alzbeta managed to get her whole body weight into it.

It was typical that he had a young, attractive woman enthusiastically moving a mile of mouth on his cock, when he didn't want one. Wasn't she going to get tired? Bored? Her head banged away, her breathing was controlled, her posture relaxed, her focus perfect—she wasn't getting tired. She wasn't getting bored. She was waiting for him. Jim realized that with a performance like this, it was going to be downright rude not to offer a fluid bravo. Sadly, it was as exciting as watching it happen to someone else; no, it was nowhere near that exciting. It wasn't exciting at all. It was mildly pleasant, like being in warm water. The bed was more seductive, alas, than Alzbeta; despite her dedication, he detected the encroachment of sleep. He reached into the drawer of fantasy, glad that no one would ever find out what he took as a booster in his effort to shoot.

Alzbeta dutifully attended the last spurt and then sprinted to the bathroom, where her gargling fought it out with the spluttering of the tap, and then the wavering wail that came from Katerina in the garden.

It was a wail that no one wants to hear, a wail every person, every animal understands: when life is pressing far, far too hard.

Portrait of the Artist as a Foaming Deathmonger

Your first murder deserves consideration for a long time. I didn't give it any consideration, but then not everyone can be lucky enough to have my talent, and the method you choose says a lot about you. My first victim died of a blow to the head from that suitcase of words that is the *Larousse Gastronomique*, strangulation by her own tights, a stabbing from a Sabatier carving knife, and the snipping of her parachute rip cords immediately before she went over the tailgate.

A bomb can be extremely effective and can get you right up there on the scoreboard; but that requires expertise and access to materials that can't be found in a corner shop. Do you really know anything about that? Don't fall for this nonsense about throwing a match onto a pile of fertilizer. Unless you've had professional training, it's a tough one to pull off. Besides which bombs almost always have an air of pretension about them, as well as being mechanical, impersonal, and usually signal tedious political hang-ups. The best sort of killing is intimate; you ought to feel that last breath on your cheek. That's why guns don't really work either; they're much harder to get hold of than you'd imagine, whatever the newspapers say. And even if you're shooting close enough to put powder burns on your target, you can't get over the detachment involved. You don't want to be lumped in with soldiers and Whitman, plods only in it for the pay.

No, your genuine ghostbreeder does it for satisfaction and uses the two hands, as artists have always used them. Mr. Dexterity from Dexterityshire, that's me.

Remember, you only get a first murder once. Don't mess up.

There are so many things to sort out. Do you want to know the victim or not? How will you get access? What are you going to do with the body? Do you want to get caught or not? Or will you do the whole thing *vers libre,* damning reflection and seeing how it pans out?

Let's be honest here, because honesty is the only substance that should be found in the bloodways of an artist. Bumping off the missus, your boss, your father, the newspaper boy puts you in touch with nature, but it also strongly suggests that you are only going to put up with so much shit from fellow members of the community. That's the problem; we can all think of good reasons for reaching for the homicide.

To step up the honesty to genius strength: deluxe killing is one-way. Men doing women (or, naturally, men doing men who are serving as women) for fun. It is akin to the difference between going down to the pub and killing someone who spills your pint (unlikely anyone will spill your pint again) and killing someone who was minding his own business (you will really get noticed next time you go down to the pub). Offing for offing's sake. Admittedly, there have been some impressive practitioners on the other team: black widows cashing in dozens of insurance policies or those toxic tyrantesses who hemlock their way to a throne. But the gratuity isn't there. When you strangle a beautiful woman with an item of her expensive lingerie (don't miss that irony), you're saying, it doesn't matter, I can easily get another one, even if you keep a few body parts in the fridge to make some jewelry out of them or for postmortem whoopee. This is finally about going down, and putting a woman six foot under is the ultimate prostration.

It's your choice, but you have to live with it.

And then there's the question of when does a bit of snuffing get upgraded to serial killing? Kill one person and people won't pay much attention; a piece of steak out of the fridge too long, a child's roller skate, a wasp's sting could do the same; any accident, flash-in-the-pan can do that job. Killing two, well, that could be a fluke. But three, three is the Cain club. Any more than that, however, and you have got to be careful; otherwise you'll be taken for a rock 'n' roller, a real goer like the Wests, Gacy, Bundy, Dahmer.

I had to take care of my girlfriend because she was getting turkeyed elsewhere. What! you cry, after this lecture, a bog-standard *crime passionnel*? You're boring the tits off us. No, this is advanced stuff (notice how clever I am). Frankness comes in several strengths. How much ham does a sandwich need to be a ham sandwich? And just because something looks like a ham sandwich doesn't mean it is. When I confess to being the cause of her death, I do it in a way that ushers in a doubt. Did I just wig out after a bad-hair day, or was it a good ghostbreeding opportunity in circumstances I knew would get me a few years off if it got to court?

The same suspicion applies to my bumping off her partner in turkeying. Was I really that *passionnel,* or was I in the mood for fun? And when the pizza-delivery boy turned up and got shredded, that's when it gets almost impossible to believe I simply couldn't help myself.

I'd do your killing in the provinces so that when you get to London, it will be assumed your activities weren't properly reported.

I've always been pro-excitement and anti-dinge. Breeding outs. Happiness was a great concern of my mother's, and anti-dullness was her trade. If I inherited anything from my father, I don't know (and I don't care), but anyway I wouldn't have needed it. I got it all from my mother, especially the patience. She would wait for up to four months before we would pack up and move somewhere new to look for happiness. From the age of eleven to sixteen, I had thirty-two different art teachers, and I made sure I produced bad work for all of them. I didn't want any of them encouraging me and then taking credit for my eventual triumph.

From the moment my mother gave me some crayons, nothing else was on my mind but being an artist. For a long time I thought my name, John Smith, would be a hindrance. I was young and foolish. It should be your art that makes your name colorful, not the other way around. Nevertheless, there is enormous discrimination around. You only have to look at the record; despite our numbers, there has never been a prime minister called Smith. The ranks of great artists have no Smiths. Did they choose a Smith to walk on the moon? Where are those Nobel statuettes on Smith mantelpieces? Only one conclusion can be drawn from this: there is a well-organized conspiracy to keep Smiths from success. Look at the London telephone directory. Twenty pages of Smiths. But when your enemies line up in opposition to you, you should thank them, sincerely and lengthily, because they're helping to make your imminent victory all the more splendid as you hack through their assorted limbs.

Instead of getting into the rat race at school and filling my head with all sorts of knowledge surplus to being an artist, however, I spent my time thinking up a new name. I knew I was too young to produce great work (an artist should always have his eyes wide open), so this was how I started to prepare my legend. I have always been anti-rush and pro-reflection. So my waking hours were occupied with concocting an appropriate name for a world-explaining artist: Ron Astronomy, Woof Mercedes, the Incredible Conceiving Machine, Bingo Shamed, Glands and Hands, Er Dario, Sammy the Seal, Phil Lonely, Yann Vonk, Hoo-Haa in Gondar, and hundreds of others not as good, before I settled on Johnny Genius, which I felt showed respect to my roots and put across the important element of what I had to offer, but wouldn't be difficult for art students to spell when they wrote essays about my work.

Everyone knows that artists like Michelangelo, Picasso, Renoir, Dürer only really cracked it because of their names; but having invested thousands of genius-hours in the genesis of a name I could be proud of, I almost instantly realized that, brilliant though it was, it was wrong. You can only be yourself (eyes wide open), and I realized it was anti-courage to try and side-step the Smith prejudice. In any case, I had other names offered.

Oi Tosser. Gerbil-sucker. Cunt. Poof. Turbo-moron. Jhat. Dumbo. Beginner. Pauper. Wanker. Batty-boy. Sicko. Stinkhead. Dingleberry. Nutter. Bell-end. Gumby-boy. Motherfucker. Arsehole. Creep. Neo-ponce. Learner. Boombo-klaat. Turd. Stick-insect. Cocksucker. Sheepshagger. Killjoy. Pervert. Spaz. Idiot. Prick. Big Prick. Shirt-lifter. Fuckwit. Childmolester. Failurist. Antichrist. Shit. Dick-head. These are just a random sample of the things I have been called because I am an artist and a Smith. But it's perfectly natural for people to view you with contempt, to disparage your appearance, to lean out of their car windows and spit at you. When they undo their seat belts, get out of their cars, rummage in their boots, and then run toward you with a no.5 iron (or possibly a no.6—eyes wide open), this is confirmation that your apprenticeship is going well. When petrol is poured through your letterbox and there are shouts of "we've cut your phone line," these are good signs. The world is full of world deprecators.

But you do make mistakes. Everyone does. Nothing wrong with mistakes; the important thing is to stop making them and to no longer be a mistakist.

Though spotting the mistakes is much harder than you might first surmise. Sometimes the mistakes lurk under successes, like mouse-doings under a carpet, or coagulations under a coaster. Sometimes the successes are snoozing under sprawling failures, pearls hidden under those great glops of congealed snot popularly referred to as oysters.

I believe it is vital for an artist to stay in touch with the community and to see as much of life as possible; the ivory tower is an anti-healthy iron maiden. And I knew how important it was to avoid those evisceration zones that are supposed to be art colleges. That's why I became a freelance driving instructor; my own master and no bonds. You are out and about all day, and living in a car makes you streetwise (not to mention avoiding the incessant fuss of packing and unpacking your sundries); the Queen's highway was my way.

Some might find the absence of privacy disconcerting, the public having the privilege of a window on your every waking and sleeping moment, but I uphold the principle that the artist's every breath should be subject to examination; I am anti-mystification and pro-exhibition.

But this was also to give some color to my biography, as well as to give time for the Project, laying the table as it were for the great blowout of Western culture, unveiling myself as the Savior and Dispatcher of Art and the Showist of Many Everythings.

Painting in the car limits the size of your canvas, but I was fortunate in that my natural bent was the two-by-two-foot.

Finding a parking space, a costless parking space; that's not easy in London. Whole years of my still-youthful life have been spent either driving around to clients or just looking for a berth. But that's the luck of the macadam; and there's nothing like a good traffic jam for getting the juices going. A motionless motorway is better than any office or studio for doing serious work. Putting London under your wheels teaches you so much about human nature. And it's important for the artist to be independent; you should have access to crispy wonga without the twisting hand of patronage. As soon as you start thinking about selling or pleasing, you are thinking about the market and not about art. No. Art first, and inevitably the wheelbarrows dripping with precious stones and wads of high-denomination notes of respectable currencies are brought on.

There was a freedom in those years of prefame, a freedom from hassle and interviews. Love the obscurity, my young friends, because you may stumble round and fall without anyone noticing. I worked hard, and I experimented. While I could never avoid dropping some brio into my work, some pieces had more inspiration stuffing than others. Nevertheless, I stoutly skirted around the camps of art, the galleries, the clubs, the colleges, the museums, the postcard shops, because I didn't want my genius contaminated by the *E coli* of mediocrity from others' leftovers.

Some of my early highlights I would point out for special mention are: *Portrait of the Artist, one minute before being attacked by a householder irate at having his driveway blocked, wielding an arty lamp he doesn't want anymore* and my fumescape of Baron's Court, *This Carbon Monoxide Is Mine,*

This Carbon Monoxide Is Yours. Or on a more tender note, *Bored Hauler Drilling Earhole.*

But after tinkering around, you find your forte. Pictorially, I maintain that dogs have had a raw deal. The anti-canine prejudice of the present scene is wrong, and it is in this area that I have made my greatest contribution, in the cycle of paintings that begins with my portrait of a plucky Scottish terrier with deep brown soulful eyes, tongue panting, under the statue of Eros, titled *Lost in London* (a masterful mix of emotion and social comment, if I say so myself, and the brushwork on the collar alone would make Dürer burst into tears). There is the brutal impact of my depiction of a charming Yorkshire terrier staring up with deep brown soulful eyes, *Will You Be My Friend?* And moving up the canine scale, there is the bittersweet pride of the three-legged rottweiler in Hyde Park, viewed from the rear, *Monarch of All He Surveys with His Deep Brown Soulful Eyes.* Then there is the wonderful counterpoint of two deep brown soulful-eyed bloodhounds joined together by the natural sausage they were simultaneously sharing, *Pals,* the slobbering flews the most cogent statement of self-wealth I've ever seen an artist achieve. The lurchers, the pugs, the Afghan hounds, the setters, the beagles, the chihuahuas, the corgis, the Saint Bernards, the poodles all leading up to the cheeky deep brown soulful eye of the boxer, colluding with the viewer, as he takes a tinkle on a sentry box complete with guardsman outside Buckingham Palace, *Walkies.* A miniature universe and a lexicon of the far-reaching solely on his left hind paw. Close study is especially recommended.

No one knows exactly when painting began, twenty or thirty thousand years ago; please feel free to choose. But I can tell you exactly when the history of painting finished. At nine minutes past nine on the ninth of September, 1999. That was when I put the finishing touches to what I knew would be my final painting and the world's final painting. After this, my greatest painting, no more could be added. I had exhausted the world pictorially and pigmentally. (I deliberately chose a date that would be easy for future students of the fine arts to memorize; really, I had pretty much finished on the eighth, but I saved a few brush strokes for the following day and the sake of epochal neatness.)

Now I am not naive. I knew that even mind-exploding talent the likes of which the world had too rarely seen would not be enough on its own. I knew sooner or later my genius would have to be guided to exposure, the finest fruit needs a grocer, so once my ouevre was well fattened, I began to scout out the camps of the art-pushers, going in disguise. Posing as a simple, happy-go-lucky driving instructor, I sat in the Goat Tavern and the other pubs around Cork Street, clutching my copy of *Auto-Trader*, pretending not to know the word *art*, capering on the chatter around me, gleaning some field marshals of information. Unobtrusively, in quiet libraries, when no one was looking I flicked through magazines and books to discover who were the wedgelords, the massively overweight gorillas, the bridge builders of the business who could get me smoothly and effortlessly to a public and a fitting glory (the shipping and the paperwork).

It's not very likely you'll have heard of Renfrew. He doesn't need the public to know about him. Some people need to be well-known to have wealth and power, celebrities of the weathergirl ilk, the face vendors, the drivel drivers, the vacuity shepherds, whatever words you want to use, who try to sham events for the uneventfularians; and there are those who have a fortune through fortune who like to lick the cameras; but Renfrew doesn't need to be journalized to have wealth and power and is content to be known to only a few thousand people. His address book (while doubtless larger than mine) has only two categories: artists (very rich) and the willing buyers of art for centipede-like figures (incomprehensibly rich).

Not all the stories about Renfrew are frightening. Some are very frightening. The most eloquent testimony is the silence his name evokes. No one wants to say anything that might get back to him, because no matter how complimentary you think you are, he might come and kneecap you anyway. One art critic, who described Renfrew in print as the master dealer of a generation and a culture maker, found himself shorn of his career. Renfrew is the massively overweight gorillas' massively overweight gorilla, although rather thin.

You keep hearing the same things again and again. No pleasantries. No puffing. No negotiation. The hostages are shot immediately. He names a price, and the only thing you can say is here is the check. Any meandering, any comment on the weather (which might or might not look like a prelude to a haggle), any attempt to slow down payment, and the line goes dead. And it's no use phoning back a minute later with a higher bid; you'll find yourself in an endless stream of short conversations with his secretary for the rest of your life.

The stories. The stories. He has nothing to do with people. He never meets them. He never shakes hands with anyone. His staff have to take an elaborate course of vitamins every morning and are all immunized for so many diseases, commonplace and esoteric, that they could eat dung with impunity in the most unhygienic rubbish heap in any country. When his secretary needs a document signed, she holds it up against the glass partition in Renfrew's office; he okays it from his half, where he sits amid complicated and expensive air filtration systems, and then issues, from its niche, the rubber stamp carrying his signature. Outside of his purified enclave, the story is he wears a biological warfare suit.

I wondered how best to draw Renfrew's attention to my brilliance, and I decided that there could be no better introduction to me than me, so I opted for full-frontal exposure.

I had considered some clever introduction or gimmick, but I eventually rejected such subterfuges and plotting as beneath my dignity. So, destiny perched on my shoulder like a parrot ready to do the talking, I walked into Renfrew's gallery.

I recognized him instantly. Over six feet, the ash-gray suit (his Savile Row tailor never gets a fitting but simply has to send the suit—always ash-gray—back again and again till it's right), and the gaunt features (only grilled organic vegetables pass his lips). He was supervising a hanging at the back of the gallery quite openly, without any biological warfare suit, and I realized what rubbish gets generated about the influential.

Nevertheless, catching him in the open, I knew, was a rarity and was surely a clear indication of how history was rolling up its sleeves on my behalf.

"Mr. Renfrew, I am pleased to tell you this is the most important day of your career certainly, and probably of your life. Before you thank me for choosing you, let me explain what I have to offer you—"

Renfrew said nothing, but a meze of horror, distaste, annoyance, and even fear surfaced on his pale features just under his left eyebrow, which he raised, a meze that even I would have trouble replicating on a canvas.

You wouldn't expect a gallery to have security. I certainly didn't. Not security in the hackneyed form of beefy boxer-nosed heavies who silently and swiftly appeared from nowhere. Perhaps other transgressors, pensioners on a day-trip prodding a canvas, young women thoughtlessly ignoring the no-smoking injunction, received a firm but kindly admonishment.

I didn't. I found my feet an inch or two above the ground as I was whisked to the door by the two smartly dressed bruisers, each the size of a small crowd. Wounded by their anti-Smith comportment, and admiring the cut of their suits (eyes wide open), I said nothing as they frog-marched me down the road to a nearby trolley bin, which they opened and threw me into. One of them then searched around for a bag of smelly garbage to sprinkle over me, to overemphasize the message. (This needless multiple underlining is typical of a nonartist; if your message is clear, it needs no repetition.)

Rather than being seriously disheartened, I was impressed that the summits of art were so well monitored and guarded. Besides which, as an artist one should never be shy of experience, and I doubt there are many people working in the origination trade who have been headfirst in a trolley bin; it's more interesting than you'd think, and I knew it would make a golden moment for my biographers. Renfrew and I would laugh about it in the future, I had no doubt, although Renfrew's laugh would always be a little nervous. Generosity overflows in the heart of the true artist; I resolved to shake hands with his goons when Renfrew put on my show, *Man's Best Friend*.

However, as I struggled out of the bin, I realized I knew one of them. His almond-shaped head (eyes wide open) was the one I had admired as a whippersnapper because of its unique shape. I don't remember many people from school (I can hardly remember the schools, let alone my fellow pupils), apart from some of the more anti-artistic types: Fred East, who attacked me with a lawn mower, or Gander Mahoney, who, if it hadn't been for his poor coordination and lack of experience with the javelin, might have deprived the world of me.

"Peter, is that you?"

"Eh?"

"Peter, it's me. John. Johnny Genius. We were together at Thamesmead Comp."

He looked at me for a moment.

"To be honest, mate, you're a complete blank. But since we were at school . . ." He reached into his pocket and fitted a metal loop with a serrated edge onto his fist. It would have certainly hurt me a lot if this blow hadn't completely knocked me out.

But this was a necessary initiation; how would it look if I took over the art world without getting beaten up? You must always think of your biographers, and a few weeks of struggle were a small price to pay. I also had to admit that Renfrew must be the victim of endless pestering by untalented no-hopers, and he deserved some sympathy for that.

What I had to do was simply get my art to Renfrew because then everything would fall in to place. I decided that standing by the entrance to his gallery would work. He'd get out of the car, see my remarkably brilliant painting, and the history of art would be changed forever. In fact, the morning I was standing there, it was Pete who got out of the car, and as far as I could tell, art history wasn't affected at all; he made me eat a corner of my canvas at knifepoint, before taking me a few minutes' walk away to find a plate-glass window he could throw me through.

So I tailed Renfrew home to his sumptuous mansion in Highgate. Under cover of darkness, in the early hours of the morning, I carefully erected a small exhibition of my paintings outside his kitchen window so that in the dawn's sleepy light (far from ideal) as he breakfasted he could see the future and the end of daubing. Renfrew must have been aware of some modification in his garden because I saw Pete advancing toward me with a small tree that he'd procured from somewhere with a total disregard for the environment. I knew it was time to depart. For a large and tubby man, Pete was capable of an acceleration that would have done credit to a sports car, and despite the considerable amounts of adrenaline going into the old ticker as a result of my previous encounters with Pete, he would have easily caught me had he not fallen into a hole.

He had fallen through the turf trapdoor made by an artist who was hiding in the hole underneath, working on a performance piece titled *Two Weeks in an Art Dealer's Garden*, involving an unusual mixture of theory and survival tactics that required him to live in Renfrew's garden with no supplies and to record his experiences. What a saddo. Weakened by a diet of raindrops, daffodil petals, beetles, a peanut he had mugged a squirrel for, and some stale bread left out for the tits, the concealed conceptualist was no match for the enraged Pete, who, unconvinced of the gravity of the conceptualist's artistic mission, broke three of his ribs, ironically providing what was, by common consent, the highlight of the piece and a great deal of publicity through the subsequent legal action.

Thinking that I should not be afraid of being conventional, I put two of my paintings in the mail, but obviously Renfrew didn't get them or didn't see them since he failed to call me on my pager.

Naturally, I didn't give up, although I was beginning to think my biographers would have their work cut out. I've always been anti–giving up. There's more than one gallery on Cork Street, I said to myself, and more than one street in London, and more than London in our fair land. I thought my work would be a marvelous opportunity for a lesser or a provincial gallery to close the gap on Renfrew, but oddly they persistently refused to understand that.

I finally came to see the price I had to pay for my originality, and to acknowledge that centuries of oppression of Smiths wouldn't be so easily shifted. But I conceded that I, too, had been guilty of pro–conventional thinking; you must avoid the Acceptance. The Acceptance is that art is for galleries or other recognized public pictureries. Waiting one evening for my prawn bhuna take-out in that bastion of tandoori supremacy the Dawn of the Raj with a crowd of others, I recognized that this was a place where my art could be exhibited and win a public along with the Bombay mix, or in that time-honored tradition I could exchange one of my paintings for a lifetime's supply of curry and a side order of bindi bhaji.

But I had more lessons to learn about the extent of my originality and the Acceptance that take-out restaurants are there to provide people with take-out and not the launching of civilization-altering art; there was one very sticky moment involving a nasty-looking chopstick in a Chinese restaurant on the Holloway Road. But the greater your originality, the harder the Acceptance is; it's like trying to push your nose through an oak door (not that, to be honest, I've ever tried).

You have to see things as they are (eyes wide open). Unfortunately, I could see I was years ahead of my time and that all I could do was to leave the summation of painting in a lockup in Willesden and wait for the world to catch up with me.

But I'm not one to sit on my laurels; I began to look for a new medium to conquer, and it only took me forty-five minutes to create a whole new art form. I was sitting having a drink in the Marquis of Granby, when, as the place was packed, a couple came and sat at my table. I couldn't help overhearing their conversation: they were recently married, and the husband had just been posted to Plovdiv, Bulgaria, for a year. They weren't happy about it.

"You'll love it," I chipped in, not knowing why.

"You've been there?"

"I lived there for two years," I replied, or rather a reply was issued in my voice. It wasn't me that started spouting about my time working as a water purification expert in the Bulgarian countryside. It was Big Thought doing a number through me. I enthused about the warmth of the Bulgarians, the quality of the cooking, the beauty of the scenery. I taught them a useful phrase in Bulgarian, a greeting that can only be used at eleven o'clock in the morning (ideally during the final tolling of the church bell) that was considered the most beautiful and courteous expression in the whole language, so much so that people would travel the length of the country simply to be in a position to utter it to someone they held in particular esteem, and its enunciation could reduce grown men of no known sensitivity to tears. I even gave them the addresses of two friends who, I assured them, spoke flawless English and who would be happy to show them around.

Naturally, the closest I had got to Bulgaria was once picking up a bottle of Bulgarian red in a liquor store and then putting it back on the shelf. All I knew about the place was it was somewhere near Africa.

But because I had been on duty (eyes wide open), Big Thought had put me on to an exciting new form of art, which I have dubbed: the grabby. Of course, a layman or someone without the necessary degree of sophistication and discernment might mistake the grabby for a lie. A grabby isn't a porky; it's personalized fabulation, a bespoke tale. There's a world of difference between the flat denials or artless misdirections that make up the vast proportion of falsehoods ("everything's fine" or "I'll bring it back straightaway"), or sitting in a pub and claiming to be a fighter pilot or trying to sell blockheads several acres of swampland or a brick on the Costa del Sol, and what I do. It's the difference between the surgeon's scalpel and the heavy's switchblade (I am the surgeon's scalpel).

My brisk assurances had completely changed that couple's outlook. My tale of Bulgarian water purification had given them the elevation a work of art should produce, got them air-borne. Over-the-moonity for the community. Perhaps this grabby will come to a swift end in Bulgaria, but it could just as easily last a lifetime and accompany that couple to their final resting place. No work of art can cheat time forever.

And they bought me a pint. There has to be payment for art. That's how you know it's art. That's time-based life for you.

The night after the invention of the grabby, I was in the Slug and Lettuce when a woman began sniveling to me about her aunt's breast cancer. I explained that I was a cutlery designer, but that two of my aunts had had breast cancer, that they had been successfully treated fifteen years ago and were now full of beans, one an incorrigible marathon runner and the other a keen tennis player who had recently thrashed the doctor who had originally misdiagnosed her 6–love. My audience left smiling. So it went on:

IDENTITY	THEME	FEE
Cutlery designer	Breast cancer's a breeze	Bottle of Corona
Snake farmer	Tax evasion	Drambuie, pint of Fosters
Theologian	Dating agencies are in	Dry white wine, Planters honey-roast peanuts
Jockey-trainer	Sixty is the prime of life	Half a pint of cider
Cricket commentator	Fostering children is ace	Mineral water (sparkling), pork scratchings
Model railway journalist	Unemployment can be licked	No drink, half a mint

IDENTITY	THEME	FEE
Ballet dancer	Bastards *are* punished	Bottle of Rolling Rock
Gay burger scientist	You are beautiful, not fat	Had to buy her a Campari
Snake farmer	Your runaway son isn't dead, just run away	Pint of Greene King IPA
Model railway journalist	Life isn't shit	Pint of Guinness

So the grabby was in business. I was getting the attention, if not the wonga, that was my due. I was nursing a pint in the Goat Tavern, wondering how I could boost the grabby so I could have the means to get moated up in a rural idyll, when Big Thought checked in again. A Loudly snatched a stool from the table I was at.

"Put that back," said my voice, while I was only halfway through the thought that permission should be asked before even an unneeded item of furniture is removed; my voice used an impatient tone one should reserve for those much smaller and weaker than oneself.

"Or what?" asked the Loudly, as we both considered the evidence that he was not only willing but able to beat me up very, very badly. While I make no secret of being pro-fitness, my genetics have provided me with a small body, and my dedication to art has unfortunately equipped me with barely visible muscles.

"I am an artist, and I require that stool," my voice commanded.

"Or what?"

"I'll wring your neck." I must say I was surprised by this development. It was clearly a brazen impossibility; even if the Loudly had been bound and gagged and I had been incited into a state of total anti-Loudly fury, the best I could have managed would have been a firm ticking-off. Once, provoked beyond measure by a hulking bluebottle, I had boffed it with a rolled-up newspaper, but that had only made the buzzing worse. I still think with regret of several ants I stood on unwittingly in a sandpit in Margate when I was eleven.

But you should trust those dark recesses. Oh, those dark recesses!

"Why didn't you say so?" said the Loudly, replacing the stool. This just goes to show that merely because it looks obvious that something will happen, doesn't mean it will: sometimes you jump out the window and float. I have always been anti-cowardice and pro-bravery, but I have always found these policies inadequate in coping with individuals larger than me, the same size as me, or smaller than me when they have taken a shine to subjecting me to physical readjustment.

Shortly afterward, when the Loudly left, he pointed me out and said: "Watch him; he's a killer. A stone-cold killer."

Then someone walked over to me and asked me if I'd like a drink. The summary for the following week's grabbies is as follows:

IDENTITY	THEME	FEE
Serial killer	Killing people is easy (like swatting flies)	Three pints of Carlsberg, two G and Ts, Chivas Regal, spice poppadoms, chicken moglai, basmati rice, plum ice cream, filter coffee

IDENTITY	THEME	FEE
Serial killer	Killing people is difficult (overturned furniture, etc.)	Four bottles of Stella Artois, four shots of honey-flavored vodka, two packets of salt and vinegar crisps, pack of Benson & Hedges
Serial killer	How victims beg for mercy	Five bottles of Pils, two Famous Grouse, spinach fritters in a salsa sauce, lemon sole, pommes frites, tartare sauce, half bottle of oak-seasoned New Zealand chardonnay (excellent); autographed volume of poetry; invitation to a skiing holiday in Cloisters
Serial killer	Mortal remains and drains	Five bottles of Grolsch, three margaritas, bottle of R de Ruinart champagne (Paris en bouteille), smoked rainbow trout fillets with homemade horseradish, lollo rosso and radicchio salad, cutlets of marcassin on a bed of glazed turnips and vegetable macedoine, bottle of Blagny '89, terrine of two chocolates, glass of Sauternes, one Cohiba, one eighteen-year-old *Glenmorangie,* one cashmere scarf, one jazz cigarette

IDENTITY	THEME	FEE
		(Northern Lights), one line of charlie, one director's showreel on VHS-cassette, one polaroid photo of girl with telephone number scribbled on back

Even when you have a great grabby, you have to finesse it slightly to make it interesting for yourself as well as to bolas the attention of your audience. When I told my listeners that I had just got out that morning, you could see them tossing around ideas like: Should he really be back on the streets? Is this another boo-boo by the shrinks? Another easy-peasy probation board going overboard on human reformability with a fiasco in the making? Once you've been out for a while, there's a sporting chance you've got a grip on your unfortunate weaknesses and that you're not going to blot your copybook again, but when you grabby you have to balance the freshness of release from the penal system against your growing recognition. Once you and your grabby become better known, you have to drop "I got out this morning" to the vaguer "I just got out" to avoid being found out.

But there isn't too much speculation as to why you're not behind bars, rubber or otherwise. As we all know, murder these days hardly interferes with your liberty. And the good thing about hitting thirty is that it's not difficult to persuade people you've been away for ten years.

I spend most of my evenings in the Chelsea Arts Club now. On the right-hand side as you walk in, there's a snug with a couple of pro-rest armchairs and a bookshelf. I've read many of the books because I spent a lot of time there in my pre-grabby days (once I had decided to reveal my paintings) in order to sample the company of fellow artists. As my artistic mettle had been formed, I thought perhaps I was making a mistake in not seeing what the others were up to. So I would sit in the bar and address fellow drinkers: "I am a great artist. Are you one too?"

It was a slow and painful discovery that whether he seeks company or shuns it, the artist is chiefly alone on that yomp to glory.

LINE	SAMPLE RESPONSES
I am a great artist.	Good for you. I'm talking with my friend. Could you lend me twenty quid, then? Oh. I have to catch a train in ten minutes.
Do you want to discuss art?	Not really. I'm meeting a friend. Someone's sitting there. That's a dangerous question. There's 20 percent off my installations this month.

But those days of rampant anti-Smith prejudice are gone.

A fascinated circle was around me one evening as I was saying: "The most important thing is that I've forgiven myself, so that I can enjoy life to the full. You can't bring back the dead, and even if you could, think of all the legal problems to do with housing and ownership and parking . . ."

Suddenly I was aware that everyone's attention, which had been my toy, had been taken. My audience had switched allegiance to a tall, ash-gray suited figure. It was Renfrew. A hand was extended toward me. I took it, before it disappeared in a flash, leaving me with the impression of a snared animal bolting from the gin.

"Mr. Smith, I hear you paint. Is it permissible to inquire about the state of your representation?"

Fifty Uselessnesses

Both guns drawn slickly, the Kid spun them for several revolutions and then reholstered them without ever taking his eyes off his imaginary adversary. The coordination remained, and he could still do it fast (although he had to be slowing down).

He also knew something was wrong. The wrongness was breathing down his neck, but he couldn't tell what sort of wrong it was or if there was anything he could do about it.

Taking out his tobacco pouch, he rolled a cigarette and tried to locate where things had gone wrong.

He had a lot of time to think. Many years had been spent thinking, and he didn't really have anything to show for it.

The end of his career had been like that. For weeks before, he had powerful wafts of wrongness. For months, in fact, but he hadn't been able to recognize it as going off the rails.

He hadn't decided to give up his job. He could have just resigned, but no—he had to get himself fired, perhaps so he'd have someone else to blame if he regretted it later. His reluctance to chuck it all might have had something to do with the way he'd got the job. Comprehending it was high time for a proper job (suit, decent money, pension), he'd seen the advertisement for a vacancy in the town planning department, gone to the library, looked up town planning courses, and had then concocted a fictitious CV and lied his head off at the interviews. Unhampered by any knowledge and effortlessly recounting jokes, he had walked it.

He wasn't found out because although the job had been well paid, there was nothing to do. You went to meetings where jokes were welcome, and you drove about getting to know lampposts. A self-respecting town needs a town planning department, but the truth is towns plan themselves. Perhaps his easy con didn't permit him any respect for his colleagues, or five years of boredom simply got to him.

A mug of tea had started the trouble. He had a short drive to get to work, but with the heavy traffic it took upwards of half an hour. He had trouble waking up; the only way he could leave his bed was to fall off and drop onto the cold, hard floor, which gave him enough impetus to get to the bathroom. He had honed his routine so that he would arrive not on time, but three or four minutes late, so that no one could really complain but he would get more bed. He would gulp down some tea, stuff some toast into his mouth, and run to his car clutching his tie and then spend time in the jams getting to hate the familiar faces.

One morning he was so late he took his mug of tea into the car to drink on the way in. After six weeks he was strolling down to the car in his bathrobe, shaving, dressing, and making breakfast in the car. People stared at him, but he didn't care, and it was only later he realized how dangerous an attitude that was. He reached the point where he was arriving after lunch in full cowboy kit and twirling his six-guns in meetings before his behavior incurred any rebuke.

The first four months of unemployment were the hardest; after that you settled down and didn't mind too much. Like drowning, he supposed; you splash and thrash, but then the distress passes and you go with it. Anyway, by then getting dressed and washing have become work. He hadn't had much in the way of jobs before, and he certainly never had anything capable of being called employment after. Yet he wouldn't pretend that the end of his marriage had anything to do with him hanging up the suit and tie; his marriage had been on its own timer. He and his wife had sat in different parts of the house, hardly managing a row, like animals of different species stuck in the same cage by a thoughtless keeper. However, when she said good-bye for the last time, he wasn't that surprised to find himself sobbing.

Where had he taken the wrong turn? Or where had he missed the turn? As a young man he had never replied to the question "What do you want to do?" with the answer: "I see myself sitting around a lot, in an almost empty house, on a really worn sofa, like one the fire brigade would set alight for training; in short, a failure, but a failure who's not even worth talking about. No huge collapsed schemes; just a failure who rarely gets past the front door."

That was the only good thing about not having any money; it helped you to be tidy. His lounge contained one small television (that a burglar would turn his nose up at) on a pedestal of telephone directories, the sofa, a dead cactus, a rusting wok he was unsure of saving, his pearl-handled guns, and a copy of *Famous Indian Chiefs I Have Known* by O. O. Howard. He had sold, lent, or given away nearly everything in the last decade. He would have sold the guns if he could have got a half decent offer.

He looked out of the window at the sky, a great gray veto. He also saw Spring next door, helping another car to rust by taking it apart and scattering it around the car graveyard his garden had become. Spring paused in his junking to burrow into his left nostril with a black nail.

He was always getting that. Outside Birmingham, he had been on a train when, on another track, he was treated to a quick vision, as the trains pulled away, of Margaret Thatcher in a first-class compartment, getting an iron finger into the iron nose. As a lad on his great American trip, in a small bar at Phoenix airport, he had seen John Lennon drinking a Coke and excavating, which had crushed all thoughts of an autograph. To top it all, he had spotted George Best in a no-name pub near Oldham, musing over a pint in a discreet snug, thinking of what might have been and getting digital. This strange gift of catching celebrities in nasal clearance had been given to him, but he hadn't been able to profit from it.

And of course he had the fast draw, but that hadn't got him very far either. His activity as a gunslinger had got him as far as an invitation back to his old school to talk about the lore of the West.

The mantelpiece still carried a picture of them. Togged up: the Bramhall Bunch (Bramhall District Frontier History Recreation Society), all four of them. There had been others hanging around, but the core of the Bramhall Bunch had been him, Baz, Airhead, and Wojtek. They had done the fairs, old people's homes, one supermarket opening, local television.

The Wild West had fascinated him from childhood. He had hoarded every scrap of information about it. If you wanted to know exactly where Doc Holliday was standing at the shoot-out at the OK Corral, or what was Jesse James's favorite tipple, the number of gunfights in Oklahoma in 1870—he was your man.

It had taken years to work out why it attracted him (and others) so much, but as he grew up he saw it was a world where problems could be identified (they wore black hats) and solved. Problem in sight, you didn't call the police, write to your MP, or consult a lawyer; you strapped on your iron and got sorting. That was the drawback with life: nothing ever got sorted out.

Regretting how much the frame had cost, he put the photo back. He was the last of the Bramhall Bunch.

Baz ("Jolly Rancher") had gone south of the border. Baz's passion for the Wild West, he had long suspected, was only a mask for a desire to dodge his wife and kids. "The lads are counting on me," he would say to his protesting spouse, portraying himself as chauffeur, though he hardly ever did the driving because he was too drunk.

Getting away from wife and kids was something Baz worked at. He also ran marathons. "It's for charity, luv, and the lads are counting on me." His wife believed him to be going down the pub when he bounded out of the house in his track-suit and trainers, and trailed him in the car repeatedly. It seemed preposterous because he had a beer-gut the size of a twelve-year-old—but Baz could run a marathon in under four hours even in the full Dodge City issue—that was how badly he wanted to escape his dependents.

Charity and the marathon teamed up nicely when Baz did a runner to Marbella with three hundred and forty quid for disadvantaged children. It wasn't a haul that made running worthwhile, merely possible.

Baz had opened a bar ("The Red Devil") with a gorgeous young bit of fluff who must have been into the older, fatter, monolingual man kick, but who eventually turned into a wife with two kids. Early on, they had all been sent one snapshot of Baz, grinning chemically, wearing his "Born in the North, live in the North, die in the North" T-shirt, clutching a pint of unidentified beer and the sultry señorita.

The story was that Baz wanted to come back but was fearful of the child support. He had to be in the shit, otherwise they would have heard from him; he didn't care about staying in touch, but he had always believed that smugness should be shared around.

Baz was a Manc who would have to come back. Baz would be pining for the warm beer and the cold rain. The Kid doubted if he ever would miss Manchester that much given a sunny, affluent alternative. That was the irony; he had hardly ever left Manchester, but he really wanted to get out.

Naturally, he had tried to escape. When he was nineteen, he had gone out to the States to walk in Doc Holliday's steps and to find a way of staying. He had discovered that (in Arizona at least) there were two sorts of jobs: ones where you need qualifications and a green card—which went to Americans; and jobs where you didn't need qualifications or a green card—which went to Mexicans who would work for amounts of money so small you had to laugh.

Desperate, he met Pat, a man with boundless optimism and a trailer full of a thousand battery-powered toy tanks. So he and a black guy called Steve (who was hitching his way to LA for a hula-hoop championship) spent three days going into every shop in Phoenix trying to sell the tanks.

Not trying to persuade the shops to stock the tanks, but to sell them to the sales staff . . . Pat had a theory that people who worked in shops didn't have enough time to shop and were secretly dying to buy battery-powered tanks, and that it was vital that the Kid should have an assistant to demonstrate the amazingness of the tanks while he did the sell.

At the end he was left with a profound respect for the courtesy and tolerance of Americans; or maybe if you worked at a perfume counter, or in a travel agent's waiting to lure people to the Bahamas, you didn't expect someone to walk in and offer you a tank. He was also left with a complete stock of tanks, though after a debilitating afternoon chatting with a bored sixteen-year-old left in charge of a florist's, he had come close to a sale.

Pat was too experimental a businessman to make money, but he was kind enough to stand them a meal after the rout. It was the best meal he ever ate; the food was dross: powdered mashed potatoes, a rigid lamb chop in flaps of gravy, mushy string beans that tasted as if they had been in cowboys' boots for a week; this in a run-down diner that had a wall missing. But he hadn't eaten anything for two days, apart from a stale doughnut at the florist's. His plate had been cleared to cleanness and then stared at wistfully.

However, the Kid had a fixed ticket and another week to go before he could get back to England; claims of wholesale death in his family had failed to soften the airline's policy. He was going through a bin outside a Kentucky Fried Chicken when he met McGregor.

McGregor had a small pig farm and wanted a house-sitter for a week while he went to his son's wedding in Chicago. The Kid's English accent and his knowledge of what happened in Coffeyville in 1892 convinced McGregor that he was Honesty's younger brother, and so he was entrusted with McGregor's house and his collection of Uruguayan election memorabilia while a tubby Mexican was to play swineherd. The Kid was given a gleaming gun and the advice: "If anyone turns up, just start shooting."

Apart from his interest in Latin American psephology, McGregor didn't go a bundle on possessions; no books, no television, no hi-fi, no deck of cards, and a radio that either didn't work or that he couldn't get to work. The Kid had a quiet week, eating everything in the fridge (old jack cheese and older jack cheese) and having to remind himself more and more often how lucky he was. The Mexican didn't speak a word of English, and, after having watched him feed the pigs on the first morning, he realized why Frank James had invented bank robbery in 1886.

The farm was three miles from the nearest road, and there was nothing to do except watch the occasional Immigration service helicopter whupping over and wander around naked (he had a hunch that sun-kissed tackle would triple his life back in Manchester), but it was so hot he could only stay outside for twenty minutes at a time.

At the end of the week, he had a plumb-loco session, during which he went out and shot at cacti by moonlight. He felt better but was so embarrassed by the spent ammunition that he invented a story of two shady bikers driving past, which got him a hundred-dollar bonus (spent on his first pair of Nocona boots).

No one knew where Baz was. On the other hand, everyone knew where Wojtek was: Strangeways. Life Sentence. Wojtek ("The Man with No Name"—he did in fact have a name, but it was unspellable, unpronounceable, and generally too much) had always been overtly intense, in a worrying way for someone who had access to guns. He had been stranded in Britain after martial law was declared in Poland; the Wild West had two attractive features for Wojtek: it was American (therefore not Russian at all), and it had guns. Wojtek had also got into gun clubs and would spend as much time as he could afford shooting and saying things while he reloaded like, "Me and Jaruzelski, one day."

The Kid hadn't been there when it had happened, but he had sat through the trial. A Friday night, everyone out enjoying themselves (a bad start since nothing riled Wojtek more than fun). Wojtek, drinking alone, was slammed into by a young Irish carpenter and lost half his pint to the floor. Even a wholly insincere "sorry" would have been the end of it; Wojtek was crazy, but big on courtesy. The carpenter sat down with his mates—Wojtek pressed a .22 barrel between his eyebrows.

"Don't shoot, don't shoot," the carpenter had shrieked. "I'm so scared I've wet myself," he said, pouring some beer into his own crotch to simulate urination. That was the trouble: arseholing along at a hundred miles an hour, you can't stop in time. The carpenter thought Wojtek such a divot that he couldn't believe the gun was real, and probably didn't live long enough to realize it was.

Carrying the gun was Wojtek's mistake. Carry a gun and one day you'll meet someone pleading to be shot. But having got to that point, he could see why Wojtek shot him; we all need to be taken seriously.

Ironically, the Irishman was in possession of items not unassociated with bomb-making (though it never came out in court), and the police liked Wojtek and wanted to do something for him, but couldn't. If Wojtek had just shot him, the brief reckoned he would have got off with manslaughter (eruption), but because he gave the carpenter time to say "sorry," he went down on murder (premeditation).

For a couple of years he had visited Wojtek, smuggling in cigarettes and chocolate, but then Wojtek revoked his visitor's order, the most insulting and humiliating thing that had ever happened to him.

Then there was Airhead. Airhead ("Miller the Killer") designed airports. He designed them, although no one had ever used his designs (the Liberians had been keen at one point). He would do all the bookings and publicity for the Bunch. Then he had gone on holiday with a girl, and the last they heard from

127

him was a postcard from Aberdeen, where he was running a needle museum.

He was the last of the Bunch. The Bramhall Kid farted to punctuate this thought. He was farting continually, real paint strippers that prevented him from tolerating his own company. The doctor had given him the "you're old, what do you expect?" look, which at fifty-two he was only going to get more and more. Changing diet, eating charcoal, popping antibiotics— nothing impeded the flow. The digestion of suns light-years away held no secrets, but they couldn't tame his lower intestine.

Realizing it was time for final scores, he switched on the television. Arsenal had beaten United 1–0. The grayness tightened its hands round his throat. He knew instantly without hearing any of the match report that it was down to Cole. It was another one of those great mysteries, why Ferguson, who after all knew more about football than he did, kept on playing Cole, instead of owning up to the waste of money and getting Cole to do something useful like selling programs.

Walking down to his local, the Kid didn't notice, at the junction, waiting for a green light, David Beckham in a Porsche (one hand on the wheel, the other struggling to impale his left nostril), because he was thinking about success.

How close he had got to success. He had got so close to success, he had left his fingerprints on it. Brook had never really ridden with the Bramhall Bunch, but he had raised a glass or two with them because he had a thing about Injun mythology and was always telling the story of the panther that lost its dick. He had always gotten on well with Brook, and when Brook opened his first tanning salon in 1972, he had offered him a junior partnership for a thousand quid.

Normally, he never had more than a fiver to his name, and banks were more likely to put barbecue sauce on their money and burn it than lend it to him, but he had lucked out. While working as a laborer one weekend, demolishing a long-derelict house, up in the attic, hidden in bandaging round a beam, he had found a stash of Regency guineas (which he didn't bother mentioning to his workmates).

He remembered leaving home to meet Brook down at the pub. He could still remember patting the fat envelope in his jacket pocket and then the crippling horror when he wanted to hand it over to Brook, the sickening search for the vanished envelope.

Three weeks afterward, impossibly, he found the envelope behind his sofa. However, Brook had gone into business with a Nigerian, who would rip him off a treat but who would nonetheless leave him a multimillionaire as Brook "had brought more ultraviolet to Lancashire than the sun." If he had got the money to him, all he would have had to do was to continue breathing.

Instead of going into tanning, the Kid had bought his authentic, though decommissioned, Colt Peacemakers. Every time they met, Brook said: "Let's have a drink" and "I'll see if I can cut you in on something." By the nineties Brook had stopped saying that, sticking to a grin.

In his local the Kid immediately noticed a young woman, and more consequentially, that she was collecting the dead glasses. Her face was unfortunate, but her breasts rounded so much he wondered if she'd had them done, but then remembered that was what it was like being eighteen. A child supplied with breasts.

Granger said: "Kid, this is Melody. Melody—Kid." But what he meant was that the Kid no longer had any supplement to his dole. He had picked up the empties and on very busy occasions helped Granger out, in exchange for a drink or a few notes, which, along with looking after the Wilsons' cats when they went on holiday (three times a year), was the only gainful employment he had had.

He wasn't angry. He would never have changed his routine; it had to be changed for him. And it wasn't as if Granger was getting any benefit out of her; Granger was like him: not allowed to enjoy himself.

Granger stood him a pint—severance pay. He drank it trying to give each mouthful its due, but it was no more enjoyable than watching someone else drink it. He left as if he had only come down for a quick drink.

At home he took out the fifty pounds he had hidden in the oven (never used): his hope roll. In case the universe offered him a deal for fifty quid; in case Brook turned up and offered him half of his chain of tanning salons and health clubs for fifty nicker; in case a flying saucer landed in the back garden and offered him a bucket of diamonds, cheap. Most of the previous ten years had been spent shuttling back and forth between the pub and home, but he had hung on to this tube of fifty uselessnesses.

He put on his holster. The right positioning of the holster was the art of the fast draw. And practice. And talent . . . though most of the real gunfighters had never seen a fast draw. A good job for them was shooting someone in the back with a rifle from a place of concealment a quarter of a mile away.

Last March, going out to get some cigs, he had tripped over a policeman lying in his driveway. The policeman was unhappy, not because someone had tripped over him, but because he was lying on gravel in a light drizzle and he was afraid he would be shot at.

The alarm was a false one, caused by the eighty-year-old Mrs. Mortimer, who had been using a cap gun to scare off some starlings eating her grass seeds. Some booby had seen her firing and called the law. When he had been young, it had been different. People had known each other. They didn't necessarily know each other well, and they didn't necessarily like each other, but the siege of Mrs. Mortimer's house wouldn't have happened. Tension had risen to hazardous levels as the police's megaphonings were ignored by Mrs. Mortimer, who was deaf.

He was lucky; when he started to think about how to attract the police, hammering began. Spring. He was always hammering, sawing, scraping, thumping, sanding, drilling. In the twelve years he had been living next door, he had done enough do-it-yourself to build five houses. When he wasn't doing that, he was pulling cars apart and then forgetting about them.

When Spring opened his front door, the Kid was there, hand outstretched, cocking his gun. Spring slammed the door—the Kid almost getting satisfaction from his fear.

Then the Kid walked into the middle of the road and emptied both guns into the air.

Back inside, he took an envelope from the Water Board (the comfort of an unpaid bill) and addressed it *For the policeman who shot me* and slipped in the fifty quid. On the other side of a church circular, he wrote: "You know." Then he added after consideration: "I want to say it was all my fault. I did everything to make it look real because I needed some help. Please have a good time on me with the enclosed. Deepest apologies from the Bramhall Kid."

As he loaded more blanks, he reflected again on the West and its offer of growing your own bigness.

When he heard his name being called, he walked unhappily toward the door, ready for his last fast draw.

Then They Say You're Drunk

The morning's nutter was there.

Brixton, Guy decided, must have more headcases per square inch than any other place in the world. He had sojourned in the great cities of the continents, had seen some sorry, deformed, trashy sights, but for multitudinous loonies Brixton was unassailable. It was a pity he couldn't find a way of profiting from it; then it occurred to Guy that since so many of them ended up in custody as clients of Jones & Keita, he did make a few quid off them.

Today's guest nutter was black and massive. Could easily bounce into any bouncer's position. That was the other thing about Brixton, not only plentiful in barkers, it had the biggest barkers he had ever seen.

Walking up to the bus stop, Guy reflected that someone with his trousers around his ankles, trying to eat his shirt, wouldn't normally have troubled him much. It was the size of the shirt eater rather than his activity that was perturbing. Six three and big, big, big; they obviously didn't spare the carbohydrates at the bin. What concerned Guy was that if the shirt eater wanted something to wash down his victuals, and mistook Guy for a can of Tennent's and tugged firmly on his pull tab, Guy couldn't do much about it, apart from croaking pathetically. The shirt eater was huge enough to do anything he wanted to.

They were very keen on taking off their clothes. A week ago, Guy had peered out of his window and spotted another whopper obsessing outside. Guy found using the window very stimulating; it was an eventful view: riots, accidents, robberies. The strapping loony had been fastidiously garnering items from dustbins and then arranging them in the interior of his neighbor's car; having installed the objects, he climbed in and joined the rubbish, sitting there peacefully in his pinacotheca.

Phoning the police was the usual concomitant to looking out the window. Working for a solicitor and asking the police for help was a mite odd; it seemed unnatural. Guy had been especially reluctant to phone for the law on that occasion because he hated his neighbors, and the owner of that car in particular.

Whether it was his job or merely living in Brixton, Guy found himself painfully short of warm, goodwill-like emotions. He'd watch his neighbors and get extremely annoyed by the way they walked. He hated Brixton, he hated his neighbors, he hated the clients, and, the truth be told, he wasn't too keen on himself.

Although he had been longing for the refuse arranger to cause some expensive damage to the car he was in, because the nurse's car was next to it, Guy had phoned the police. The nurse was ensconced in duodom, but you had to plan ahead. If the refuse arranger wanted to extend his display to the adjacent car, there was nothing Guy could do about it on his own, and bearing in mind it took the police half an hour to turn up (the police station was ten minutes' walk away), it was best to book in advance.

Two police officers appeared: a policeman (five seven, tops) and a policewoman (five six) with nothing in the girth department. Guy estimated that between them they could just about restrain one limb. They tried reasoning, not having much choice. Guy had time to make a cup of tea and another phone call while they implemented mateyness and coaxing. The refuse arranger refused to budge and responded by pulling off his clothes. Guy observed the policeman speaking into his shoulder to summon reinforcements. Four larger policemen dragged off the refuse arranger, while the original pair retrieved the strewn clothing.

———

On the bus, one stop closer to Peckham police station, Guy watched the drunk attempting to buy a ticket; Guy wasn't late yet, but the drunk had been fiddling in his pockets for four minutes in search of a coin, holding everyone up, until the passenger behind him volunteered to pay his fare.

Guy had been convinced that the drunk had been sent to multiply the unpleasantness of his trip to Peckham, but the drunk latched on to an African woman sitting toward the front, and leaning forward in the confidential manner drunks have (despite their shouting), battered her with his breath. The woman tried for the wrapping-all-her-senses-in-one-spot technique; however, the drunk was so on that Guy was sure that even sober he was unbearable. "But I don't want to BOTHER you with MY PROBLEMS," the drunk promulgated with projection that would have got him a contract at the theater.

In his coat pocket, Guy checked for his knife. Despite being overfamiliar with the law on offensive weapons, he had started carrying a switchblade. Not in case of being mugged. If anyone wanted his money, they could have it. He wasn't going to risk injury over a few quid. No, what worried him was being selected for pull-tabbing by one of the barkers.

The longest he could go now without encountering a barker, once he was out the door, was twelve minutes (the time it took to get to the tube where there was a minimum of one on duty).

The shortest time had been thirty seconds, one morning when he had stumbled out to get a newspaper. As he was carrying out the phenomenally onerous task of paying, he was shoved in the back, shoved in that very definite and violent manner that tells you someone is shoving you deliberately. Guy had turned round to see a lithe black teenager wearing a T-shirt with cut-off sleeves and an Arab headdress. "You should be more careful," he said to Guy. Virtually asleep, Guy realized it was going to happen; he could see other people in the newsagent's staring at them with the keen interest that presages a splash of blood. He was going to be beaten up multiculturally. Wonderful.

They shoved each other for a while, Guy struggling to work himself into a rage. Then, without a word, Arabhead walked out of the newsagent's, crossed the road smartly, and went into a greengrocer's, presumably to find someone to shove there. Four minutes later, when Guy was fully awake, fully furious, and fully armed, he had gone into the greengrocer's looking for him, but he had vanished.

After that, he resolved never to go outside untooled up. If he had to use it, he would say he had just found the knife on the street and was on his way to hand it in when . . . Guy didn't see why the role of the only honest person in the United Kingdom should fall to him.

———

As he got off the bus, an elderly black man spat at Guy. The comet of phelgm trajectoried a couple of inches past Guy's chest. Then the man grinned at Guy. If it had made contact, Guy would have been forced to do something about it, but this wasn't worth it. If you stopped for everyone abusing you or gobbing at you, you'd never get to where you were going.

Guy entered the reception area of the police station. And waited while the constabulary deigned to acknowledge him. In the streets, in the courts, in the newspapers, they might have to take it, but here, here was their domain. "Solicitor's rep," Guy announced when they felt they had let him ripen enough, "in the matter of Scott."

With most of the clients, you discerned a batting average in favor of criminality, that there would be a few months of good living before they got arrested; he always had the intention of asking the Scotts why they did it, because they were always caught. They were dependable clients and had even started asking for Guy by name.

Part of the reason why Guy hadn't asked the Scotts why they did it was because, despite their always being caught, they always claimed they hadn't done it.

In an age where family bonds were often sundered in ugly fashions, or simply didn't exist, it was rare to see a father and son so close. Scott senior and Scott junior were unusual in other ways. Street robbery was suited to the nifty. It was an offense much favored by failed athletes, those who hadn't got it right at county level, but who were happy to have a chance to put their training to use.

Scott junior wasn't right for this line of work. So fat he wobbled like a water bed (born too late for success in freak shows), you couldn't imagine him crossing even a bathroom with speed. This was where Dad came in, providing a chauffeur service.

Peckham police station, after one of their early (if not initial) forays, was where Guy had first encountered them. No charges were filed because Scott junior had attempted to snatch a bag from a lady who turned out to be his former PE teacher. (He obviously hadn't recognized her from behind; otherwise he might have recalled her judo classes.) His PE teacher did recognize him and, apart from loudly naming him tautophonically and clinging to her bag, she had thrown him to the pavement and, having pronounced "This isn't school, sonny," knowingly started to kick him senseless. Dad piled in and simultaneously joined his offspring on the pavement.

The Scotts were rescued by the police. Scott senior's version was they had been assaulted by a demented woman, and he was outraged that a number of witnesses maintained that Scott junior had made a grab for the bag. Taking their contusions into consideration and the feeble nature of the snatch, they were reprimanded.

In one respect, the Scotts fitted the profile of street robbers—they were exceedingly dim. Bag-snatching was not a crime that attracted the calculating or imaginative. There was some craft in finding the right sort of victim in a favorable environment: small, skinny females with no fondness for the martial arts or a predilection for carrying concealed weapons—in a badly lit car park or sequestered side street or secluded subway. The technique didn't require much study: the handbag was grabbed and the victim pushed or thumped to the ground (though there were those who esteemed the method of shoving the victim to the ground first and then grabbing the bag). If nothing else, you could envisage Scott junior excelling at the shoving part.

Then came the Balham high street job. Scott junior plucked the bag cleanly, leaving bagless lady gaping, and jellied his way to the car. The Scotts sped off chuckling and, turning the corner, drove into a police checkpoint (a biannual event). No tax. No insurance. No license. No brake lights. No tread on the tires. Arguably, they might have brazened it out if it hadn't been for Scott junior sitting in the passenger seat with the contents of the crocodile skin handbag spread out, scrutinizing a powder compact.

Patiently, Guy had listened while the Scotts had protested that the bag had been thrown into the car by a mysterious stranger who had hotfooted it out of their lives. They had just been making their way to a police station to hand it in. They were stumped as to how the woman's description fitted Scott junior perfectly, down to the "Whip me and cum on my tits" logo on his T-shirt.

Out on bail, they had another whirl. The snatch went okay, the getaway was okay, but the car broke down on the way home. By the time they returned by bus, the police were waiting for them, after surmising from the description furnished by the victim ("out-of-work Sumo wrestler") who the culprits were. The Scotts: setup, victimization. The jury: guilty. The judge: suspended sentence. Moral: get good wheels.

Though you could go over the top, Guy concluded, remembering Palmer's smash-and-grab on an antique shop (which had been staked out by armed police, presumably on a tip-off, which was bizarre since Palmer had never been known to think more than fifteen minutes ahead). Palmer had been transported to the scene of the crime in a bright red Ferrari, just stolen by his friend, who was driving.

According to Palmer, he had visited his friend, who had offered to give him a lift to another friend. When, during the journey, it had emerged that the car was stolen, Palmer had instantly demanded to be let out. The car came to a stop coincidentally in front of the antique shop, where, incensed by his friend involving him in a criminal act, Palmer altercated with him and directed a brick at him (which had suddenly come to hand). The brick had missed the friend but had hit the antique shop's window. Palmer had been solicitously examining the

goods in the window for damage, when the guns had materialized.

There were a few clients with whom you developed a matey
rapport, with whom you could have a chortle. Guy had thought
about voiding the thought: "You don't mind if I laugh, do you?"
But Palmer wasn't the sort of client who encouraged levity; he
was the sort of client who would bite off your ear if he detected
the slightest diminution of respect toward himself, no matter
how much legal training you had had. Palmer was a nonlaugher;
he had been absolutely earnest about his line of defense.

Guy had excused himself, left the interview room, laughed till
he cried, composed himself, and had returned to resume taking
instructions.

Sadly, Palmer was another devoted client, although no one
wanted to handle him. Most clients had their territories, their
proclivities, their patterns. Not Palmer. Palmer did everything:
moody money, arson, plastic, burglary, molesting young girls.
He was an all-round entertainer. Handling cases like Palmer's,
Guy couldn't avoid coming to the view that if he had any moral
fiber he'd be doing something to sabotage Palmer's defense, not
that it was needed in the antique shop matter. Palmer was looking at some bird, all the more if he demanded a trial, though
there were judges foolish enough to give him probation.

Reading Palmer's palm, as it were, the future was easy to tell:
he'd revolve in and out of jail, blighting lives like botulism until
he unloaded a major viciousness, a rape or murder, when even a
judge would be forced to put Palmer away long enough to study
for an Open University degree.

Someone out there was waiting for Palmer to excise the happiness from their life.

———

Finally admitted, Guy had a word with the arresting officer,
who had that very jolly bearing that policemen have when they

have a perpetrator on the charge sheet within hours, and have the perpetrator so well sewn up that the entire legal profession working in unison (having resurrected and roped in every lawyer that ever lived) couldn't do anything about it.

The Scotts were improving; they got the bag, got rid of it, and got home without incident. They went unrewarded for their improved efficiency since the crime had been recorded by a new high-quality color security video-camera, and the Scotts had been instantly recognized by the investigating officer.

The Scotts were very popular. There was nothing the police liked more than criminals who caught themselves. The officer was very chatty, revealing that the Scotts had disposed of the handbag but luncheon vouchers had been found on the sofa and (here the policeman gave a contented snigger) the victim's credit card had been discovered in a coffee jar.

Guy instructed the Scotts to go *no comment* because that was usually the best policy, doubly so with the dopier clients, who would invariably create more work for counsel if they detoured from those two words. And it was a stance you couldn't be faulted for; it might not always be the best, but it was never wrong. You could always talk later if necessary. The Scotts would be better off putting up their hands in light of the video-tape, the handbag's contents making themselves at home in the Scotts' home, and the victim's vivid recollection of Scott junior's "Kill them all and let God sort them out" T-shirt.

Yet the Scotts clung to their innocence like a pit bull to a favorite leg; somewhere, by someone, a long time ago, the Scotts had been advised never to cough, and this motto had stuck in their minds, like a hunk of hair blocking a drain, blocking out any prudent assessments of their predicament.

There were, Guy reckoned, three main categories of stupidity. There were the nervy types, who still reverberated from the shock of school and who liked to keep out of people's way in case anyone asked them to add up something or tested them on the capitals of South America. They only got involved in crime by accident since they knew they would fail. Then there was the more practical group, who realized what their limitations were and worked round them. Lastly, there was the category that the Scotts were domiciled in, those too stupid to realize they were stupid, those who spent all their time wondering why everyone else was so stupid.

The conference with the Scotts was affable, apart from their inability to comprehend why Guy thought bail was unlikely.

———

The Scotts had fitted in with unprecedented convenience. Guy strolled down the hill leisurely, with time to kill before his appointment at Brixton prison. He popped into a shop and bought some cigarettes for Bodo. The Scotts had been disappointed that Guy hadn't been able to offer them a smoke. Guy usually carried ten Benson and Hedges, but it had given him a surge of pleasure to have been without them.

Farther down the hill, there was a fresh drunk (unlaboring Irish laborer variety) with the question-mark posture of the profoundly inebriated. He held a can of blue-label, and guttural in the gutter was declaiming, "and then . . . and *then* people say to you, you're drunk . . ."

They were relaxed at the prison. They normally were unless someone had gone over the wall in the previous week. Guy sat down in the interview room and waited for Bodo (currently the favorite client) to appear. Bodo's problem: close association with seventy ks of marijuana.

From Augsburg he had come to London to play guitar. Short of readies, he had met a man in the pub one evening (no, he really had). The man got chatting with Bodo and offered him three hundred quid to make a delivery. This was one of the reasons Guy liked him, it was such an easy mistake. Bodo knew perfectly well what was involved, but had thought, one run, three hundred quid. Guy sympathized with him; he had been in a similar situation when he had met Gareth, who had persuaded him to try outdoor clerking for his firm. He could easily have met the man in Lewisham who had hired Bodo.

Duly arrived at the rendezvous, Bodo had found an edgy van driver who wanted to rid himself of the bales as swiftly as possible. Bodo had been flabbergasted to find the transfer being conducted in the open, to wit, the car park of a McDonald's, and that the bales weren't even disguised, just wrapped with a few shreds of newspaper. Bodo was greatly worried about the sloppy packaging since only a few of the bales fitted into the trunk of his car and the rest had to be stacked up on his passenger seat.

Shaken, Bodo started off for the address he had been given (verbally), having been also told a car would be following him. Bodo watched as the red Lotus, which had been cruising twenty feet behind him, sped past after he had been pulled over by the police, who wanted to talk to Bodo about the red light he had run. ("I didn't even notice the light; I was checking the map.")

The prospect of Bodo, sweating in conditions close to freezing, and a car replete with gargantuan bales of marijuana roused the suspicions of the police officers:

"Can you tell me what these packages are, sir?"

"A very long jail sentence, I think," replied Bodo in the way to win policemen's hearts.

It didn't look good for Bodo. He had put his hands up, though in a situation like that it didn't do you much good. One kilo, you could pretend it had been planted or that someone else had left it there, but with seventy, you just had to start shopping for a good five-year calendar. Bodo had barely had room to drive.

It didn't look good at all. He had all sorts of disadvantages. University education. Undivorced parents. No history of sexual abuse. No history of substance abuse. No history of alcoholism. No illegitimate children. No criminal record. Flawless English. Skills. Nothing to mitigate whatsoever. The judge would throw the book at him.

In he came, wearing his "Legalize it" T-shirt. "Wie geht's?" asked Guy, always eager to exercise his one German phrase, because it made him feel European and because that night with a German girl in a youth hostel in Rennes hadn't been in vain.

Bodo was trying to be tough about his forthcoming sentence and being partially successful. He was settling into it; though he had some problems: he wanted to try for bail, but the only people who had that sort of surety were his parents and he hadn't shattered their serenity yet. Essentially, Bodo wanted bail for a last fling with his girlfriend. He wasn't fooling himself that she would be waiting for him when he emerged a much older and wiser man.

They discussed bail and other business. There wasn't much to discuss. Guy had attended mostly for Bodo's sake, to try and cheer him up; he knew there couldn't be much to occupy him in HMP Brixton. It wasn't as if he could learn anything: a virtuoso guitar player, a Ph.D. in astrophysics, and he spoke and wrote better English than anyone else in the nick (the governor included).

Bodo was focusing on the future. "I will go back to Augsburg. Teach guitar. No more big cities. No more adventures. Everyone will know me as that boring Mr. Becker, and no one will believe I did crazy things in London." He pulled on his cigarette with laglike intensity. "You know, by the time I get out, it probably will be legal. Perhaps I should do something to speed up the campaign."

They got up and waited for the warden to collect Bodo. "I was looking at the moon last night," Bodo said. "You can see it very well from my cell. I was looking and I thought, one day there will be people there and they will have jails there, because they will have arseholes on the moon. Wherever there are people, there are arseholes. Be careful, Guy, you never know when you may turn into one. Look in the mirror often."

He got home and ran the bath. Guy locked both the locks on the door and placed his longest kitchen knife (with a nice serrated edge) on the toilet seat cover. It was unlikely, almost impossible, for anyone to get in, but Guy found it hard to trust the universe these days.

He missed the police.

They had turned up the night Guy had complained about the noise next door. It had been four in the morning, and Guy had learned there was something outstandingly annoying about a mighty salsa beat passing through a wall. Most styles of music he could handle, and he had nothing against people having fun, but this jarred. The police had the same effect as him: none. Either the neighbor couldn't be bothered to answer the door, or the music was too loud for him to hear the furious bangings on the door.

The police officer had commiserated with Guy, who had resolved to reciprocate the gift of insomnia by going out and slashing his neighbor's tires after the police had gone. The police officer had looked out of Guy's window. "You've got a good view here, haven't you?"

So Guy had found himself with a surveillance unit in his front room. His citizenship wouldn't have gone that far normally, but there had been early mention of a few quid being thrown his way for inconvenience.

It was the hairdresser's they were interested in. It had impinged a little into Guy's thoughts too. The hairdresser's seemed to be closed more than was generally considered beneficial for a business, with its shutters firmly pulled down. Even when open, it didn't seem to be doing any better than when it was closed. Nevertheless, parked around the premises were a number of cars that shouted affluence.

"Is it drugs?" Guy had asked.

"We don't give a toss about drugs anymore," the officer had replied. "They're flogging guns." The police left after a week, looking dissatisfied. Dissatisfied, Guy gathered, because nothing of a definite nature had been attained, and because while they had been doing some close-up work in the White Horse, Guy's flat had been burgled and their cameras stolen. Guy lost nothing; they didn't take his television or video, which was rather insulting. They were old but serviceable.

The most grating thing was that his door had been kicked down. Guy had spent time and money fitting extra locks on the door. The locks had resisted admirably, but the door itself had disintegrated into toothpicks.

The company had been good, though. Guy had enjoyed swapping tales of iniquity and vileness.

He was pleased to see his reflection in the mirror. He was going to Hampstead; that should give him a break from all this.

———

Strolling to the tube, Guy watched a Tennent's drinker lob his empty can onto the top of the entranceway of Lambeth's Housing section and then proceed to urinate lavishly against the building while his girlfriend gazed on in a my-hero fashion. You got tired of people distributing rubbish everywhere and dispensing substances that were not intended for public inspection, but it had to be acknowledged that it could never be wrong to hose down a Lambeth council office.

At the tube, Guy broke through the cordon of evangelists (chiefly Christian, but with Islam closing the gap, some equipped with luggable speakers) and the selection of purvey-ors of politics (chiefly communist). Brixton underground sta-tion had a mysterious quality, the trait of congregating people who wanted to change your life, mostly noisily, by taking your money. And people who wanted you to change their lives, by taking your money.

In a corner of the concourse, a stonehenge of drunks and barkers was laughing at the funniest joke in the world. The king of the dossers was holding court.

The king, to Guy's knowledge, had been at the tube every day for the last five years, on a nine-to-five basis (a much better attendance record than any of the employees of London Underground assigned to Brixton). People still gave him money—perhaps it was his unkempt demeanor.

Because in fact the king wasn't a street person; he lived in a council flat around the corner from the tube, the new estate that had been built by the railway line after the rioting in '81. He had a variety of natty outfits and seemed to enjoy working the tube. And why not? The concourse was warm, dry, furnished with hot and cold beverages, snacks, a newsagent, a photo booth for shooting up in, and catchy rhythms pumped out by the music shop.

———

The king fancied himself as profound; when giving the litany of "spare change, spare change" a rest, he would sire full-volume observances such as "Persons! Persons! Where are you going?" With a suggestion that he was trying to elevate them to a higher plane of being.

Through the ticket barrier Guy was confronted by a black sunglassed Walkmanner walking up on the first segments of the down escalator (in effect, on the spot), drink in hand. Guy paused for a second to see whether the pacer wanted to walk off or whether he would work out that he was supposed to go down. But he carried on striding happily as if the underground station were his private gym, a perception provided by wonky mental machinations, or perhaps a simple craving to infuriate those who wanted to descend to the platforms.

Guy didn't care what cortical flamboyancy had licensed this. Living in Brixton gave you a superb ability to distinguish between irksome eccentricity and hazardous lunacy. The drink was a complete giveaway—orangeade. Everyone knew real nutters and lovers of GBH drank Tennent's. Besides, he was quite small. Guy shoved him out the way without bothering to add "sorry."

On the up escalator, an Australian surfing expertly on the handrail glided past Guy.

With the train rattling away, Guy opened up packets of annoyance and determination. He was annoyed because he had been thinking for months now how attractive Vicky was, and how despite her being agenda'd, he wasn't warming up her skin.

He hadn't been able to understand how she had been able to go out with that twentieth-century nonentity, Luke. Despite taking pride in his amorous resources, Guy recognized, there were males who were stronger, richer, tanneder, excitingly employeder; he wouldn't have liked it if Vicky had been dalliancing with one of them, but he could have understood it. He had wanted to say, "If you're not interested in me, fine, but at least let me fix you up with someone proper."

Patience was Guy's speciality. He was prepared to wait; a rebuff or two wouldn't put him off. He was prepared to stay in touch without any physical remuneration; he wasn't disheartened by polite conversation.

However, Luke had gone back to his hometown of Ipswich for what had been billed as a long weekend, but hadn't come back. What had appeared in his stead was a piece of wedding cake in a flowery box, with an invitation for his wedding to old childhood sweetheart (who Vicky had long assumed relegated to the sporadic Christmas card league), accompanied by a short note: "I think it best if we don't see each other for a while."

What had amazed Guy was Luke's cruelty. Or humor. Both had seemed beyond him. Luke, a sound engineer, seemed to have such enormous respect for sound, that he hardly ever uttered a word, and it wasn't even as if the words he did utter carried extra pith to compensate for his long silences. Over and over again, Guy had been through his long silences. Over and over again, Guy had been through his memories to verify his impression of Luke as tedious and nondescript. He took up about eleven stones' worth of space; that had been his chief characteristic. Though of course the most vivid memories of Luke were the ones he didn't remember but could see, those of Luke grimacing and groaning as he compressed Vicky's buttocks.

Vicky had discovered that she had been matrimonially out-flanked on Monday; Guy had discovered that she had discovered on Wednesday. Congratulating himself on his diligence and the efficacy of his intelligence network, Guy had phoned instantly, ready to supply commiserations.

To his shock, he had found Vicky far from disconsolate, but about to move to Hampstead, where she had acquired a position as house-sitter in a four-bedroomed wonderland (sauna, jacuzzi, gymnasium, satellite TV) as well as some chef from a Korean restaurant who was taking her for long walks and who was talked about in tones that conformed with someone who was verging on a buttock-compressing situation.

She had sounded very chirpy; indeed the only rain cloud that appeared in her vocal firmament was when Guy proposed a meeting. She reeled off excuse after excuse, so it was only now, a week later, that Guy was getting his slot, since Vicky was having a drink with two Dutch female friends. Guy was buoyed up by the idea of the company, although he was rather worried he was falling in love with Vicky.

Guy found them in the pub, and noted that Vicky greeted him with that total lack of interest that too often signified a total lack of interest; similarly, the two Dutch girls were perceptibly unexcited by his presence. Far from feasting on his words, as women who are intent on a holiday liaison would, they scarcely paid more attention to him than to any of the other people in the pub.

Studying Vicky, Guy surmised that he was part of a batch-job, that she had had to take the Dutch out for a drink, and he had been tacked on to kill two birds and one out-of-work actor with one evening in the pub.

Guy bought a round just in case the ladies were aroused by generosity, and then they sat down at a large round table that had already acquired a hardened pubber (old single ex-door-to-door salesman variety), who sat there serenely with the tools of his trade, the never-diminishing half-pint in a pint glass, the roll-up with almost a cigarette's-length column of ash, alcoholic hair, and a smile that was confident it knew what was what.

The conversation rolled on without any aid from Guy, who was sitting next to the pubber. After a couple of minutes, the pubber, with the ornate diction of someone trying to disguise their drunkenness, asked Guy if he had a handkerchief. Guy replied that he hadn't, because he didn't. The pubber then tripped up the girls' conversation by canvassing them for a handkerchief. They were unable or unwilling to provide one.

A few moments later, the man asked Guy again for a handkerchief, with a trifle more urgency and an intonation that insinuated that Guy was holding out on him. Guy repeated with bonus firmness, a firmness he hoped would penetrate the boozy padding, that he didn't have one. What was beginning to irritate Guy was that it was a three-second walk to the bar or the toilet, where, if his need were that great, a tissue could be obtained. The man seemed determined to annoy someone into fetching a handkerchief.

The Dutch girls were now listing with Vicky (rather insensitively, it seemed to Guy) which actors would be most welcome in their undergrowth; the actors they named didn't have more talent than he did, Guy felt, but they did have advantages such as immense fame and wealth. He'd like to see how they would fare opposite the girls shorn of their celebrity and riches; probably the same as him. This enumeration of carnal preferences boded badly for him, since the girls clearly felt they were among girls—it was the soundtrack of a failed evening—when their mouths ran out of words and Guy was aware they were staring past him with the blanched visages of road-accident viewers.

He glanced over his shoulder. The reason the man had been pleading for a handkerchief was now abundantly clear. A strand of snot, a foot long, dangled like a dipstick from his right nostril. The pubber's hooter was huge, which doubtless empowered the well-racinated extension.

For any Brixtonian this was rather elementary stuff, and Guy wasn't hugely bothered. Unexpected in Hampstead (what was the point of paying millions for your home if you had someone growing mucous tendrils in the local?), but in Brixton they would have tried to lasso you with it. The pubber was progressively more and more amused as the pendulum parabola'd over a larger and larger area.

"Am I upsetting you?" he chuckled. It wasn't upsetting, Guy analyzed, but it was incredibly irritating. He hadn't traveled all the way across London for this, and he wasn't giving the pubber the satisfaction of knowing he had added another layer of unpleasantness to the evening. Guy shut him out of his mind, having checked that the pub (which wasn't that busy) had no other rump havens.

Shortly after, alerted by the extra work of the revulsion muscles on the women's faces, Guy revolved to witness the pubber escorting, with two fingers, the strand onto the carpet. This eased things a bit since he no longer had to worry about the swinging adventures of the snot.

However, when Guy was tactically agreeing effusively with Vicky about the importance of a united Europe, he espied horror having another outing on her face. Guy lifted his gaze to perceive a three-incher worming its way out of its hangar. There was another request for a handkerchief.

"Why don't we go outside?" suggested Vicky.

They went outside and sat at a plastic table. It was the end of May but not cold. Not cold enough to prevent them from sitting outside, but cold enough to prevent them from enjoying it. Guy didn't see why they should be outside catching a chill. This was all too English for him; someone inconveniences you, so you help them make things even more inconvenient for you.

Things weren't right. There had always been revolting drunks, the insane had always been partial to public transport, but Guy recalled in his teenage years it had been out of the ordinary. You saw one in the street, and you went home to say "There was a really revolting drunk in the street" or "What a nutter we had on the bus today." Now it would be striking if half the passengers on a bus aspired to civilized behavior. Though perhaps he should try moving out of Brixton.

Guy's reverie was terminated by the figure of the pubber lurching out of the doorway, the man with the metronimic catarrh. We're in for a reprise, guessed Guy.

"Hope you're . . . enjoying yourselves," he said as he zigzagged past with an inflection that broadcast that was the last thing on Earth he would want. Perhaps he had been on course for home because he took a few more steps, but the group's provocative lack of response caused him to tarry. He established himself a short distance away from their table (but more than a flob or a fist away) and started emitting abuse. They tried not paying any attention, but this didn't impede the invective, which was delivered in stock, blunt, and unimaginative terms, but with a remarkable hatred.

And here we are, mused Guy. In a dying city. Where else would you spend your day being polite to morons whose only talent is burning up others' money in benefits and legal and penal costs? Wading through beggars, spending an hour cross-ing the place, only to be ignored by women and end up sitting in the cold being sworn at by a man whose secretions are no longer secret?

On one Dutch face Guy saw a look that said the man needed help and understanding. On his own face Guy imagined there was an expression that maintained that the man needed to be kicked in the head vigorously, ideally until he was dead. He was close to snapping. The trouble was that the inveigher was old, puny, and drunk; Guy would simply be beating him up. In a way this was the most galling aspect—that the pubber was shelter-ing behind their notions of decency. Furthermore, Guy's familiarity with the law conjured up charges of assault or man-slaughter.

Besides which, the ladies wouldn't approve of any laying on of hands. Women were funny about things like that. And there was no point in reciprocating the insults; that would only fuel the harangue.

"Some people aren't very nice," continued the pubber, "some people are . . ." He went on to use the verb that has proved most popular on city walls since city walls had come into being.

They opted for drinking up. Guy wondered if there was a country anywhere where individuals like the pubber would be executed and if he could emigrate there. However, just as they were getting to the bottom of their glasses, the pubber shuffled off.

The Dutch contingent was staying with Vicky, and Guy accompanied them back home so that if anyone else wanted to swear at them he could assist them in ignoring it. In addition to which, Guy prided himself on not giving up. The possibility of the three girls unrobing and having a yearning for aromatic balms to be kneaded into their flesh existed. But as so often happened, it didn't happen.

A minicab was called for Guy. Having missed the last tube, he was now rounding off with an expensive trip down South. Guy had barely been in the car ten seconds when the driver, a Jamaican, asked him if he could seek his advice. The driver recounted how, back in Jamaica, he had met a girl, got married; he had brought her back to live in London but she had absconded after a week. "So me had 'er deported." All well and good, but then he had been back in Jamaica again, where he had patched things up, and now he wanted to bring her back again. He was thinking he should ring the Home Office.

Guy could see the Home Office relishing the call. Guy could see the driver walking into the office at Jones & Keita and asking for advice; like most of their customers, he seemed to be in contention for some international award in imbecility. The driver must have had an age with a four in the front, and Guy could see the wife with an age that still had a one at the start; a young lady no doubt older and wiser after her deportation who would either fit in her supplementary intubations while her husband

was out on the road, or who would do a more thorough disap-
pearing act next time.

Yet, perhaps because he was feeling tired, it glinted less like
stupidity; it was simply part of the ongoing. What people do.
And apart from the airfare, what was the difference between
going to Kingston or Hampstead?

"Give it a try," said Guy.

"Dat's what I say, give it a try."

The minicab broke down halfway along Acre Lane. Guy
waited patiently for a while in case the driver had the ability to
revive it; then he paid, ready to walk the last ten minutes. "Good
luck with your wife," he said, surprised that he meant it.

He looked up for the moon but couldn't see it anywhere.

Ice Tonight in the Hearts of Young Visitors

We were waiting at the border. It was dark and cold. Hardly cold for December, but not much fun.

We had been waiting all day, along with the other journos. Nagylak had been struck by a hurricane of newsworkers; everywhere you looked was three-deep with freebooters, misery hounds, expense wizards.

We had got the last Mercedes in Budapest. When I had hired it at the beginning of the week, the company had been delighted to get an earner like the Merc out on the road. "Can I take it out of Hungary?" I had asked. "Of course," they had replied, offering me extra insurance with a big smile. It had never occurred to them that anyone from the West would be crazy enough to go to Romania—what was happening in Timişoara then was at most a disturbance. By the end of the week, they were denying cars to anyone suspected of involvement with news or demanding deposits five times the cost of the car.

A pack contains privileges. I didn't have to bother doing anything. If I had been solo, I would have been fretting about missing something; I would have been pestering the Romanian border guards, trying to get them to open sesame. Instead I put my feet up, drank a beer, and thought about how I was quids in.

In the next lane was a Volvo limo, serving three German freelances (I assumed they were freelances because they didn't seem capable of getting proper jobs) who were attempting to give a Hungarian hotel bill to the Romanian border guards in the belief it was a visa application form. I eavesdropped with pleasure as their repertoire of languages (which didn't include Hungarian or Romanian) failed to get them anywhere.

They were still issuing visas at the border, although no one was being let in. It was a Friday evening, three days before Christmas, and ahead of us in the blackest of darkness lay something that fitted the description of a revolution. Sixty kilometers over the border was Timişoara, the town where a demonstration in support of a pastor, László Tökés, had been fired on, killing dozens. Dozens, hundreds, thousands, no one knew. No one knew what was going on in Timişoara. No one knew where Tökés was or whether he was alive.

Zoltán was sitting quietly in the back of the car in the way an interpreter with nothing to interpret does; he knew all about shutting up, as a former member of the Hungarian minority in Romania. We listened to the radio and heard how it had all gone pear-shaped for Ceauşescu in Bucharest. No one knew where he was or whether he was alive.

Szabolcs was scurrying about, sniffing for scraps of fact in the way a journalist should. He was a lawyer, though, if a highly unemployed one (as a result of his having taken on the Hungarian authorities), and currently my driver. For a long time, when I had needed a driver I had gone for thuggish taxi drivers, who could be relied on to get the most out of the roads.

I had made Szabolcs's acquaintance because as a champion of
the poor he had become my pipeline for unfortunates; he was
always rustling up consumptive rent boys or bewildered gypsies
for me to quiz.

I had tried him out once as a driver because, with an expec-
tant girlfriend, he had been desperate for money. From then on
Szabolcs had always been my driver of choice because he could
exploit a car with a ruthlessness that was frightening and the
complete opposite of his dealings with people.

In the trunk I had a bag full of clothing, toiletries, food,
maps, Romanian phrase books and bribes, and worryingly only
one spare tire. (Having driven in Romania before, I wanted
more than a single spare, but they hadn't had any spare spare
tires at Avis.) When I had told Szabolcs we might be away for a
few days, he had brought five packets of cigarettes and a ther-
mos filled with coffee that gave no quarter. He was such a
Budapest intellectual, it made me want to cry.

I had been hoping we could knock off for the night and go
back home, when, suddenly, all the engines started up and the
barrier was raised.

"Timişoara?" Szabolcs asked.

"Timişoara."

Was the beast called revolution lurking in the night, eating all
the rules, twirling order around like a majorette brandishing a
baton? What was waiting for us? Jubilant revolutionaries?
Snipers? Hot drinks?

The Romanian guards watched us rolling in, a "you're mad as
fuck, you are" look on their faces. We were the fourth or fifth car
across, and I was very happy about that. As we motored on
steadily into the blackness, I was half expecting to see a flash of
explosive power as one of the cars preceding us got zapped—a
drawback of having an imagination.

Our headlights provided the only information: eerie. We had a map but no idea what the road would bring us to. I wondered if this was the biggest mistake of my life. My mind harped on the hundreds of thousands of Kalashnikovs in Romania, if not millions (dictatorships never stint on weapons); how each Kalashnikov had a magazine carrying thirty rounds, and how it would take merely one bullet, fired no matter how carelessly, no matter how accidentally, and no matter how devoid of malice, to fly through the Mercedes as if it hadn't been there and to clean out my universe.

A few moments into the doubt, we see figures blocking the road. If I had been driving, I'm not sure I would have carried on. The people closed in on us and started banging on the sides of the car, an unsettling sensation—but they were cheering. This was my first lesson in what a revolution means; it means everyone out on the streets, even if you live in a village five minutes' walk from the Hungarian border, it's almost Christmas, it's pitch dark, and the released fervor can only disperse tracelessly into the night.

Weaving our way through the celebrants, we drive on to Arad, the main town before Timişoara. By the time we get there, I'm very bullish because I've been in the country for twenty minutes and no one has tried to shoot me. Arad was dull; it was like any small provincial town anywhere late at night. A few pedestrians, a few cars, some lighting, but nothing worth the effort of putting it in your memory. The dullness is both reassuring and disappointing. I'll live, but with nothing to say.

Like tourists, we get lost in the one-way system. On our fourth lap of Arad, we accost a woman for directions. She volunteers to show us the way since she and her large bags of foodstuff need to get to Timişoara. Zoltán translates her chatter: she lives outside of Timişoara and has no idea what's happening in the town; she just came to her relatives in Arad for supplies.

We drop her on the outskirts of Timișoara, and quickly there is a change; whether on account of the ugliness of Timișoara's suburbs or because of something sinister on the loose, I can't say. But we sensed we had left the everyday.

A tall woman in a long raincoat and two men stand in the road; this will be the first of many roadblocks we will encounter. They are unarmed. How effective can a raincoat be against someone carrying a gun and not interested in stopping their speeding car? Nevertheless, every able-bodied Romanian citizen will insist on taking over a slice of thoroughfare and running his or her own checkpoint irrespective of its usefulness and regardless of what is happening in the country.

After a curt interrogation, we were waved on, though Zoltán was deployed several times before we got to the city center, which was peaceful, although there was an overturned bus and grains of glass everywhere. People were milling around, alert but unexcited.

It was wonderful to be able to say, "Take me to your leader." After a number of exchanges, Zoltán and I were directed to the Opera House, which we were assured was serving as the headquarters of the revolutionary committee. After more negotiation and repeated frisking, we were led up and down and around and around the building for an improbably long time. Finally, we were ushered into a large chamber where . . . eight people were watching television.

This wasn't how I had imagined the hub of a revolution. One person was out on a balcony talking to half a dozen people below in the square, but it was only a chat, not an inflammatory address.

Zoltán and I rotated around trying to figure out who was significant. How do you start interviewing a revolution? There was a switched-on-looking man on his own in a corner. I offered him a packet of Kent cigarettes and a talk. Kent cigarettes weren't actually used as cigarettes in Romania; they were a currency. In the past I had opened a closed restaurant in Bucharest with but one packet of Kent. Cartons would circulate the country never to be opened, and three, it was claimed, would get you a medical degree.

I was confident I was in the purity of a revolution when he refused the packet, but, suffering from the most excruciating tobacco deprivation, he ripped it open, took one cigarette out, and lit up. Then he positioned the open packet invitingly on a table so that others could help themselves.

The smoker explained that the revolution had triumphed in Timişoara but they didn't have a clue what was happening elsewhere. No one could say what the Securitate was up to. No one could say how many had died, but certainly thousands.

The others we talked to ditto'd this; no one was in charge. No one knew what was going on. No one had been involved in the fighting, and there was a curious absence of weapons in the Opera.

Was this right, or was I talking to the wrong people? I hoped the other journalists who had gained the sanctum weren't lucking on to knowers or doing business with atrocity merchants. It was like being a teenager again and believing everyone was having a better time than you.

A stringy student in a bobble hat rushed in and announced in English for the benefit of the member of the press: "Helicopters are coming. Helicopters are coming. We will die."

No one paid any attention. If those present had started screaming and jumping out of the windows, I would have done likewise. But since no one acted concerned, I contented myself by slyly studying the walls and assessing how they would cope with the assault of heavy machine-gun fire or missiles.

I came to the conclusion that I no longer had any need to stay in the Opera. Outside the stars were comfortingly tranquil and unmarred by helicopters.

Back at the car Szabolcs had amassed a small entourage.

"Let's go," I said.

"They can take us to the bodies," Szabolcs responded. The Romanians nodded with alacrity. When it had all started in Timişoara, as was obligatory in revolutions, the unarmed demonstrators had been fired on. Szabolcs explained that not only did no one know how many people had died, but no one had known what had been done with the bodies. Thus a search had been initiated and a mass grave uncovered.

I wasn't keen on seeing the bodies, but I wanted to see if I could take it. And I had to bring back something approaching news. We distributed the edibles we had stashed in the trunk, and one of the locals got in the car to direct us to the disinterment.

"Come back and see us some other time," said one of the women to whom we had given chocolate.

The massacred had been buried, in a place both appropriate and yet perhaps hoped to be too obvious for anyone to consider, the town cemetery, which, however, was more like a messy building site than a cemetery. It occurred to me that I had never been in proximity to a corpse, and I hoped I wouldn't do anything unseemly.

Our guide was conducting Zoltán and me across the muddy wasteground, when Zoltán stopped. "This is too much," he announced. "I'll be in the car." I didn't protest because inspecting corpses hadn't been a condition of his employment and because his bowing out made me feel incredibly tough.

We walked on a few more yards. We smelled them before we saw them. There wasn't much light, which was fine by me. A dozen bodies had been exhumed, mostly naked and smeared with soil. My first thought was digging up these bodies was a job I could never be persuaded to do.

The one body I vividly remember is that of a broad, middle-aged woman, with a very young infant laid on her belly. Not much was said. It was hard to imagine anything worse than this, dumped in the wintry ground with a double desolation (abandoned and unreachable) and a double blackness (sightless in darkness). One couldn't imagine a more potent expression of the lesson that warmth is all.

I had a good look; then I conceded that, journalistically and morally, there wasn't anything else to do apart from standing around appalled. Returning to the car, I found the helicopter spotter wandering about exclaiming: "The Securitate is coming. The Securitate is coming. We will die."

We drive back to Hungary so I can report. The emanations from the bodies dally in my nostrils, and I have to jam a packet of coffee against my nose so that its powerful aroma will bury all traces of the dead.

In sight of the border, a tire goes. While we change it, the radio is on and we hear stories of Securitate agents hitching lifts and leaving clandestine explosives in journalists' cars. From Arad there is a live feed from a reporter hiding underneath a radiator, describing how the town is being shot up by the Securitate.

I am perplexed why so many depictions of hell have hordes of sinners clambering over each other, roaring in roaring flames, spit-roast or pitchforked by imps as they burn. If I had the chance, I would be buried in the center of the sun with some pals, because I assure you if there is a hell, it will be the most solitary of confinements and cold.

Bookcruncher

He pushed open the door marked STAFF ONLY. He took a look at the noticeboard to see if there was anything new. There wasn't.

A number of shoplifter alerts were posted with crude characteristics: smelly, Irish, steals atlases. Or: horn-rimmed glasses, long overcoat, sandwiches, fond of gardening. Some sales and turnover stats. Vacancies at other branches. He opened the cupboard where he knew the coffee would be and got the kettle to boil. Into the jar that served as receptacle for coffee money, he counted out the change, two dimes and a nickel.

Not caring about coffee was a feat he congratulated himself on. What the reputable brands were, he had no idea. He didn't waste a second fussing over coffee, how many spoonfuls, how much water, how much milk, how much sugar. Coffee was something many people could get worked up about. He had one over them.

He shot through some new books and then tried a few phone calls. But no one was there.

So he sipped his coffee and enjoyed the comfy chair.

He felt okay, he told himself. Truthfully, no, not okay . . . more than okay . . . he felt good. At ease. He spent fifteen minutes thinking how unimportant birthdays were. Then several minutes considering whether he might be wrong. Followed by half an hour pondering that sitting on your own in a bookshop office on your birthday with a couple of bananas and half a loaf of half-dry bread for supper, although he felt fine about it, might seem wretched to others, and was he worried about looking miserable? Did what other people think matter? Eventually he got tired of thinking about it.

There was a pleasant atmosphere to the room. Snug. It was a pity he didn't work here, but anyway, he had to get to work.

———

The next morning, he emerged unobserved from Natural History and walked out and made his way toward Port Authority.

As he was crossing a quiet street, a skinny black man approached him: "I've got something for you."

He made no response and strode on in that unlistening way that forms big cities, sensing his failure to look poor, crazy, and dangerous enough to repel contact. The poor and crazy he was pretty good at, but he was not getting anywhere near dangerous. But he stopped when the black man offered him an elephant.

He looked into the trailer, and irrefutably it was an Indian elephant. A young elephant, young enough to fit into the horse trailer, old enough to look disgruntled and tired of the elephant game. Shaking his head, he carried on.

"You need this elephant," exhorted the salesman, transmitting such urgency that, for a moment, he experienced the conviction that what he did indeed need was an elephant, this elephant. This emotion vanished as quickly as it had come. That was what it was all about essentially: people telling you you needed things, or that you enjoyed things, and then discovering that you didn't.

"A hundred dollars. A hundred dollars is all I'm asking." A bargain. Too good to pass up. But he didn't need an elephant, a dodgy one to boot; that much he had learned in his thirty-three years. He tended to be defined in the negative: he was someone who didn't need an elephant. The salesman was, almost by definition, a more interesting person since he needed to sell an elephant, although more desperate. Above all, he didn't have a place to put the elephant, since he didn't have a place to put himself. But perhaps that was the greatest gift, the knack of allowing yourself to be convinced of the imperativeness of a purchase and staying that way.

He went to his locker and rummaged round. He liberated the Bookcruncher T-shirt from the grip of other apparel and changed.

He didn't like the T-shirt anymore; he found it embarrassing. "Bookcruncher" in a bold arc at the top, the first two lines of *The Iliad* in the middle, and underneath, in lowercase, "fear me." It was the kind of item you had made when you were young and belligerent. A woman who had started lecturing him on dress sense in a diner despite his flagrantly reading two books to deflect her had been horrified to discover, when, under interrogation, he had calculated that the T-shirt was twelve years old. Genuinely horrified. But he didn't throw it away, since he never threw anything away, and like most unwanted items of clothing, it was indestructible.

Now he had the option of going round the corner to the Paramount Hotel for a quick wash or going to Sylvana's for a more comprehensive job; he was on for a shower, but the deal with Sylvana was doing the washing up and dusting in exchange for towelage. Sylvana had a lot of books that were phenomenally difficult to dust, and since he had now read all of them he found it hard to get involved.

He strolled over to the Paramount and entered the Gents, where he stripped to the waist, freshened up, flossed lengthily, and realized he didn't feel very industrious. He went there regularly and had never been bothered. Unintentionally, he supposed, he managed poor and crazy as done by the rich and foreign.

Afterward it was the Cuban restaurant and the special. He always ordered the special; this relieved him of the duty of studying the menu, and the staff of the duty of trying to unload the special. He was up to 1884, and he reached for his copy of *The Remarkable History of Sir Thomas Bart*, which was remarkable only in being boring, and *The Story of Charles Strange*, which wasn't strange but boring.

The garlic chicken and rice with black beans came after only three pages. As he made the first incision, he wondered whether his father was dead.

They said you only became a full man once your father died. One afternoon, would he suddenly feel a surge of power out of the blue and know? That would be the only way he'd get any news about his father.

He wondered how often he had that thought. Once every day for ten years? Twice every day? Three times every two days? How much time was it that he had wasted? For five minutes a go? Ten minutes? You wasted so much time with the same thoughts. People complained about having to do the same things, about having to eat the same things, about having to wear the same clothes, but they never had any problem thinking the same thoughts. He realized this was another thought almost as frequent as the preceding.

In the booth opposite him, a man in a porkpie hat reading a newspaper complained about the special.

That was the one thing he could thank his father for: he could and would eat anything without a murmur. It was not so much that his father had been a bad cook, but when his mother had left, the food had always been tasteless and stunningly unvarying: sausages, black pudding, and pork chops. Other carnal effects in danger of going off in his father's shop had been thrown in very occasionally. He wondered how often he thought that. Every time he saw someone fussing in a restaurant or leaving their food. Mealtimes, he had learned a long time ago, were something to be crossed.

You were granted immunity to your own thoughts, he decided; it was close to impossible to bore yourself. If you had to sit next to someone who would regularly say *that's one thing I can thank my father for* and *mealtimes are something to be crossed*, you would be gibbering within two days. So maturity is: when you stop having new sermonlets and you just drive ceaselessly round the roundabouts you've already built.

Nevertheless, he relished the rice pudding, bruised with a little cinnamon, and the coffee; it was good to go wild periodically. He mostly avoided the final thought of the paternal package—what was sad was not that they hated each other, but simply that there was nothing there. He had sonned adequately, and he wished his father could have pretended a little. After some years he had been granted a partial understanding of his father, when, on a train, he had seen one of his friends from school. He had not talked to him for five years, but he had not gone over to chat to him; he had nothing to say. It was funny, was it not, in a world where a satellite could tell your brand of toothpaste, where you could blast a million words ten thousand miles away in the lowering of a finger, where you could wallow in sitcom from any continent, where there was no hiding and no silence, he didn't know where his father was and he had nothing to say to him?

"You read a lot," said the behatted kvetch, indicating the two novels he had open. He nodded, because there was no denying it and because he didn't want to put up the ante for a conversation.

"Books aren't life."

"No, they're better," he replied and flipped through the thirty-two library cards in his wallet to remove his one credit card to pay.

This was twenty-first century vagrancy. An ocean away, in the rain, small sums of money carrying his name made the pilgrimage to a bank in Cambridge; meanwhile in London, small American debts trudged to an address where a check would be signed in an acceptable approximation of his signature by Elsa, giving him the right to plastic.

He felt good. Rice pudding and coffee goodness. And a no one else in the restaurant was doing what he did goodness. No one else in New York. Probably no one else in the world.

On his way to the public library, he stopped off at the post office to see what had appeared. One check, three months late. A book to review; that would be three hundred words saying what it was like, and three hundred words saying what it wasn't like; fine. An invitation to a conference.

Several letters from Elsa—a birthday batch of correspondence. These days, he always suffered from a temptation to put her letters straight into the rubbish, because over the last few years there had been nothing new. She had the same job, the same flat, and she employed the same expressions of concern and coaxing. He would have thought she would have got as tired of writing these sugardrops as he was of reading them, but no; they were her roundabouts.

But then Elsa was tenacious, and that was only one of her virtues. *Crunchy, you can't expect me to make the first move* was a phrase that turned up every fifth letter and was, he surmised, totally unironic despite Elsa having made every move from one to a thousand, and having used every weapon in the feminine arsenal from the smooth pebble to the shoulder-launched missile.

A wake of pink envelopes, cabinetloads of cards and other affection-heavy baubles had trailed him around the world: marzipan hippos, beanbag lions, furry diaries, a Bible keyring (surely the peak of incongruity since he had nowhere to live), chocolate breasts, tins of baked beans, inflatable lips, wind-up walking miniature Christmas trees—all bearing the message of softness. During periods of intense activity, she wrote almost every day; the bestial incarnations of the heart hunted him down: smiling bears, cheery dolphins came with the messages *for someone special, thinking of you makes me happy*. Along came the dejected rabbits, lugubrious moles, and forlorn kittens with the tag *missing you*. Elsa's supply of any object or animal capable of an alliance with endearment was apparently endless, despite her being a university graduate, thirty-two, a woman of good taste, and half of her communications failing to reach him.

No real reason why she had chosen him He knew his chief merit was that he had no demerits. He wouldn't beat her; he wouldn't go chasing after other women; he wouldn't drink or blow their money at the bookie's; he wouldn't make her watch football on the television, or defecate on the floor. Like the legless tortoise in the joke, you would find him where you left him. He had been tempted by Elsa's repeated insistence that there was room aplenty in her flat, that he could do his work there. He wouldn't take up much space, and his upkeep was minimal. It wouldn't be a bad arrangement.

The only reason he didn't take it up was that he didn't want it; and he knew if he yielded it would remove the possibility of her finding a proper happiness. Was it nobility or just recognition that he would be nulling her life?

Every now and then, silences of a few months' duration opened up, while Elsa's unsuccessful romances would be digested. A male silhouette would be spotted peripherally after Elsa went off on a holiday. A one-off reference to a forester met on a beach, a promoter met on a cruise. Her liaisons seemed to be only as long as hotel beds.

It was good to see that Upstairs didn't just punish the freaks. While Elsa's looks would never stop traffic, she was intelligent, employed, considerate, a good cook, had a job in which she met people all the time, but she still spent nights prowling a double bed, although all she wanted to do was to hose a man down with tenderness.

He never understood those who thought being different was stimulating or valuable. Anyone who has been on the outside knows how cold it is.

He went over to the public library, found a quiet corner, and loaded up. In the right *Three Weeks in Mopetown*, in the left *If I Were God*. Other readers often looked at him, but no one said anything.

The academic roundabout came, as it did nearly every day.

Why hadn't he got an academic job? Probably because he didn't want one. But he loved stepping out of the dark and shooting profs in the back. Repeatedly. He loved the unfairness of it.

He would start off by mentioning something obvious, so they hoped they had an audience worth showing off to. Then he would usher in something rare, to show he was heavy, to get an eyebrow raised. Finally, something truly obscure, only one or two copies in existence. To really scare them. It was easy. He did the nineteenth-century people by going back to the eighteenth; he did the eighteenth by using the seventeenth, the seventeenth

thing for sex, that her interest in him had nothing to do with
, and that everyone gets one free fuck.

When she had seized him, he had almost shaken her off
ause he had books to read, but he was glad he had got that
of the way.

hen there was the party when, just as he was regretting not
ing in the library he was so bored, two women stripped off.
felt like applauding but hadn't. The bafflement of the other
les was interesting, and it took him a few years to diagnose
t was going on; the unattached either were intimidated by
audacity of undressing or were unconcerned by women
ose genitalia were common knowledge; but inevitably, there
Kev from Belfast who did both of them over the rickety
ing board in the laundry room. Kev was the only one apart
n him who didn't complain about the college food. It was
n even then who was going to get on.

He picked at a bit of bean on his Bookcruncher T-shirt,
ch had fallen in and coalesced with the gable of Achilles' *A*.
But he had dedicated himself to reading everything.

hen, on reflection, he realized he couldn't do that. But
rything in English. Everything in book form. He had read a
d amount; he had been averaging three or four average
ks a day since eleven. Although some time had been
ted in irrelevant topics. He knew more about Chinese his-
y than was healthy for anyone but a Chinese historian, for
ance.

He had never explained his mission to anyone, because he
n't want anyone to know if he failed, and because he wasn't
e what the point was. He sensed there was an answer at the
, but he had no idea what it would be or what he would do
h it. Perhaps he would write something original. After all,
can you write something original if you haven't read every-
g before?

clobbered by the sixteenth. It was easy; you only had to move a
mere ten or fifteen years out of their fief to unsettle them. Then
some would smile with relief and say it was not their beat. How
could you understand writers if you didn't know what came
before, what they read? What the people they read had read?
With those who took refuge in their era, he would go back and
strafe their turf to show them that was no protection. That's
why he did the reviews.

He put down *If I Were God*. Eighteen eighty-four and counting. Getting the books in the right order was impossible, and he
couldn't be as neat as he'd like to be. He had to zigzag.

The Idea had come to him thirteen years ago on the third
floor of the university library, reading a letter by the extremely
dead Pope Pius II: "Without letters, every age is blind." And he
wondered what you would see if you had all the letters, if you
had read everything ever written. He was already living in the
library by that point, which was perhaps the start.

Or had Paris been the start? He had backpacked there with
Tom. Short of money, deeply uncool, they wandered around
hoping to accrue chic and excitement. They had been amazed at
the number of hotels in the Quartier Latin and how full they all
were. After two hours of walking around, they found one that
had a free room, but they didn't have the money. They were
offered a lesson in why people booked rooms at the height of
the tourist season.

Three times they had walked past the bookshop; he had
astonished himself with his self-control. The fourth time, he
suggested to Tom they go in.

He had known about Shakespeare & Co. and what it was. He
had been young then, fairly ignorant, but alert enough to know
about Joyce and Eliot being bandits. Once inside, he was
disabled by the choice, but Tom, who had no time for books,
went up to the counter to ask the crumpled man for hotel ideas.

They had never been in Paris before, let alone the bookshop, but the man had clearly seen them a thousand times.

He sighed: "If you're really stuck, you can stay here for one night. That's one night."

So he spent his first night in Paris in a bookshop, or, more significantly, he spent his first night in a bookshop in Paris. Tom went out to have a kebab and then returned to talk to two American girls who were also in for the night and eating yogurt, while Shakespeare & Co. became his favorite bookshop. He didn't eat and he didn't sleep all night because he was so fascinated by the American editions he had never seen before.

He had watched the sun come up over Notre-Dame and remembered how supposedly Faust had arrived in Paris, his baggage bulging with newly printed Gutenberg Bibles to sell, and how he had been encouraged to get lost by the Parisian manuscript guilds, who didn't want their action cut into.

It had unstoppered him. You didn't have to leave when the bookshop closed. You stayed and carried on reading. He was already spending so much time in local bookshops that he was pegged as a shoplifter, but now he realized, he could spend many more hours in bookshops. But he hadn't sensed it was the start. Just holiday fun.

The start had been in attendance that evening in the university library, when he had been accidentally locked in. Then he had started staying in occasionally throughout the night because he didn't want to leave. He was never discovered; the staff came round at closing time, but it was easy to hide in the nocturnal stacks of a quiet top floor and then emerge unremarked in the morning.

True, the phone call from his father had been part of the start. After his first term, he found himself cut off. His father had missed out on university; had at sixteen, as he often publicized, gone straight into butchering. The encouragement he

had received to go to university, he discovere[d] encouragement to go. He found himself adri[ft] change to fill a trouser pocket.

Hardly the greatest cruelty the world had s[een] found a job, but he decided to cut his expens[es] room, putting most of his stuff into stora[ge] library at night, reading most of the time, th[en] the college in the morning, where he would u[se] munal bathrooms; followed by some shoppi[ng] back to the library.

He had none of the standard student expe[rience] anywhere. From arriving at Cambridge till [he] leave, apart from once accompanying Elsa an[d] countryside foray for pubs. He didn't go to th[e] bing. Buying clothes was out. Eating properl[y] books was out. Boozing was out. There was th[e] arship, and the hardship fund. He did some w[ork] sity library during the holidays, so everyone [knew] him around. And his life wasn't just the UL; [the] other libraries for some variety and a change [of]

An uncomfortable awareness touched him [that] one else who had his tastes: that he was a part [of] was constantly friendly to him, but they h[ad] Nevertheless, he had some fun. One afternoo[n] up in Silver Street and conducted back to a be[d] who worked as a cleaner at the hospital. "Unc[le]" addressing him as he struggled to loose her gri[p] to remember whether he had ever seen her bef[ore] ing you here; why not come back to my place?"

Some great passion, he had imagined, was e[ver] a week he tended only amorous poetry, but of c[ourse] could be found on any street at any time. He le[arned] of things: he cottoned on to why most people [were]

The numbers are daunting. A few hundred books to 1500. Some ten thousand to 1600. Eighty thousand to 1700. Three hundred thousand to 1800. Then things go crazy. Much of it was recloaking. Much of it was dross. Much of it was brief. But if he hadn't come up with the two-book technique, simultaneously reading one book in his right hand and one book in his left, he wouldn't have got anywhere.

It occurred to him that he might appear pitiful. After he had been living in North London bookshops for four years, subsisting on reviews and marrying Japanese women who wanted nationality lifts, although he felt fine, he could see that people might think spending your whole life in either bookshops or libraries was wretched. He decided he couldn't spend all his time in bookshops in North London since he didn't want his horizons stunted. So he started touring: France, Germany, and finally America.

What had he learned so far? Motion looks like progress. German bookshops had champagne, but only in American bookshops could you get frappuccino.

And hope. Hope. Books were made of hope, not paper. Hope that someone would read your book; hope that it would change the world or improve it; hope that people would agree with you; hope that you'll be remembered, celebrated; hope that people would feel something. Hope that you would learn something; hope that you'll entertain or impress; hope you'll catch some cash; hope that you'll be proved right; and hope that you'll be proved wrong.

Unfortunately there was the problem that even if you read everything you don't read it as the same person. When he first read *The Iliad*, the opening was just the opening: an explanation. The anger of Achilles: people always thought it referred to Achilles' rage at losing his favorite slave-girl or his sidekick Patroclus.

When he had read it first at eleven, he hadn't read it. At seventeen, when he reapplied, it was beginning to come into focus.

Yet only when he was thirty and he had been stuck in a lift, and he had gone in for the third time had the meaning dripped through like portly raindrops infiltrating a roof.

It was no accident that the first word in Western literature was anger. Achilles' anger. He now saw it was anger at being alive, anger at having no choice. *The Iliad* was the truth, *The Odyssey* the sales brochure, where you dally with tricky women, get home, and slaughter all the people who have been giving you grief. *The Iliad* was the scoop: stuck in a war you didn't ask for, working with chumps who couldn't even find Troy in the first place, unable to forget that your mother left you and that a centaur made you eat entrails, no choice, no challenge, and the knowledge that you're not going home and that nothing is going to make you feel better.

When he read reports of spree killers topping themselves, he saw it wasn't because of remorse or desire to dodge the penal system, but despair because their actions hadn't made them feel any better, that they had leaped over the edge and the anger was still there. And it ran all the way through. Gilgamesh was angry. Jahweh was angry. Moses was angry. Pharaoh was beside himself. Electra was incandescent. Oedipus frothing. The Ronin were hopping mad. Hamlet was miffed. Orlando was furioso.

The problem was Upstairs . . . Karma. Kismet. Destiny. Fate. The Fates. Parcae. Namtar. The Norns. Doom. Fortune. Providence. Luck. Cosmo. Allah. Book of Fate. Threads. The words turned up again and again; they were the clichés he read over and over, not because the writers were unimaginative but because there was no other way of putting it.

Fulhams were what you got. The dice were loaded, but you had to throw them to see how the numbers fell.

———

He strolled to the Barnes & Noble on Union Square.

Generally the bigger they were, the easier it was. You found a quiet stretch of shelving just before closing time and made yourself scarce until everyone had gone and you could get bookcrunching. He hadn't been caught very often. Over the years he had only been apprehended four times and had been let off.

They had looked at him in a way he didn't like to think about, which suggested that he was either a failed burglar who couldn't get it right, or too failed an individual to want to be close to. Only the woman in Nuneaton had called the police. "I'm calling the police," she had hissed. He could easily have run off, but he waited, not understanding why the woman had said that, since if he had been possessed of criminal intent or a guilty conscience it would have primed him to get going or to get heavy. He hadn't run off, chiefly because he had nowhere to run to. He had read twenty pages of *North and South* before the constabulary showed up. They weren't able to get very excited, with no sign of damage, forced entry, or theft. "We'll say no more about it this time," one said, since there really was nothing to say.

It was not being prepared. You would fumble for a sentence in your pocket and come out with what was there or carry on fumbling. Walking home from school when he was eleven, two girls his age, whom he had noticed regularly walking home the other way on the other side of the street, crossed over. "Is it okay if I hit you?" the blonde had asked. He had been thinking about the question and an answer, when the blonde's fist impacted unpleasantly on his jaw. He then thought what he should do. He smiled and walked away.

Without preparation, it was sticky. In Portland once, he had been deep into Phlegon of Tralles's *Book of Marvels* and the emperor Hadrian's centaur, so engrossed and not expecting anything since it was a humid summer two o'clock in the morning, sleepy in a sleepy town, that he hadn't registered another presence in the bookshop.

His attention was disturbed by the owner, a large man clutching a camp bed, pleading not to be killed. "Please don't kill me," the owner repeated, sinking to his knees; puzzling since he was only armed with a 215-page paperback and the incident with the girl had taught him he didn't have a fearsome aspect.

"The air-conditioning packed up at home. It's just too hot. I have money here; I'll show you. I won't tell the police anything. Just let me live." He had wanted to roll out his standard story of having been accidentally locked in, but he never had been any better at lying than he had been at telling the truth, and the owner was having none of it. Taking the money was the easiest option, so he did and went to a hotel with enough books to get himself through the next day. He could see how he might be perceived as criminal, but he couldn't fathom how he had made it to dangerous, yet the incident left him splattered with interestingness and power.

As Barnes & Noble closed, he hunkered down in Politics and waited an hour for the building to clear of sounds. There had never been a book that hadn't contained fibers of other books; to write, you have to read first. Could he be a person that had nothing of others in him? Was there anyone else who worried about no one eating fish in *The Iliad*? And who remembered the thirty-three terms of abuse for tax collectors gathered by Pollux of Naucrates? At the same time wondering if Apuleius's lost novel *Hermagoras* would ever turn up? While not forgetting to ponder if the *De Tribus Impostoribus Mundi* had ever existed?

He then made for the luxurious armchair that had endeared Barnes & Noble to him so much and plunged into (on the right) *Singularly Deluded* and (on the left) *The World's Desire*.

He got tired of it sometimes, but he kept going because he had gone too far to go back. A bout of weakness had made him take a job for two months, but it hadn't made things better.

His concentration couldn't have been that good because he heard coughing. For a few moments he sat motionless as if that might change something. Faintly, he detected it again. He thought about letting coughing be coughing but couldn't get back into left or right.

Reluctantly investigating, on the first floor, he could see a thin woman dressed in mixed black. Attractive. He knew she wasn't staff; he was familiar with the assistants, and also she had an . . . unstaffy manner. She was reading.

Not only was she reading intently, but she held a book in her left hand and another in her right.

His steps startled her. Promptly, she closed the books and slotted them back into the shelves. "You must be closing," she said in an appealing way. Her skin was pale, her lips gotcha red.

He wanted to say that he didn't work there.

"Don't look at me that way," she snapped.

She set the alarms off as she left.

He concluded that he felt okay, but he feared he would feel bad, and that the badness was on its way.

I Like Being Killed

He had asked her to come for lunch that day.

"We haven't had lunch together for a long time," Owen observed. He was peculiarly insistent about it, and Miranda would have been quite happy to accept, but she already had a rendezvous. Strictly shagging. A strictly shagging engagement on the other side of London.

"I'm a bit under the weather . . . I'll give it a miss, but thanks for asking."

Owen urged her to come. She said she was feeling very ill and would have to stay in bed all day. He said it was very sudden, and she said yes it was.

"What is it?"

"Don't know."

"Do you want me to get you something?"

"No."

"Sure?"

"Sure. You go to work; I can die peacefully."

So he went to work, and she waved ailingly at him as he strode down the road.

Then she had a shower, got dressed, and spent an hour and a half getting across town to Headstone. She had never been to Headstone before, she had never heard of it before, she didn't know anyone who had heard of it, and she was confident she would never go there again. An encounter with an out-of-work actor two days previously was taking her there; among other things, they had discussed computers. He had one he wanted to sell; Miranda wanted to buy one. "Come over to my place and have a look," he had said. Nevertheless, he had known he wasn't going to be selling, and she knew she wasn't going to be buying. Despite all sorts of latitude, you didn't say, "Come over to my place at half past eleven, and we can go at it hammer and tongs."

Miranda did have a look at the computer. She could see it from the bed when they did it doggy style, until pleasure deprived her of vision. Her satisfaction surpassed total, despite the actor's breaking off twice to instruct his solicitor about suing one director who hadn't given him work and another who had.

As Miranda left the flat, she walked into Owen, who was coming out of the flat opposite. Owen had never been to Headstone before, he had never heard of it before, he would never go there again, and he had spent an hour getting there from his office to see a client. To underline everything, the actor, in red boxer shorts, rushed out to present her with her bra, which she had forgotten.

"I was going to propose," was all Owen said.

What were the odds? She couldn't add up very well, but mathematics had always fascinated her. Greater London has seven million people, not counting the tourists, the illegals, the commuters, nonspecific interlopers. What were the odds? Two hundred million to one? Five hundred million to one? Two billion to one? It was a meteor strike. A lotteryless lottery win.

She wasn't embarrassed because she never was. But she was sorry for Owen and regretted hurting him. He was into the couple deal in a way few men were; he didn't expect her to sit patiently at home with the hot food while he attempted to upend as many women as he could. And his desire for pairing wasn't, as it so often is, out of desperation (no one else will ever talk to me). He was good-looking, intelligent, funny, considerate, and a great lay with more party invitations than he knew what to do with. He talked of how you had to work at living together and make sacrifices—and it wasn't razzmatazz. He even *liked* washing up.

Miranda saw she had been selfish, that he was too good for her, and that he could create happiness elsewhere. Being with Owen was like using a Ming vase as an ashtray: wasteful; or, as she swapped simile, a vegan winning a lifetime's supply of prime steak: unnecessary.

After Headstone, she came to three conclusions: if everyone else enjoyed it as much as she did, there would be no civilization; that everyone in London has a Headstone story; and, finally, it was a mistake living with someone you liked, and that she would never do so again.

$$\Sigma$$

Trying to define *comedy* and thinking about how to hold the mike had occupied Miranda all afternoon. They lived on the third floor, so pondering out of the window, she spotted Tony walking home in good time to get back into bed and to affect a lackadaisical air. She did this for two reasons: because Tony was inclined to believe that, if he found her in bed when he came home, she hadn't disembarked all day (this imagined indolence really got to him), and because she didn't want him or anyone else to find out how much sweat she did put in.

He located her in the bedroom.

"Hard day?"

"Mmmm."

"You haven't forgotten we're going out?"

"Mmmm," she responded by pulling up the eiderdown. He retreated to the kitchen, and after a few minutes she shuffled to the bathroom for an outrageously long bath. She had no trouble being punctual, but Tony got so worked up about being late that she couldn't resist it. As she splished and sploshed she could hear him restraining himself from pacing up and down, and swallowing admonitions. Miranda emerges in a towel.

"You haven't seen my tweezers, have you?"

"Aren't they in the bathroom?"

"The tweezers in the bathroom are the rubbish tweezers. I'm looking for the good tweezers."

"Can't help you then. Could I say at this point, in a non-pressurizing, non-nagging, and generally non-annoying way, that we should leave in ten minutes?"

"Do you think saying that's going to do any good?"

"In that case, I didn't say anything."

Miranda stares at Tony attempting to appear as if he's reading a magazine and not waiting for her. Not looking up, he says, "I didn't say anything."

Not for the first time, she rates her dislike of Tony. Tony the Pony. Reliable. Steerable. Forgettable. But that's why she lives with him. Why can't men be men? Why doesn't he just slap her around the face, so she could go to dinner with a black eye? The thought pleases her, although she also recalls the only man who ever gave her a black eye (Irish plumber with wife and family back in Ireland who lashed out when she said she was going to abort his unintended child to avoid a career in single mother-hood) had to leap out of a first-floor window while putting on his trousers to avoid the kitchen knife she was propelling toward him.

Miranda returns to the bathroom and the joke tweezers; she got them in a free beauty kit years ago. They work, sort of, but they give no satisfaction. With the other pair, when you pull a hair it feels as if it's been pulled forever.

She puts on her black dress, pries off some lint, and takes much longer than the most demanding dentist in a bad mood would stipulate to floss her teeth.

"So what do you think?" She twirls for his judgment. Tony knows he can't win; that's the test. A hopeless outcome either way. Aware that he has already lost, will he go down fighting?

"Great. You look great."

"You're just saying that to please me."

"There wouldn't be much point in trying to please you, would there?" For a moment she thinks he will let rip, but he puts on his coat and walks out with a come-or-don't-come finality. It is a moment of small dignity, but too small to activate any admiration.

People don't change, she thought as she got in the car. Once you've had a good look inside someone, you're not going to be surprised; people weren't predictable, but they didn't change; a train can jump off its rails, but that doesn't make it a kangaroo. And that was a real problem.

"There's a really impatient man behind us," says Tony to confirm her assessment. Tony said this quite often, though sometimes he said: "There's a really impatient woman behind us," or, in poor visibility, "There's a really impatient driver behind us." There was generally an impatient motorist behind Tony since he drove everywhere at between thirty-three and thirty-five miles an hour. Miranda suspected that this would be the last time she would let Tony drive her anywhere. She couldn't bear it anymore. What got her goat was not so much that his top whack was approximately thirty-five miles an hour, because the traffic being what it was, you rarely had a chance to exceed that limit; it wasn't the slothfulness that was irritating. And if he had done it out of some excessive lawfulness kick, that wouldn't have been so bad. The unbearable part was that Tony didn't understand he was driving far slower than everyone else, and that the world wasn't full of impatient people, but that he went around creating them.

She started to tense up as they approached their destination. Tony's other line around parking time was "This space is too small." Any space was too small unless it could comfortably take three cars. Incredibly, there was a huge stretch of uncarred pavement that you could fit a lorry on. Miranda had to go back to her childhood to remember a parking gap that size. Pavements no longer seemed to come with ordinary curbstones, but with cars fixed on.

Miranda thought about house spiders. Where had they lived before there were houses? They had been around for millions of years before man. Was humanity just brought in by the arachnids to keep them out of the rain? And what about those reports she had heard that in some parts of London exterminators had discovered that mice would only eat McDonald's hamburgers. Cheese, fruit, chocolate, muesli, everything else—they turned up their noses. Was this the actual purpose of the urban abomination, providing junk food for rodents? There was something in all this. Then she recalled the two foxes she had seen the other day, sunning themselves in the back garden. They had noticed her but had been completely unbothered, annoyingly so; happy and relaxed, they had been more at ease with life in the city than she was or anyone she knew. They gamboled lazily; it was their beach holiday. Man can't handle the big city and the wildlife sniggers. There was something in this.

Despite being Tony's friends, Heather and Imran were good company. Lily and Damien were also there. Lily worked with Heather and would have been great to have had in an audience since she laughed at everything. "Good evening," "What would you like to drink?" "These potatoes are great" all cracked her up. Miranda had met her before and disliked her; mostly because she could tell Lily was like her; she lived for cock. This annoyed her because Lily was only nineteen.

Before Miranda had come to a conclusion about the only real currency in life, she had been around. She had done drugs, from the qualified and the unqualified. Education (however botched). Therapies galore. Travel. Of all sorts. She had got to her position after a journey. A decision twenty-seven years in the making. Lily's spreading her legs was nothing but spending your entire life in the same house.

Damien wasn't bad-looking. He was much older than Lily, around the crucifixion age, and was, on the one hand, having great sex (you could tell how good a couple's liaisons were), but on the other hand he was slightly uncomfortable about being with the office tart.

"I hear you're a stand-up comedian, Miranda."

"Sometimes I sit down."

"Do you make a living doing that?" Damien was an insurance adjuster, and like most straights with well-paid, securish, but essentially dreary jobs, he was terrified and aghast at the idea that someone with a profession that seemed exciting and glamorous, and one without a safety net, should also have the temerity to make money. He wanted to hear that she had to work as a barmaid or security guard to get a crust. Tony could have chipped in here with a wisecrack about how she might have made a living but he paid most of the bills. Miranda was never involved in paying rent, gas, electricity, water, food; she didn't mind spending her money on clothes. But Tony kept quiet. It wasn't consideration. Tony was a Pony, and the Pony was counting on his mix of wild oats later on.

"So far."

It was at this point people began to get worried that you might be very successful and merely reluctant to talk about it. "Are you famous?" was a question she had been asked more than once, presumably so that her interlocutor could take down her details again for future reference if the answer was yes. She hadn't worked out a really good riposte to that. Presumably if the question had to be asked, there wasn't a really good riposte. Then there was the other question, which Damien asked, "Have you been on television yet?" which was in many ways the equivalent of the first. For most people, television was the tower of importance, the name maker, the conferrer of existence. True and false; often it didn't matter.

Evidence: Catford Stan ("I should have come from Stanmore, but I didn't"). In the whole of the business, he was one of the handful to have really made it, although even in the business many people didn't know who he was; certainly no one outside the business knew who he was, although they might have seen him. You wouldn't remember him, although you might remember the jokes. Stan told jokes so dirty you feared the ceiling would collapse in disgust. Old jokes too. And not even old jokes that people had forgotten. As Stan put it, "I'm not funny. I tell jokes." A joke teller who made more money than almost anyone else, working stag nights chiefly. Unless you were playing Wembley, you weren't getting more wedge than Stan. Fame really didn't offer much. On the circuit people either weren't making it and basting themselves with rage, hatred, and any other toxins they could lay their hands on, or were making it but then were shitting it royally about how long the flight would last and whether anyone was really their friend.

Stan was happy. He raked it in, paid no tax (cash + no one had ever heard of him), bedded most of the strippers whom he compered, and never worried about whether it would last since he was also much in demand as a furniture restorer, which he enjoyed doing much more than performing. He still lived in a one-bedroom flat in Catford, and not a nice one-bedroom flat either, which puzzled people, although there was a persistent rumor that he owned an island off Cornwall.

"Say something funny," said Lily, giggling because Tony had asked her to pass the salt.

"Something funny," said Miranda, but Lily didn't laugh at that. Miranda didn't bother talking after that. She didn't do dinner parties anymore; unless she was paid to be entertaining, she wouldn't disport herself. She moved her foot up and down Damien's calf. He managed to keep a straight face. Tony talked about some of his ideas for pumping up the guilt and heartstring plucking among the citizens of Britain so they would contribute to his charity, which worked for children with incurable diseases.

She now moved her foot up and down Damien's leg in an unmistakably erective style, to make it clear this wasn't some subtable accident. She was curious what Damien would do; her breasts had been amply stared at, and, short of snorting and stamping his foot, his signals couldn't have been bigger.

Damien was beginning to sweat now. He was worried that Tony or Lily would notice. Silly, in even fifty years it wouldn't matter whether he garroted them, let alone annoyed or upset them. She tried to stretch up to his lunchbox but unfortunately couldn't. He cared about what the others thought. She didn't. Who was better off? She got tired of the game.

"I'm just going upstairs," she said as she went up to the bathroom. What would have been nice would have been Damien following her up so they could have screamy sex amplified by the tiles, while those remaining at the table would have to pretend nothing was happening. Damien didn't oblige.

Because his ideas had been applauded and because she hadn't humiliated him, Tony went home in a good, engorged mood. The prospect of Tonysex did nothing for her, but in the way a champion has to be able to produce even when under the weather or beset by tabloid troubles, she wrung his brains out. As the Pony whinnied into sleep, she lay there in the soul-smashing darkness thinking about a cover she had designed for her diary when she was eighteen. The cover had read:

> *No life after life*
> *No one will help you*
> *You are all alone*
> *You always will be*

It had an equational neatness, and she believed it was true, but she had thrown away the cover after a month because it had depressed her too much. It was her truth, but it was as much use as a light coating of petrol in a forest fire. Having the truth was on a par with having a bit of chocolate melted into your pocket, just something there, not something that had any use. Or wearing blue socks instead of yellow socks after you had jumped off a skyscraper.

There was no help; nevertheless, she needed it. And she had to stay off the metaphysics and the imagery.

$$\Sigma$$

Too much time had been wasted trying to find the good tweezers, so she had bought a pair. Not that it had been easy; the shops seemed to delight in selling dreck.

"Where do jokes come from?" Miranda asked. "Have you ever thought about that? Not the routines rehashed from television, but the jokes that pop up topped and tailed, a beginning, a middle, and an end. A flourish on an event. Something happens in the world and there's a joke. Nobody knows who made it up, nobody knows where it comes from, but it goes round the world like the sun."

"Does this mean you don't want to come?" Tony says, looking at his watch.

"I think it's God. That's why everything falls apart in the world, the famines, the massacres, the plagues, the earthquakes; he's too busy with the one-liners and the payoffs. We're his captive audience."

"Miranda, if you don't want to come, just say so. You don't have to."

Was Tony getting cleverer? This time she wasn't winding him up, but one of her favorite games was to get Tony ready to go out, then to say she didn't want to, so Tony would take off his jacket, kick off his shoes, open a beer, and settle in front of the television, only for her to say she wanted to go out again. So he would switch off the television, put the beer back in the fridge, put his shoes on again, find his keys, only to discover that she wanted to stay in again. Her record stood at seven switches.

As they went down the stairs, they found their downstairs neighbor Regina on her hands and knees, with a broom and pan, cleaning the carpeting on the stairwell, while her mother stood over her, supervising. Miranda had heard stories from her friends of their mothers turning up and raiding their dirty linen, rearranging their cutlery drawers, getting on ladders to check the tops of bookshelves for dust, or even sneaking into their flat and redecorating it a color more to their taste while they were away on holiday, but this was a landmark. It would be a hard job with a vacuum cleaner, let alone by hand. It was one of those chores that was supposed to be shared in the house, so, of course, it never got done.

"The dirt out here's terrible," Regina's mother commented as they passed. Regina came from Bolton, and her mother was clearly convinced that the capital had corrupted her daughter, and a sure sign of it was her indifference to the helixes of dust, mud pellets, ash, and leaf fragments partying in the stairwell. Regina smiled cheerily. She had obviously gone for the do-as-you're-told policy of mother-handling, with a she'll-only-be-here-for-another-day forbearance. Regina was a harpist, and her mother's anxiety over outlaw particles harming her daughter's welfare was incongruous as Regina made most of her money working for an escort agency. Regina didn't consider herself good-looking, but "a fake tan and a low-cut top—they work." Miranda had nodded. Men in the main were easier to deal with than budgies. Or her boiler. The boiler had three controls, and she had had more trouble operating that than most men.

Regina specialized in businessmen from the North who only wanted someone to laugh at their jokes, agree with them about how awful London was, join them on the dance floor, look like a young prostitute, and come back to their hotel rooms so they would be thought of as hard-living sensualists. Regina's limit was hand-jobs for very well-behaved clients under forty, for which they were extremely grateful.

Finally, Miranda didn't get to the event in Islington. The fund-raising flare-up came as they got across the barriers at the tube. She was a little ashamed of herself for needling Tony about his job; it was too easy and too well trodden a route. A new instrument of torture should have been created, but she had got him to melt down by charting how all the money his charity raised was rerouted to Swiss banks or lesser despots in the countries he was trying to help.

"You're right," shouted Tony. "It usually is a waste of time trying to help people. Money's stolen. Messes get messier. The wrong stuff is sent out. The fucked-upness is so intense sometimes you think your head will explode. It may be what I do doesn't remove a second of pain for one child. Perhaps. But at least I'm trying to do something for someone else. You should try it, just once, for the experience."

Tony's rage impressed her, but she didn't show it. Was she goading Tony into developing some character? She doubted it. Trains didn't become kangaroos. Miranda let Tony storm off into the night. She hadn't been keen on spending an hour in a room full of affluent people who had just purchased a tasteful perspective of themselves as justice dispensers. The Pony would canter home on his own, thinking of his nosebag of wild oats. Instead, she went down to Soho and killed time by drinking coffee, misdirecting tourists, and phoning up the Top Dog in several voices—Polish matron, American geologist, Italian cyclist, Welsh ecowarrior, Glasgow roadie, and her favorite, the Iraqi dentist—to ask about the brilliant Miranda Piano, what time was she appearing tonight, and were there any tickets left?

From having two hours to kill, she managed to arrive late. But there was not much point arriving early. You'd have to sit in the prep room, doing some jealousy and hatred with your fellow performers about the performers who weren't there, while Annette the wrong barmaid brought you the wrong drink. Annette came from the Australian outback, and there was something particularly fine about someone coming all that distance to annoy people in London. If you asked for bitter, you get lager. If you asked for draft, you got bottled. If you asked for brandy, you got Scotch. If you asked for coffee, you got tea. She had tried asking for a brandy when she had wanted a Scotch, but she had got a brandy. There was no way round it. Miranda had complained once, and Annette had slapped her round the face. Everyone had got together and written down their choices on a piece of paper. "You think I'm stupid," Annette had said. "You flakes think I can't remember a couple of drinks. Whose idea was this?" There had been a severe soundlessness and much observation of shoelaces. Annette had refused to serve them any more drinks until Miranda had eaten the piece of paper and everyone had bought her a drink. It was a lesson.

As the room was crowded, Miranda chose not to fight her way to the prep room but to lurk with the punters. She was looking around for somewhere to sit (there weren't many chairs—the management weren't optimists) when a beanpole in a turtleneck, who was sitting chatting intently with a girl, noticed her scanning and leaned over to the next table and persuaded them to release a chair from its coat-holding duties. He then picked up the chair and lifted it over for Miranda. Miranda was shocked at his courtesy and worried for him. He wore glasses, and glasses could be fashionable and admirable, but his weren't. They, like everything else about him, transmitted the message: beat me up. He would clearly have been the first choice for a kicking at school. His companion, who was quite attractive, was clearly not going to sleep with him. Miranda wanted to tell him not to be so concerned with other people, not to lay himself open like that, but she knew it would do no good. She thanked him with a nod.

Captain NoGood was already into his set, which Miranda had seen half a dozen times. There were some people whom you could watch doing the same routine half a dozen times and it actually got funnier, but this didn't apply to the Captain. He had a reputation, though, because at a gig two years before, someone had dropped dead. It couldn't be proved that the audience member had expired from an overdose of mirth as people died from heart attacks all the time, in churches, in police stations, in hospitals, in their sleep, in lectures, but it was no use pretending that taking out a member of the audience wasn't eye-catching.

In any case, the Captain was three hundred years of fun compared to the star attraction, Arthur Leech. Leech was a cult comedian—that is, he wasn't funny at all. When Miranda had started to work the circuit, she had been astonished to discover that there were turns who weren't funny at all, not a little bit. Not a question of a bad night, or rough material, or a stiff audience; they were not funny. Then she had reflected that there were lawyers who knew nothing about the law, doctors who knew nothing about medicine, businessmen who knew nothing about business; why shouldn't there be comedians who weren't funny? Leech had been at it so long, he kept on being employed because it never occurred to someone not to book him and because he was assiduous in licking arse.

She also disliked Leech because he was Scottish. What bored her about the Scots was their inevitable ranting about how effeminate Londoners and the English were, how they couldn't play football, how great Scotland was, invariably when they were propping up a bar in London.

As Miranda stepped out to solid applause to begin, she realized she didn't feel like performing, and that she didn't want Leech, who was on after her, to have an audience. She decided to drive them out. To destroy the audience.

There were about thirty people, and they had been warmed up by Captain NoGood.

"Before we begin," Miranda said, "I'm sorry, but I have to vet the audience. I won't perform for any old Tom, Dick, or Harry. This is a top-flight comedy and is suitable only for sentient human beings."

They laughed at that.

"I don't want anyone stupid in this audience."

She walked up to a girl in the front row who was enjoying herself too much and inciting others to merriment.

"You. What's seventeen times twenty-three?" Miranda had no idea what it was. So much for her two years studying math at Middlesex University.

The girl shook her head. Miranda called over to Mussa, the bouncer. Mussa was Senegalese, a doctor, and she knew he had been mugged by two twelve-year-old girls on the Railton Road. "We're twelve, and we're going to mug you," they had said. Mussa emphasized that the girls had been large for their age, and armed with some object in a brown paper bag they said was a stun gun. Mussa had no idea what a stun gun looked like or what it might look like in a brown bag, so he took their word for it. Nevertheless, he was six foot two and looked the part, although he smiled too much. At her insistence, Mussa escorted the girl out, playing along with her. The audience loved this. Even the girl seemed amused.

Miranda tried to be perfectly serious. "Let me tell you about life, the universe, and everything. The universe is there to provide me with hard, curvy cock. Life, let me tell you about life. Here's how it works. Life turns up and asks you what it is you want—fame? riches? shagging? happiness?—and says: 'Fame: Okay, I can do you fame in one thousand hard payments.'

"And you say, 'So, that's fame in one thousand hard payments.'

"Life says, 'No, that's half-fame I'm offering you in two thousand hard payments.'

"And you say, 'Wait a minute, you said fame in one thousand hard payments.'

"Life says, 'You're not listening, I said a quarter-fame for four thousand hard payments.'

"You say, 'Okay, whatever. I'll take it.' But life's gone. And that's everything."

She has reduced one man to a donkey. He brays ceaselessly, which the audience find funnier than what she's doing. She has destroyed this audience. But not in the direction she had been aiming for. Two people in the front row have creased up almost fetally.

"You'll laugh at anything, you lot." Miranda went to the bar and looked for a telephone directory. She started reading. They started laughing. She had hit a seam of pure comedy. Some moments you only appreciate ten, twenty, forty years later, but she knew instantly that this would be the best audience she would ever have; even though she didn't want it, when there would be no record of it. Just the thirty people present who would let her lead them anywhere.

Embarrassment was her next tactic. A notion existed that harvesting your own life, plucking and opening up the blacknesses, was a sovereign source of material; but only certain sorts of painted confessions were in demand. Nearly everyone worked hard, nearly everyone was in the shit, and when they paid money for a night out, they wanted a laugh. Like a bag of chips, they wanted a bundle of laughs. Bitterness about your husband leaving you for an older, worse-toothed, poorer woman or about your younger sister dying messily of an incurable disease was a turnoff. Because people didn't want to hear, and they didn't want to hear not entirely because they wanted amusement but because they didn't want to be reminded that they had sympathy.

"I have a problem," announced Miranda, convinced she could trample on their grins. "I've been to lots of shrinks. My mother committed suicide when I was twelve. My problem is this. I miss her. Can anyone help? Is anyone here clever enough to solve the problem?"

Miranda could feel an audience's mood, like a fruit. The audience fruit had a surface that informed her instantly of impatience or enjoyment burgeoning, a surface so candid even in an audience of thirty, one person unwilling or nodding off could be distinguished. The audience happily forsook comedy, eager to see where she would take them.

"I thought not," she said after a long silence. "I'd give twenty years of my life to spend five minutes with her."

Then Miranda walks off. A trickle of applause which detonates into a half–standing ovation follows her. Leech, significantly, has walked out. Captain NoGood gives a what-the-hell-was-that?-but-whatever-it-was-it-was-great grimace.

Outside, the expelled girl is waiting anxiously. "Is it okay for me to come back in?"

A nineties Soho standard male, number-one cut, chic glasses, and a black leather jacket, struggles up to Miranda and asked for her number mysteriously. On the basis that she didn't see why she should give her number to some unidentified tosser, she did. She didn't collect her money. It wasn't that the Top Dog didn't pay, but it didn't do anything to make it easy. Jack the promoter didn't flee the country, but he wouldn't be anywhere in a five-mile radius. He was always there at the beginning of the evening, so newcomers assumed they'd get their lolly at the end, but by then he'd be gone. She'd catch him at lunch tomorrow.

She'd learned something; all she had to do was figure out what it was.

$$\Sigma$$

"If you're using the tweezers for some strange sexual purpose, you can tell me now," Miranda urged.

"I'm not. I am not using the tweezers for any sexual purpose, strange or otherwise."

Tony was trying to read some fund-raising document, so she didn't want to let him. He only needed fifteen minutes' concentration to do it, and she didn't want him to succeed.

"If you confess to being homosexual now, I'll forgive you."

"I'm not."

"I can tell, Tony. You're into turd-burglary big-time, aren't you?"

Tony threw down the papers, realizing it was the moment for a last stand. Suddenly, she felt guilty about the unfortunate children, the expiring orphans her needling might be doing out of succor. But she couldn't back down now. Hit hard, fight dirty.

"I never see you trying to sleep with other women."

Tony reeled, totally blasted by the outrageous accusation. But back he came.

"Perhaps you could set something up for me?" he retorted. He was learning to like punishment. "You could watch."

"But you're the one who always goes on about true love, Tonee," she said, trying to throw him with a hundred-and-eighty degree turn.

"And you're the one who always goes on about sex. No matter how you look at it, there's nothing more important than fidelity."

"Shagging."

"That's a momentary pleasure."

"You have a point, Ton-eee, but if you get enough momentary pleasure, and lay it end to end, you get constant pleasure. You don't care about me; Damien was staring at my breasts the whole evening, and you did nothing about it."

"They're wonderful breasts."

"I think Damien's attracted to me."

"Why not? You're very attractive. I'm always telling you how beautiful you are, but you refuse to believe me."

"That's because you have a perverse fixation."

"I suppose that's what love is," he yelled, kicking the table, doing neither party any good.

The phone rang, instigating a time-out. She had put him in his place; that was the main thing. A man was on the line claiming he had seen her set last night and that she had given him her telephone number last night.

"No I didn't. Who are you?"

"Ha-ha," said the caller. He actually said it. Then he said he was a television producer and wanted to see her.

"Phrank, you must he stupider than I ever imagined to think I'd fall for this."

"My name's not Frank, it's . . ." She decided it must be true. The voice was too boring. It was the voice of someone who had worked all his life in a dole office. Phrank would have given himself away by being too colorful, too mannered, having thought too much about the motivation, overelaborating a story. Nothing as plain as come to my office.

She watched Tony examine the table for damage. So there it was. You do an unfunny act, and someone you can't remember offers you work in television as you're in the middle of putting the Pony on the exercise wheel. She'd have to go to the library to see if there was anything on this.

"*You* . . . are my lord and master," she said, pointing at Tony and popping out her left breast, endeavoring to give it a plaintive air, sure she could bring Tony back from impotent fury to venereal frenzy in under thirty seconds. Tony knew she was being ironic, but he had no conception of how ironic. There wasn't a man in the world who couldn't detect some sincerity in that statement.

Σ

She got out at Oxford Circus and occupied herself with looking for somewhere where she could buy a decent pair of tweezers, and wondering whether she was good enough for television yet. The definition of comedy, which she had been hunting for three years now, was as elusive as ever. Trying to reverse-engineer the laws of laughter, she had pulled apart thousands of jokes, because once she had those laws she would have a factory that could produce unlimited comedy on any subject. But the wff hadn't turned up. Perhaps she wasn't that funny. Now that was a worry that blemished the horizon repeatedly. It was one she had never discussed with anyone, because once an idea escaped from your mind, it could spread. She wasn't that funny, it was true; she wasn't as funny as she would be, she was still learning her trade, but she was as funny as most of the people on the box.

Miranda weaved down Oxford Street, never hearing English unless it came from a very stupid face.

If you stopped any of these pedestrians, she doubted if one in fifty could explain even electricity, let alone the Boolean stuff. The better the machines, the less the thinking. People were up to pushing buttons. Clicking. A clicking nation, clicking machines made in far-off countries. Soon all we'll have is our accent, or our imagined accent since the mixture of slang, patois, and subrap that was actually spoken the Americans wouldn't want to buy. We'll be swinging through the concrete trees, playing games on computers infinitely superior to the players.

As she made her way down Wardour Street, Miranda saw her sister coming down the other side. They stood smiling at each other for five minutes, waiting for a break in the procession of cars and messengers. She hesitated as she saw a lacuna coming;

should she cross, or should she hold her ground and make her sister cross? It was a weakness even to think about it, she resolved, as she stepped out firmly in the wake of a truck.

"It must be three years," said Patricia.

She worked it out. "Four." She was good on dates.

For fifteen minutes she and Patricia chatted well. Miranda admitted to herself it was a terrible thing not knowing where your sister lived. Not talking was one thing; not knowing where not to talk was another.

"And have you heard from Dan?" Patricia inquired.

"Yes."

Miranda did hear occasionally from Dan. Her brother; known in the family almost from birth as Dan the Disaster Man. He had provided her with a vex-filled childhood and some of her best routines. She had, coincidentally, been thinking of doing some Dan for the producer round the corner. All routines fail sooner or later, but the Dan was as close as you got to infallibility in the comedy world.

Dan's calamity CV: At fourteen he burns down the important parts of his school (unintentionally; intentionally would have been fine). At seventeen he writes off the family car, something he does again the following year. At nineteen he gets the first girl he sleeps with pregnant and falls prey to a disease so rare he is discussed at conferences: he develops a series of United-Kingdom-shaped rashes which come and go at will. At twenty, after two years of unemployment, he manages to hold down a job for three hours, writing off the managing director's car, which had been entrusted to him for parking purposes. At twenty-one Dan announces England is carrion and that he is tired of having his life stifled by the collapsing layers of a decomposing nation. He goes to America: within a week he has written off a rental car and is in jail since the Americans are convinced his passport is false and that he is a well-known counterfeiter; the misunderstanding is cleared up after a few days, by which point he already has contracted hepatitis without health insurance.

Thence to Fiji, where Dan meets the most beautiful woman he has ever seen. For reasons never divulged, the woman agrees to go back to Dan's hotel room (she drives). Dan is, understandably, looking forward to this since "it would have been the first time I'd gone to bed with someone I found attractive." They disrobe; Dan regards the nudity in his bed and has time to think "this is what life's all about" before a marble-sized meteor steams through the wall and burns a seam down his left leg, carrying on through the floor and embedding itself in a trouser press in the room below. If Dan had got hold of the meteorite, he could have made some money, but the hotel claimed it and charged him double occupancy. No health insurance.

After this there is some mystery, because someone advances Dan two hundred thousand pounds to open a hi-fi shop. And if there is one thing Dan knows about, and it probably is one thing, it's woofers and tweeters. Dan launches his sonic paradise in Kuwait City, three days before the Iraqi army invades; the anguish of his stock being looted makes the ordeal of being a human shield almost tolerable.

So, inevitably, Dan returns home. But he does so with five kilos of the best Afghan heroin padding his body. As the plane commences its descent to Heathrow, he is suddenly granted a moment of unwelcome clarity, a profound insight into his nature. He is, he realizes, the man called by his sister "King Fuck-up the First." His sneaky ciggy behind the bike sheds at school had been responsible for millions of pounds of combustion. When dinosaurs had ruled the earth, an asteroid on the other side of the universe had singled him out for chastisement.

He had, out of his own pocket, provided the Iraqi officer corps with mellow sounds. He had formed junkyards of totaled cars. What was he doing, thinking he could be a smuggler?

So severe was his panic, he was unable to do anything apart from hiccup uncontrollably and whine intermittently. He collapses at passport control, where they give him a glass of water. Unable to comprehend why he hasn't been apprehended, Dan slouches round the corner into the customs hall to give himself up. He stands there for two minutes wanting to give himself up, but there is no one there. Gradually it dawns on him how stupid he would look if a customs officer appeared. He shuffles out.

It is the best morning of Dan's life by far. The grayness and rain of London are delightful. On the tube he applauds the worst guitarist in the world who has made the Piccadilly Line his venue, and he chuckles as large Indian families tread on his toes and Danish backpackers give him an opportunity to press his face into their rucksacks. He goes to the address he has memorized near the Old Kent Road to deliver his cargo.

He understands his life. He has made a vast advance payment of misfortune precisely in order to get away with this. He has been given his turn to use the good luck.

A pub is on the corner. Years have passed without a real pint of bitter, so Dan goes in to have a celebratory drink. He has proved them all wrong; he vows to do something for deaf children or something. As he sips his pint, a scruff sidles up to him and offers to sort him out. Dan finds this hilarious; he has five kilos of international heaven in a bag, and some scorbutic loser wants to offload some overpriced worthlessness on him. Generously, he slips the scruff a tenner for a tab of acid.

The police find Dan cowering in a phone booth, sobbing into the receiver, "My heroin's beautiful, it's so beautiful. Don't let the Martians get it; they're armed with meteorites. Please send help," while the operator tries to console him. The police offer their protection to Dan, and the recording of his call makes the Emergency Services' Christmas compilation tape.

Miranda visits Dan in jail, more because she has never been to a prison than out of any desire to see Dan. "Grass big-time" is her advice. Dan pleads guilty to possession but goes for the mysterious-man-in-a-pub-asking-him-to-do-a-job routine and is hazy about anything that might constitute a detail or information. Astonishingly, he gets bail for a hundred thousand pounds because their father is ill. The first thing he discovers on release is that his Turkish employers, without him even saying a word about them, have all been arrested. He fears for his continued well-being.

Miranda's last sight of Dan is watching him pore over an atlas. With unprecedented naïveté, she had assumed he was planning his future after his stretch in prison.

"I've got three ideas. The Scilly Islands. Mexico City. Or Turkey."

"The Scilly Islands?"

"Do you know anyone who's been there? Anyone?"

"No."

"Exactly. I was thinking about the Outer Hebrides, but it's so miserable up there and the Scots get on my nerves. The only trouble with a small place, no matter how out of the way, is that if they come looking for me, they'll find me. So we come to Mexico City, so big it would be impossible to find anyone."

"And how does Turkey fit in?"

"Double bluff. The last place the Turks would think of looking for me is in their own backyard."

"That's not a double bluff; that's just a straight bluff."

"It's a double bluff because it's so fucking outrageous. What do you think?"

It was the first time Dan had ever asked her opinion on anything.

"I think you shouldn't have dropped that tab of acid in the
Old Kent Road."

Dan blew. Whether her forthrightness influenced him or not,
he flitted. Their father's health was not helped by losing his
home. Miranda had been surprised. Dan had always been an
originator of trouble, but he had never done so deliberately
before.

Dan phoned her up from time to time, nevertheless. She
moved around a lot, so she assumed he must have spent days
and a small fortune phoning around the comedy clubs to track
her down. He didn't tell her where he was. He didn't tell Patricia
where he was either because he was afraid that she might blab to
her and that she would grass him up. If it hadn't been for the
extremely remote possibility of the Turks caring where he was,
she would have been keen on contriving a stint in chokey for
Dan. But it was the only thing, when all was said and done, that
she had any respect for: life. She had had that respect ever since
the age of seven when she had taken some fruit to the bottom of
the garden and tried to give a pear some soul by fitting it out
with what looked like to her to be internal organs, nuts for
brains, grass for intestines.

Their last conversation had been typical:

"Hallo?"

There would be a telephonic hiss, which would continue
until she realized who it was.

"Oh, it's you. Broken your leg or been struck by any interesting lightning lately?"

"No. Nothing like that happens to me now. I've changed my
name."

"So?"

"Everything's changed." She knew that there were benefits to changing your name. One of the reasons she had changed hers. "I'm doing very nicely. No meteors. No sign of the Iraqi army."

"So what do you call yourself now?"

"I am not telling you. You were the one who christened me Dan the Disaster Man." Miranda strained to remember; it seemed inconsiderate not recalling ruining someone's life. There were so many things that had been so important at the time—meals wolfed down when you were ravenous—that she'd forgotten, it wasn't that surprising she couldn't remember something unimportant.

She pulled a Dan, not saying anything, hoping the call was costing him a bomb.

"Hallo?"

"Why do you phone me, Dan?"

"You really want to know?"

"Get on with it."

"Because I want to hear you bleat. You've always been the hard case of the family, but you'll snap one day. I want to hear you on all fours, bleating. You'll put on a brave show, but one day I'll phone up and I'll be able to tell."

"I'll bet you're fucked, Dan."

"Not at all. But you, you're on the bus to Completely Fuckedsville. You've got the ticket for that, all right. Maybe next time I phone, someone'll tearfully inform me that you've taken your own life."

"Old Kent Road."

"Edinburgh."

"Kuwait."

"Edinburgh."

"Kuwait."

"Edinburgh."

She was equally astonished at the level of their exchange and determined not to be the first to give in. But in her efforts to put more Kuwait into the receiver, she accidentally cut the line.

Σ

"Well," said Patricia, "why don't you come round one evening?"

The chat had been enjoyable, more than Miranda cared to admit.

"No. Let's quit while we're ahead." That sounded harsher than she had intended, but she couldn't retract. She did take her sister's address.

She found the office, which was womanned by a receptionist who, as so many, didn't want to be a receptionist. The receptionist didn't believe that Miranda had an appointment, a theory which gained credence as there was no trace of the producer. This reassured Miranda. It would have been unnatural for the producer to have been there waiting to hand over the keys to fame.

"You can't just walk in here," said the receptionist, who was French. Exponential anger blasted through Miranda. The British, finally, weren't much good at being rude; they could be crude, bad-tempered, unhelpful, noisy, and often violent, but true rudeness was beyond them. Whereas dazzling contempt came effortlessly to the French, and for some reason no one had investigated (to her knowledge), Frenchwomen were the rudest of all.

There were three basic postures for tackling life: first, the Bendy Wendy, rag-doll technique of gloving the fist that hits you, contouring yourself around any challenge or attack because you could thus avoid ulcerating frustration, and through submission attain a victory. It sounded quite good, but Miranda couldn't get much fun out of it.

Bendy Wendy was opposed by the ninja-gun-slinger-Viking-death-match–supreme-warrior-thousand-sit-ups-a-day school that maintained you attacked every challenge with everything you had, because you should never back down or shy away from conflict, even something as insignificant as a snotty French receptionist, because to do so was an injection of weakness and a fracturing of your fighting spirit that would lead to utter ruin. Cannonading generously, Miranda had learned, though more satisfying, didn't always produce desirable results.

Then there was the midground: the keep-your-powder-dry school. You didn't open fire on the first target that came along; you waited for the big antlers.

Miranda had come all the way into town. She'd sit down for a while. She considered sleeping with the producer, blitzing him, wringing his tiny brain out by lozenging his nuts and extravagantly overpraising his prowess, enslaving him, and having the receptionist fired. Except that wouldn't make any difference. In London, you can always get another job; it might be menial, wretched, and poorly paid, but you could get another job.

Plus, she was not going to sleep with the producer to get on television. She was going to get on television because she was so good. While she couldn't deny that she had had some odd, prof-itless, and silly couplings, intimacy with someone you couldn't remember was a bit off. And you grew up, minutely.

She chose to sit down for half an hour, to see if the producer turned up and to see whether she could get the receptionist to melt down.

"You should smile. That's the secret of being a good recep-tionist." Miranda saw the receptionist quiver with rage. "If you can't smile, you should be doing something else. Teeth, teeth, teeth." She opened a magazine to indicate that she was staying put. Precisely thirty minutes later, as the receptionist was calling the police, she rose. "And above all, I think French mathematicians are rubbish."

She fought her way down Oxford Street, almost impassable with tourists. Walking down Oxford Street was the most depressing thing she knew; it was on a par with watching children being bayoneted. You couldn't walk down Oxford Street and have any hope for humanity. Tourists buying trashy papier-mâché policemen's helmets or the "My parents went to London and all they bought me was this lousy T-shirt" T-shirt. The bookshops full, of Germans and Scandinavians. Then the Asian clans selling jeans—incredibly smug. If the only thing that mattered to you was money and you were making money, here was paradise. Dim ex-cons selling rubbish on cardboard boxes to dimmer passersby. The auction shops that were tarted-up replays of those transactions where some customers actually thought they could buy a worthwhile television set or a CD player for a fiver. The beggars with their dogs on a string and their sleeping bags, the sleeping bags they stayed in even when it was twenty-five degrees in August and they looked laughable.

She wished she could go to the bookie's and put money on a prediction: the twentieth century would be the last one with any space. History would be categorized Was-Space or After-Space. We will be living in a Post-Mind country in the After-Space world, Miranda thought; the world won't end with a bang or a whimper, but clutching a games console and your face stuffed into the arse of Paulo from Genoa.

The tourists coasted around, seeking. Looking for something they had read about. London was cool. Why? Because the Americans said so. Intrinsically, London had all the charm of a sooty Victorian brick. Everything in London was built upon piles and piles of the dead; everything was third-, fourth-, tenth-, hundredth-hand. It had been populated out of all character. An ashtray full of historical fag-ends.

Miranda thought about stopping off at Waterloo on her way home, but she had the wrong clothes for begging, and her sign, HOMELESS AND HUNGRY, was back at home too. The sign was a must. Businessmen scurrying for their trains would think of offering her money for sex and then, ashamed, would throw a pound into her carton.

She went into a shop to buy some running shoes. At the very bottom of the Oxford Street sewer along with the tourist tat were the sporting clothes emporiums. The assistant who served her grunted. He grunted affably, but the entire process of fetching the running shoes, trying them on, purchasing them, and parting company was accomplished by grunts. She wondered if his grunting was a political gesture, a rejection of everyday parlance as a protest against an abundance of injustices, whether he had had a heavy night, or if it was merely a demonstration of how irrelevant even language was.

That was the way it was going. Soon the Germans would run everything, and Britain would be nothing but a testing ground for new computer games where people would be chucked computer-designed drugs to get out of bed in the mornings and to remind them they existed. It would be worth the trouble for the Germans because it would enable them to pretend they had partners.

The surest sign was that no one had any interest in mathematics. She hated London, and she could never leave.

$$\Sigma$$

The next day, she made the trip in to the producer's again. Irritatingly, she didn't irritate the receptionist anymore, who now evidently classified Miranda as insane. To further the annoyance, the producer was not around and had left no message for Miranda. However, as she narrated expansively the dismal performance of French mathematicians in the last hundred years, the receptionist got up, put on her coat, and walked out without a word.

Was this a lunch break or an inability to cope with the failure of French mathematics? Miranda waited another quarter of an hour, staying off the temptation to rifle the drawers in the office for information or money.

Viv had arranged to meet her for a cup of coffee, and Miranda strolled over to Aroma puzzling about what to do about the producer and where the hell her latest tweezers could have got to.

She ordered two espressos and wondered how long her friendship with Viv would last.

Nearly everyone was a hate keeper. They stored things up: late buses, disappointments, insults, betrayals. There were very few people who could swallow pain and misfortune and just let them out the other end. Viv was one of them. Without being spineless, she was relaxed. She had the right amount of beauty: enough to attract any man she wanted without straying into the realm of forbidding beauty; long legs and conic breasts condemned you to the most repellent of self-absorbed shits or the unhinged.

She could have disliked Viv for her buoyancy, but it was that very quality that was endearing. She was going to make it, and it was good to know that someone decent was going to make it to the other side. As Viv stirred the sugar into her coffee, Miranda saw Viv's future: she was having her fun, but she would settle down effortlessly but ruthlessly one day, becoming a devoted mum, fussing the right amount, and a valued wife, nagging the right amount. Her equanimity wouldn't be unscathed, but it would endure. When she peered toward her own future, Miranda could only see turbulence, screeching, unforeseen impacts.

"Why do you always call your brother a disaster?" Viv asked. "Dan the Very Unlucky Man would be more like it. You can't say it was his fault he got pranged by a meteor."

"I can."

"And it was his fault that Kuwait got invaded?"

"Plain as the nose on your face."

Viv's shopping was discussed. She had been searching everywhere for a suitable stand-up lamp.

"There are only three shops in London," Miranda announced. "That's why it's so difficult to find anything, not because there's so much choice but rather because there isn't."

"What?"

"There are only three shops in London. Whatever you want, whether it's a CD of yodeling classics, unscented soap, or a washing machine, if you haven't found it in three shops that ought to stock the desired item, you're not going to find it. Count next time. You know how they get crowds for films now? They shoot half a dozen people and then clone them up to fill the rest of the space. London's like that; it's more sameness, not more choice."

Miranda suspected that the true answer was actually three and a bit: 3.142 et cetera. Pi was in on it, but she didn't outline her hypothesis to Viv, because Viv had the right amount of intellectual curiosity and got restless whenever mathematics was raised. Miranda felt proud to know someone who was in line for happiness.

"I did find a lamp I liked, but it's three hundred quid. It looks great, but it's nothing but a tube of metal with a lightbulb attached and they want three hundred quid for it."

Viv was a nurse. How appropriate to the city's ghastliness that someone who processed people's shit, blood, and pain and who guided them through the Great Terror couldn't afford to live there. Know-nothing consultants could go to companies that did nothing (usually a nothing they were notably know-nothing about), where they would talk and earn Viv's annual salary in a day. And they weren't even funny. All sorts of professions that did nothing but create pain and misery coined it: skip deliverers, lawyers, sommeliers, television producers, architects, computer salesmen, human resources managers. Miranda had once met someone who advised people about swimming pools. He didn't build swimming pools or maintain swimming pools; he simply advised people about how they should go about thinking about building a swimming pool. His phone had rung three times while she talked to him. He earned Viv's annual salary in a week. Tony farted round in an office gibbering about helping people, spending most of the money he managed to raise on filing cabinets; he earned more than Viv. Miranda herself was the only person Miranda knew who earned less than Viv, but then she didn't know anyone else who earned as little as she did.

Viv only managed to survive in London because she lived rent-free. Her landlord had an arrangement with her: She didn't pay rent, but he was allowed to come into the bathroom whenever he wanted, especially if she was having a bath. An accommodation ostensibly bound to end badly, to degenerate into intolerable creepiness or at least not to last very long; but Viv maintained her landlord was an old-fashioned gentleman who was a model of courtesy, who would discuss dispassionately his role in the Korean War and respectfully pass the loofah when he visited her, once every month or so during sudsing time. "It's knowing he can pop in for a chat that's important to him," Viv would insist.

Viv had lived at her current abode for three years, but the loofah passer had been providing costless accommodation for members of the nursing profession for twenty years. Viv had just the right amount of hardness to be able to handle life without completely excluding it; like a good bouncer, she was tough enough to keep out the real trouble but willing to have a laugh. Miranda knew if she were a man, she would marry Viv on the spot. Viv was twenty-six. In two or three years, she could see that Viv would splice down nicely, and she couldn't shake off the knowledge that she wouldn't be there to see it, and that made her sad.

After obtaining more details about the lamp, Miranda got up in a going-to-the-loo style but once clear of Viv's line of vision, veered out of the café and over to the top floor of Liberty's where she instantly recognized the lamp, instantly wrapped it up at a deserted counter, and instantly walked out with it.

"There. For you," Miranda said. "It's your wedding present."

"Am I getting married? No one tells me anything."

"One day you will, and I want to be the first to give you a present."

"You're mad," Viv said. "You haven't got this sort of money. It's so sweet of you, but I can't accept it."

She doubted Viv would stay a friend till the end. With the right amount of good sense, she could imagine Viv realizing that her behavior was not colorful but diseased and doing a runner.

"If you don't want a wedding present, let me present you with the Miranda Piano Award for having a Together Life."

Uneasily, Viv did take it. On her way home Miranda saw a classy pair of tweezers, and although she had left a good pair in plain view before going out, she thought she would outsmart the tweezer-eating phenomenon that had taken up residence in her flat by buying it as insurance. She also lifted a white T-shirt. She noted down the lamp and the T-shirt, their cost, and their provenance in her book. She didn't approve of theft; she'd

pay them back when she got big, which would be soon. And if
not, too bad. . . . She didn't like shoplifters, as she had discovered the time she was arrested and taken to the police station;
the pros were human cockroaches, with no interest but themselves, the most unpleasant people she had ever met, and she
knew many, many promoters.

Σ

> **What do you give a man who has everything?**
> **A smack in the mouth.**

Her back got a tonguey wake-up call from Tony. For Tony, this
swabbing with his tongue was an arousal barrage, whereas, for
Miranda, shedding sleep, it was an uncomfortable dampness
between her shoulder blades. You could write down a joke,
complete with instructions about pauses and intonation, and
give it to two performers; the same joke could be howlingly
funny or dismally wooden. Similarly, a tongue proceeding along
your spine could be the forerunner of distorting pleasure or a
nuisance akin to a dripping tap, depending on who was operating the tongue.

"Go and get the paper," she muttered into the pillow. "I'll
have woken up by the time you get back."

Tony bounded back. "Look what I've got for you," he said, not
referring to the newspaper. Men persisted in delighting in their
manhood only doing what it was tasked to do. Every time, they
were like a boy with a new toy; every time, it was the biggest
thing in the cosmos. Every time, they ran a gauntlet of the great
and the good slapping them on the back, heroes of all time
whooping approval in a frenzy of global high-fiving.

"Too late, Tony. I couldn't wait for you."

"I've only been gone five minutes."

"Sorry. I had to have a spot of self-service."

Tony's breath sauna'd her neck; he was looking for a good place to plant his teeth in what he considered his other infallible lust unleasher.

"No, Tony. Too late," she said, rolling over and covering her head with the pillow. Tony, impaled on his own rigidity, let out a cry in which rage and frustration battled for supremacy. He understood her no contained no wavering; he had only been overinsistent once. She had placed her thumb and index finger on either side of his left testicle and had squeezed as hard as she could. You only had to do it once.

"You're crazy, Miranda, you know that," he said, leaving for the office.

She did. There was a major division in the world. Those who were consumed with the dread of being dreary, the terror of being ordinary or boring; a blender who disappears into the woodwork. The blenders, who could camouflage themselves anywhere, snatched furiously at flamboyance, sought out the epithets "out of my tree," "off my trolley," "it was mental," "barmy army." Those who weren't headcases wanted to be so they'd be invited to parties or be able to collect debts, and those who were spent all their time wanting to fit back into those standard slots, would give everything to be a tranquil cashier in Guildford. When Miranda had met a DJ at a gig in Hackney whose stage name was the Fucking Mad Bastard, she hadn't been at all surprised to discover that he was an assistant to a tax inspector during the day. He had to be.

With Tony out of her hair, she spent an hour trying to define *comedy*, but she couldn't concentrate; she was thinking about helping others. What had she done for others? She had done favors for Viv, but they couldn't really count. That was friendship. She had given marathon blow jobs. Whatever that was, it wasn't charity. There had been an occasion when she had tended to an old woman who had collapsed in the street, and listened to her drivel about her twenty-year-dead husband for half an hour until the ambulance pulled up. The crew apologized for taking so long; they had attended a block of flats where a man complained he had a new girlfriend but he couldn't get it up for her. But Miranda hadn't volunteered to provide support, she hadn't penciled it into her diary, she had been walking past when the biddy had folded, she had not been callous enough to walk past, so that didn't count.

Then Heather phoned up. She had a friend who was desperate for a baby-sitter right away. The no was on its way out of Miranda's mouth when Heather said, "They'll pay a hundred quid." Out-and-out desperation, Miranda reflected. She had no qualifications for baby-sitting other than she would probably notice the house burning down.

The mother made no secret of her disquiet at leaving her child with Miranda, which she found slightly insulting. If you're dumping your kid on an almost complete stranger, at least act as if you're happy about it. Miranda was now annoyed at having agreed to do this, even for a hundred quid; she had wanted to turn the flat upside down to see if she could find any of the six tweezers that had now vanished into thin air.

The baby was only three months old but was very adamant about its unhappiness at being left by its mother. She had already forgotten the baby's name. She tried to solve the problem of comedy but couldn't. The wffs weren't coming. This was why women didn't get anywhere: have a kid and you can go to a field for some stoop labor or run a bank, no problem, but you can't think. She tried moving the baby into another room, then down to another floor, but the screaming and its disturbing of her thoughts continued.

"I hope I can teach you a valuable lesson about screaming," confided Miranda as she carried cot and kid into the garage. She put both into the Volvo Estate, closed its door, closed the garage door, and settled in the kitchen, which was now blissfully quiet. She drank some tea, which she hoped was expensive, and tried to think of the formula for comedy. This was the only thing she was interested in: defining comedy. Unlimited comedy beckoned.

It was alarming that nothing else really concerned her any-more; but she didn't mind concentrating all her energy on that because the evidence showed you didn't get anywhere without hard work. Newton, Leibniz, Gauss, Hilbert, Ramanujan were accused of all sorts of vices except one: laziness. They went all the way. She didn't care about anything else: culture, happiness, food, you-name-it. That's what worried her about this project. If this went, there was nothing else. The problem of comedy was her last honorable link with the world. Okay, there was that. But that wasn't an interest, and it wasn't always honorable.

There was something funny about the baby being in the car. The propulsion of most jokes was a crash of truth and absur-dity; the fuel was different here. It was in the image of coddling the mother was carrying in her mind face-to-face with the aus-terity of the garage.

At quarter to four, Miranda retrieved the cot from the car, changed the baby. At five past four, the mother returned. "She looks sleepy," she commented.

"We had an educational afternoon; it's never too early to start," Miranda responded. The mother paid by check, denying there had ever been a promise of cash. It was the usual thing: when you need something, you promise anything; once you have it, you start the squeeze. Miranda feared the check would bounce, not because the family was short of money, the whole place shrieked loaded, but because the mother was one of those juggling career women who fucked everything up. All the money would be in a savings account, and she'd have to spend a week and a dozen phone calls getting the money out of her. Finally, you never regret the cruelty.

On the bus home, Miranda pondered the truth that if you found someone who would even cross the road for you without any expectation of payback, you were doing well.

Tony didn't do things for her: the things he did for her, he did for himself at a distance. She was probably the best-looking girl he'd had in her bed, and she had no doubt from the tussle between awe and gratitude on his face when he came that the Pony's oats had never been so wild.

But he had got to her, she realized. She would do something, something for someone she didn't know, for someone on the other side of the world who was in deep shit, someone who could never do her any good, someone whom she probably wouldn't like.

Tony was in the kitchen showing off with some haddock when she got back.

"You're on, sunshine," she said.

$$\Sigma$$

Why did the crocodile cross the river?
I don't know—you ask the crocodile.

Miranda, after some phoning round, discovered there were two Burmese comics who were under arrest. She had only made three phone calls, and that suggested destiny was on board. Two fellow mirth makers in the clutches of a good old-fashioned dictatorship with funny uniforms. A deserving cause that was hard to top. She strongly suspected that the funniest thing about them would be their names, that they would have a weak line in crocodile-crossing-the-river jokes, that they probably beat their wives, and that the military regime, which was probably struggling providing for an ungrateful population, was indubitably fully justified in locking them up for all-round defectiveness. Still, no one could accuse her of being in it for anything. They weren't mates of hers. What could they do to repay her? FedEx her a bowl of spicy rice? Give her an open mike in the jungle canopy?

It took her an afternoon to set it up. About a dozen phone calls. This made her uneasy. Of course, although it was a business where everyone was remarkably selfish and lazy, usually both, it was precisely because of this they were keen to sign up for acts of philanthropy. There was no money in it, and no one really wanted to do benefits, but the most galling thing in the world was not to be asked.

Miranda had only been asked to do a benefit once. It was a relief to have been asked because you weren't part of the scene if you didn't do benefits, but she hadn't been able to go because it had been in Carlisle, beyond the wall of fire. The benefit had been for strikers at a mattress factory; it had been on a Sunday, two days after the workers settled their dispute with management, but no one had told the organizers of the benefit, who instead of raising any money ended up thirty pounds down as a result of the drinks for the performers.

Her first call was to Phrank, who would agree to do anything, come round and hoover your carpets, let alone a benefit, and then the others slotted into place like a well-oiled jigsaw puzzle. She phoned up a new venue in Brixton that was desperate for attention, and which happily offered its space. That was that.

Was it that doing good was just easier than pushing your own career? There was something fateful about this she didn't like. It was alive. She could feel some extremeness in the offing. This was going to be either a débâcle or an explosive success, both of which worried her. She didn't want a dud attached to her career, but equally she didn't want to go into history as Mandalay Miranda. She had discovered that Mandalay was in Burma when she had opened an atlas to see where Burma was. But the only way forward was forward.

She phoned everyone she knew to invite them. Twice. Then she phoned people she didn't know and waved concern at them. Great. And Tony was paying the phone bill.

$$\Sigma$$

The size of the audience was something that had never worried Miranda much. Thinking about that was always a mistake; you had to worry about the quality of your performance; you had to give as much, perhaps even more, when there were six people and not sixty. This time, though, it was different; she had invested weeks of her life in drumming up trade.

The evening was about to begin, and there were only ten people; there were supposed to be twelve stand-ups on the bill. Miranda had overbooked, knowing that the impairedness prevalent in the industry would guarantee a no-show by a number of the participants.

She peered at the audience and tried to work out who they were: one obvious city refugee, some skunk-skinning squatters who saw their triviality as a massive blow against intercontinental iniquity, one sour academic with long fangs of hair hanging from his pate, a groovy doctor (divorced gynecologist who clubs), three indistinct women who were so unmemorable she forgot about them as she looked at them (the padding, always the padding), and an elderly couple who looked like the parents of a performer. Not a single journalist in sight. No television producer. She began to wish she'd allowed Tony to come. She'd made him buy five tickets, but she never allowed him to watch her perform.

At moments like this, Miranda thought about her ideal job. The ideal job would be for her to have a small room attached to a gym or sports facility where a queue of attractive (or at least not unattractive) young men, strong and dynamic, would service her all day, as a sort of winding-down from their workouts. Climbers, boxers, and swimmers were her favorite sorts of bodies. It was a tempting concept but also frightening. Tempting because it would iron out all thought, blot out everything else. Frightening on the same grounds; she was worried she wouldn't get tired of writhing about all day, although, practically, you probably couldn't carry on for more than three or four hours. You heard all sorts of stories and boasts, but the limit was somewhere there. Fine, you could spend a whole weekend fooling around with intermissions and pit stops, but for true bump and grind, that was it.

They waited another quarter of an hour, and by the time Phrank went out to talk about his briefcase, there were another eight hands to give him applause. Phrank didn't mind small audiences. Phrank would do his act for himself. He was impressive in that sense. He was a great MC, possibly the MC's MC, which meant that everyone liked him; amusing without being too funny or successful.

Captain NoGood was introduced, and by the time he said "hello" for the second time (very old warm-up trick), the audience surrendered, just like that, and bayed. A good deal of booze and dope was knocking about out there, but the response perplexed Miranda. Had he developed a funny walk, or had he gone for that old comedy standby of getting his dick out?

His best routine was claiming his penis could do impersonations. Putting a tea towel round it: Yasser Arafat. Slipping a pair of sunglasses on it: Stevie Wonder. Carefully inserting two half toothpicks under the foreskin: Dracula. Model of a wheelchair: Stephen Hawking. Dentures: Jaws. Copy of the Koran: Ayatollah Khomeini. Ice cream cone, without the ice cream: Statue of Liberty. A wad of fifty-pound notes: any Euro MP. Wristwatch around it: Big Ben.

It was a routine that had got him barred from several clubs and badly beaten up, the ultimate comedy accolade. Once by a group of Arabs, and once, intriguingly, by a group of Israelis. The only drawback to having a routine that had people either walking out or having the best laugh of their lives was the danger of handling very funny material: it made less funny material even less funny. It had been a moment of genius for Captain NoGood, but his only one.

But Miranda saw he had just hit a comic mine. As had happened to her the other week. The audience was only capable of one thing: side-splitting laughter. Captain NoGood generally liked to be farther up the bill, but he said he had to get home as his wife was ill. Deciding where to go on the batting order was irksome. No one was keen as a rule to go first, when audiences might be frosty, but it was often as dangerous to go toward the end, when there was goodwill but also higher expectations.

Bearing in mind she was in a roomful of comics who were about to play to a house of fourteen, she didn't get much stick. This was because professional or would-be professional comedians didn't see the point of being funny without payment. Juicy Lucy had disappeared. Johnny Bright and Mark Grant had had a punch-up at the tube over who got to do the custard pies (both had independently come up with a custard pie routine).

But no one minded hugely. The whole point of doing it was to say, "I've done a benefit for some Burmese comics," whether or not it benefited the Burmese or there was anyone there to witness it.

Zia was bitchy: "Why don't I go and sit out front? I swear I'll laugh like a drain at your set. That'll do more good."

Ned said: "Quisquilious deblaterations."

Captain NoGood wound up, and Phrank introduced Ned. Miranda tuned her ears from listening to the green room to hearing how Ned would do. Ned was the only stand-up she had ever seen have things thrown at him. Physical heckling. A very large spanner had been hurled at Ned, one which would certainly have smashed his skull if it had hit. "That's to help you tighten up your act, you slack cunt," explained the thrower. This incident had provided Ned with the only funny material in his set; that he owed it to an assailant didn't bother him.

"There's a word that can be written but can't be said. It's not difficult to pronounce," explained Ned, "it's a very simple word, but you can't say it. Here it is. Simon is out on the river in a boat, having a good row. His sister Samantha, on the other hand, is at home, having an argument with their mother, a blazing row. They're both R-O-W-I-N-G."

The audience went for this. The first audience ever to do so. Not uproarious laughter, but they were amused. They seemed to think it was leading somewhere. That was the thing about audiences, even audiences in comedy clubs; there was always this assumption that the person on stage has something to offer, that the person knew something, could offer some improvement, if only a nano-improvement. Ned was also the only comedian Miranda had seen who had provoked people into asking for their money back; dissatisfied customers usually contented themselves with hurling abuse or spanners. Ned had been booked to make everyone else look good, not to start winning fans.

She resolved to destroy the audience. Their bad taste infuriated her. Ned said, "Quisquilious deblaterations," and they laughed. Fine, she had asked them to come for a benefit, and as hostess it was bad form to be upset about them laughing and to clear them out, but she found it intolerable. She noticed also that the Irish blarney merchant with Jesus hair was fascinated by her breasts. He was rising fast on his own hot air at the moment; he had come to London a few months ago and had already overtaken her. Rave reviews backed up by jostling television producers.

Phrank came in and started talking about the briefcase.

The briefcase with a life. Ten years ago Phrank had found a briefcase on a train. The briefcase had contained a life in the guise of thirty thousand pounds in twenty-pound notes. Phrank had wanted to keep it. He had considered what he could do with the money: a hefty deposit on a house or flat, a start-up sum for a small business, a year of comfortable world travel. Ten years ago Phrank had been less wrinkly, but he had been as thin, as broke, as unemployable.

He had wanted to keep it, but he resolved to take the money to the police station the next day, because he had always believed in honesty. If you couldn't be honest yourself, you had no right expecting others to be honest, he said. He knew that if he spent the money, he would be ruined. The dishonesty would rot his soul. He had always hated dishonesty more than anything, whether it was restaurants overcharging or lying politicians. His act was based on denunciations of dishonesty, but it wasn't an act. He cried himself to sleep.

In the morning he took the bus to the police station. He rocked back and forth in front of it for a while, then went back home and spent the day sniffing the notes. "I was trying desperately to be a hypocrite. I was giving it all I'd got, but it wasn't happening." The next day, he walked past the police station twice before he had enough courage to get through the door. His distress was increased by the police's reaction. "You know, it would have been nice to have had some respect for being a top citizen, but they just looked at me as if I was a stupid fuck." The pain continued when the owner of the briefcase, an Iranian jeweler who had been out of his gourd on cough syrup when he had left it on the train, phoned up. "You know, a reward would have been nice, even if it had only been a tenner. But he doesn't phone up to offer me a bung. A warm thank-you, that would have been nice. You know what he says to me? 'Mr. Jones, you must be a very stupid man.' He phoned me up to tell me that." Phrank had also reported his good citizenship to the local paper in the hope of a plug but had been disappointed to find that they had gone with a story about a squirrel biting a milkman.

Phrank drank. He would have drunk uncontrollably, but he didn't have the money for that, so he drank uncontrollably intermittently. When Miranda had first heard the story of the briefcase, it had been a funny story; now it had become a tale of such rancor she didn't like to be in a confined space with it. Phrank lived with an old Spanish woman in an arrangement where both participants made no secret of only doing so because they couldn't get anything better. Phrank was an odd toy boy; a bunch of fortyish knitting needles in a sack, usually seen holding a glass; but then she was a sugar mommy with no sugar. Phrank got a roof over his head and the occasional cooked breakfast. As Phrank would say, cryptically and frighteningly, "Very little is very much more than nothing, and only the young and foolish think otherwise."

Phrank had been on the circuit for fifteen years. It was a profession where, in the space of a lunch, you could go from being a scrofulous, inconsequent drunk in a twenty-year-old suit that hadn't been much to begin with, mystifying half a dozen people who wished they'd done something else with their evening, to a man who was paid a well-appointed house or two to endorse beer. But it wasn't going to happen to Phrank. There were people who got everything they wanted out of the lifestyle, grafting for a few drinks, parading for half a dozen people, who had no truck with laughter, but regrettably for Phrank, he wasn't one of them.

Ned, having gone on twenty minutes longer than stipulated, wound up, and Phrank went out to prep the audience for Miranda's set. He picked up a handbag belonging to a girl with a backward beret. It was a very old trick, even for Phrank, but bullying always worked well live. Phrank had started out doing the handbag search as an easy source of laughs, but it was no longer amusement but humiliation he was aiming for.

Miranda again caught Jesus Hair staring at her breasts. He was four years younger than her and had only been in the business six months, but was headlining everywhere. It was annoying that he fancied he could just stroll into the business, because he could. Even more infuriatingly, he was causing a commotion in her loins.

He was the next one after her. The audience had enjoyed Phrank's excavations and was lying there like a huge dog waiting for her to scratch its stomach. An all-consuming desire to annihilate the audience came over her, to obliterate the terrain and leave no shelter for the Irishman.

She deliberated for the unfunniest thing to say.

"You're all going to die."

There were some sniggers.

"You certainly are," jeered Zia from the back as he walked out unreturningly.

She fell silent. For the audience this was the worst thing, when it became conscious of its fidgeting and its self. She looked directly at one of the lead laughers and pushed the humor out of him. Quickly, fear grew that she wasn't pausing, wasn't hiding a punch line, wasn't fingering alternatives, but had corpsed. Minutes passed, and the embarrassment dripped down and spread like a bloodstain over the audience. People didn't want this; awkward time was what they got at home and at work.

But they didn't know how to counter her freezing. She was crushing them completely, when it occurred to her that a puzzled and annoyed audience might respond even better to the next act than a well-laughed one.

So she changed tack and took off her white T-shirt, which had a curtain-raising effect. The unleashing of breasts was largely regarded by the women as cheating, but all in all, the audience had no doubt a performance was on. Miranda talked about how one breast was smaller than the other, and how men, although they spent their entire lives gawking at them, didn't notice this. She didn't like using the word *notice* because along with the expression "why is it?" the phrase "have you ever noticed?" usually portended the most meager offerings of observational comedy, but it slipped out. That the ratio between the circumference of a circle to its diameter was one of the most important in nature and that it seemed to be imprecise, transcendental, that no one knew what might be lurking at the end of Pi was her finale. The audience didn't find this hilarious, but then it was a benefit. "Good night. Quisquilious deblaterations," she said.

A bemused Phrank came on since he knew she could do funny, but he had no problem with tits.

"The beauteous Miranda Piano there doing for mathematics what Pythagoras never could. Quisquilious deblaterations to one and all. Miranda, you don't mind me taking advantage of the memory of your knockers later on, do you? I'm asking because I couldn't be so unchivalrous as to have an assist for a Barclays Bank without your thumbs-up."

Miranda used a popular gesture, and as she brushed past Jesus Hair, she whispered in his ear: "I'm going to shhk your kuu all night."

Whether she managed to snooker him with this prediction or whether she had overtaxed the audience's understanding, Jesus Hair waded about in difficulty, doing the Irish jokes that only the Irish were allowed to do now, although he was solidly sedate about his failure. The only worthwhile chuckle he got was when he inquired, "Does anyone here know what quisquilious deblaterations are?"

The others didn't do much better, and by the time Phrank went out to wrap up the proceedings, he started a ramble about the only thing, he claimed, that had given him any true pleasure in life: having a Barclays to a photograph he had cut out of a magazine when he was sixteen of a bare-breasted girl. "I have to drink, but I don't enjoy it; I have to live with someone, but I don't enjoy that." He asserted that this relationship had lasted thirty years and wasn't just physical. He had always carried this photograph around with him in a wallet, but he had lost the wallet a fortnight ago and was never going to enjoy himself again. There had been no money in the wallet, just his donor card, the folded-up picture, a repeat prescription, and his address. He had retraced his movements, been to shops, neighbors, police stations, but there was no trace of it. Phrank recounted all this for forty minutes despite the last member of the audience bolting twenty minutes before he stopped.

Miranda had watched the audience dissolve as she had a drink with Jesus Hair. Punters in general weren't hard; they weren't eager to do you favors, but very few people liked to hand out hardness. She had watched them whipping up the courage to leave as Phrank droned on. She wondered if Phrank was doing it as a prank to see how much tosh they would put up with before escaping. She had seen the same thing in the streets when people had given money or cigarettes to beggars and had then stood there while instead of saying thank you the beggar would hold forth voluminously on his or her philosophy of life, and the donors wouldn't have the gumption to say: "You are a contemptible piece of shit, and I have already given you money; don't expect me to listen to your addled platitudes" precisely because the beggars were contemptible shits with addled platitudes and they didn't want to do anything that might cause the beggars to be made aware of this.

Ned sat clutching a bottle of lager, frequently discharging a "quisquilious deblaterations." Everyone's attempts to hijack his catchphrase hadn't disturbed him. Ned had two reliable qualities. First, he was never voluntarily at home. He was always the first to arrive at a gig and the last to leave. No one talking or listening to him, or the most hideous groupies ignoring him, left him unoffended. And he never stopped using his catchphrase.

Miranda had no idea what it meant. Perhaps Ned didn't know either. Perhaps he did and was desperately hoping he would be asked what it meant. Miranda had thought of having a trawl through a dictionary once, but had discovered she couldn't be bothered. The words might be invented, but even if they were gibberish, it was indisputable what Ned intended by them: disapproval. Arguably, you could go through life as long as you had a term for disapproval and approval, and in a pinch, if you had a term for disapproval, by withholding that, you could indicate approval. Indeed, in extremity, you didn't need any terms at all; take the grunting assistant in Oxford Street. Grunting was not perfect if you had a horror of being misunderstood, but overall, being misunderstood was probably no more harmful than being understood.

And finally, the unfunniness of Ned's catchphrase wasn't an impediment; truly, that was the hallmark of the catchphrase, the automatic pilot of comedy. The uncatchiness might be. Or it could be that he was going for broke; invoking the comedy law that if you repeat something often enough, it becomes funnier. Miranda had seen it done; it was the comedy equivalent of doubling your betting at roulette to recoup your losses, and it took balls to attempt to resurrect a joke that had died because you had to keep going a long time sometimes before the audience caved in. Ned had a long, long way to go. Miranda surveyed the room, shocked that this was her life.

Jesus Hair was boisterous and warm, as men usually were when they believed astonishing things would shortly be happening to their penises. He was taking the trouble to get to know her, filling in her background to help preclude the charge of anonymous sex. He was also tuned in to Phrank's forty-minute sentence and was unable to make up his mind whether Phrank was a trailblazer, ten years ahead of his time, the envoy of a new laugh, a humor-free comedy for the twenty-first century, or just someone who would shortly be tying a noose around his neck. Uncertain whether Phrank was a friend of hers or not, he made no comment lest it jeopardize his forthcoming ejaculations. Miranda and he discussed the clubs, which ones they liked most, and the promoters, which ones they hated most.

Phrank had unloaded his message or got tired of not having an audience and came to join them. A few minutes later, the girl with the beret on backward reappeared and accused Phrank of stealing five pounds from her purse.

Miranda got up to leave. Jesus Hair got up in an accompanying manner and followed her out. In the street she turned to him and said definitively: "Good night."

"But what was that you mentioned ... about your ... and my ... ?" he mumbled.

"I was joking," she said, walking off. He wasn't bad-looking, and there had been a time when she had had sympathy for everyone in their regiment; they all faced the same dangers. But the situation now was too serious for camaraderie.

They had lost thirty-four pounds during the course of the benefit. It wouldn't do. The Pony was in for a hard night.

Σ

Miranda couldn't stop fuming about how even the local newspaper had led with a story of a cat being rescued from a church roof, not giving the benefit so much as a mention. She wasn't a quitter, she repeated to herself as she and Viv got out of the taxi and made their way across Trafalgar Square, struggling with all the equipment.

She walked toward Nelson's Column as if she had no intention of climbing it. She felt it must be obvious to everyone from the dreggy tourists to the pigeons what she was going to do, but she tried to block it from her mind.

The important thing was to get out of reach before the police turned up. She took off her clothes while Viv speedily unpacked the gear and set up the ladder. Viv had said she was crazy, several times, but was backing her up; she had the right amount of loyalty and wildness.

Miranda used the ladder to get on top of the plinth, crusty with pigeon's droppings. Viv then vanished, taking the ladder, as Miranda started prusiking up Nelson's Column. Up close, the granite exuded a chilly menace, and the whole magnitude was frightening. Frightening in a way she didn't like. It wasn't too warm, especially since all she was wearing was a pair of climbing shoes, a belt, a backpack, and a pair of sunglasses.

Progress was slow. She had done some rock climbing before, and she had spent the six weeks since the benefit carefully preparing or as carefully as you could in six weeks. But climbing up Nelson's Column naked was a great incentive to keep going; no one likes to give up when everyone is watching.

Thirty feet up, she looked back and saw a gratifyingly large crowd and gaggles of cameras, some policemen puzzled as to how this should be policed. That was the last time she would look down. She had decided to take her clothes off since she didn't want to do the climb and then find out afterward no one was interested. Climbing Nelson's Column to publicize the plight of two Burmese comics was one thing; a young naked woman doing it was another.

She had also dyed her hair blue, affixed a rub-on tattoo of a dragon on her left shoulder, and had shaved away her distinctive diamond-shaped pubes. She wanted the world to pay attention to this, but not to her. As she had explained to Viv: "You can only be famous, really famous for one thing. Archimedes—the bath. Christ—getting crucified. Genghis Khan—pillage. King Canute—the beach. Godiva—clothes off. Newton—the apple. If we can only have one hit, I'm buggered if I'm going to be remembered for shinning up Nelson's Column in the buff."

Halfway up, her hatred for the Burmese comics was almost burning through her skin. Wherever they were, she prayed someone was kicking the shit out of them. The overhang above terrified her; every muscle in her body ached. She wanted to give up more badly than she had wanted anything in her life, and it was only this realization that made her go on. She was lucky with some holds, very lucky.

It took her nearly three hours to reach the top. One hundred and eighty-five feet.

The view was stunning, but she didn't give a shit. Fear of the descent was already plaguing her. Like everything she supposed in life, by the time you get there you don't really want it. She reached for the mobile phone and started doing interviews in the voice of a German musicologist.

Looking out over London, she saw an enormous mess. Ramsey's Theory: complete disorder, it implies, is impossible. Ramsey was another one of those reedy Cambridge arse-bandits who ran the twentieth century. It might look like a mess, Ramsey says, but that's because you're not looking at the big picture. Of course, ideas like order and disorder were profoundly human; human as in Stone Age. What were you supposed to do with the sizzling new thinking in math? A homemade snowflake that lives in 196,883 dimensions and has billions of billions of billions of symmetries? Those who had erected this column would find the modern world inconceivable.

She had never been able to get beyond the nineteenth-century stuff. Even as an inhabitant of the twentieth century, she couldn't really tackle the math, although she had tried. God knows what was waiting in the next century with its 196,883-dimensional snowflakes. Miranda looked at London and had no doubt it was a mess. Faintly on the horizon, she could see the great wall of fire.

This was the hardest thing she'd done. But effort didn't count for much, really. She thought of poor William Shanks, who had published his calculation of pi in the nineteenth century. To 707 decimal places. It had taken him most of his life to work that out. A moron could now rocket that out in one second with a Mickey Mouse computer rescued from a junkyard. And to top it all, Shanks messed up—the last 180 digits were wrong. He was a celebrity only in math circles, and for only one thing: putting his life down the drain.

Well, maybe I won't make it to posterity, but my buttocks certainly will, Miranda thought. Did I do any good?

$$\Sigma$$

Tony was the only one who had recognized her. The blue hair and all the ropes around the house: bit of a giveaway. He was speechless, absolutely bankrupt wordwise.

A month later, she got a phone call from Captain NoGood. He was booked in for the Edinburgh Festival, but his wife was due to deliver their first child so he didn't want to risk not being there. Did Miranda want the slot?

People had noticed that she never did gigs outside of London. She had turned down Liverpool, Glasgow, Brighton, Manchester. They assumed she was just an inveterate Londoner, and didn't guess that although she loathed London, she couldn't leave.

But Edinburgh. The festival was it. It was where she had first seen stand-up live thirteen years ago, and it had been the place where she had seen the prospect of a career. Edinburgh didn't matter that much if you were triumphing in the clubs of London. But it mattered to her. Dan knew both about the wall of fire and how much she wanted to go to Edinburgh to do it. But because she hadn't hustled for a slot, she'd never been offered one.

"That's kind of you. Yeah, I'd love to do it," she said to the Captain, giddy at her own audacity.

When the day came, she went to Euston with her overnight bag, full of trepidation. She was surprised at Captain NoGood not going. It was only one gig, and during the festival if the audience made it to double figures you were doing well. But was it a sign of weakness on his part? Because you never knew. Just

because the audience seemed to be composed of four deadbeats
didn't mean they were just deadbeats. They could be four television producers. Or four people sleeping with television producers. Or four people dealing drugs to television producers. Or
four people who had gone to school with television producers.
Or four people sleeping with people dealing drugs to people
who had gone to school with television producers. Individuals
or even an individual who could pass on the news of comic
mastery to the right place.

Or as in the case of Catford Stan, there could be someone
who enjoyed your show so much he might leave you fifty thousand pounds in his will. One show could change everything.
Nine hundred and ninety-nine times it didn't, but you never
knew when that one was coming. Captain NoGood was demon-
strating signs of unworthiness; if you put your wife's well-being
first, did you deserve to make it? Shouldn't the prize go to those
who would do anything for it?

She was sweating as she approached the train. She felt as
if she had already been walking for five years. Simply getting on was almost beyond her. The other passengers looked
bored, dreading the five hours' travel to Edinburgh. No
human had ever yearned for boredom as much as she did
in that moment. She had considered getting on and then
just knocking herself out with pills, but she wanted to be
awake when she hit the wall. She sat in her seat, every muscle tense. It was taking all her will just to stay seated. She
didn't mind what happened too much, as long as she didn't
start blubbering.

The wall of fire had appeared when she started doing comedy. She had been in a car heading for Windsor when she had
suddenly been seized by an unmanageable panic as the car
neared Heathrow. She saw a wall of fire ahead, like a red tapestry

hung on the horizon; without telling anyone what she saw, she demanded that the car stop and she got out on the hard shoulder and started walking back to town. Several other sorties had ended with retreat as she had established that the wall went all around London, ten, twelve miles from the center. The flames weren't hot; they were full of fear. Most sorts of fear she enjoyed; this one she didn't.

As the train started to pull out, she closed her eyes to allay the faintness. If she was going to die, then she was going to die. No one lives forever.

Σ

The first thing Miranda did after she shakily got off the train was to go and buy a pair of tweezers. She had planned to lift them, but when she walked into the chemists the assistant said hello and meant it.

It was a shock after London, where strangers only talked to you because they wanted to shaft you in one way or another, to see that in Edinburgh courtesy was still going or at least the citizens were friendlier.

Miranda had been so preoccupied with the train journey that it was only in the last hour that she had started to fume about what must have been the eighth pair to go AWOL. Was Tony hiding them as a sort of practical joke? He had them hidden bloody well, because she had now spent days investigating the recesses of the flat without success. Was there a burglar breaking surreptitiously into their flat and resisting everything else except the good pairs of tweezers? Was an alternative universe opening up a tweezer-sized entrance in their bathroom from time to time? Was she suffering from some bizarre form of amnesia, which resulted in the disposal of her favorite tweezers?

She checked into the hotel, got ready, slipped on the unworn white T-shirt. There was a purity you got from a shop-fresh, unworn, unwashed T-shirt that you could never recapture.

Although she had a map, she gave herself twice as long as necessary to get to the venue, introduced herself to the manager, had a sandwich, and waited. She quizzed the manager how the other gigs had gone, and he said "fine" in a way that suggested they had been disasters. Truth didn't get much of a look-in in this business.

She watched the audience saunter into the tent that was her venue. Even ten minutes after the advertised start, there were only five people inside. There had been a time when she would have done the full fireworks for five, but now . . . It was like getting to the top of Nelson's Column; once you were there, you just wanted to go.

"What are you expecting?" Miranda asked her audience. There was a woman who was Middle Eastern, who had a clipboard, paper, and a pen and looked anxious as if her career depended on all this. Mr. and Mrs. Sensible Nordics, either Germans or Scandos, with sensible clothes, sensible glasses, sitting sensibly, and two local schoolgirls. They all looked terrified. It was a pity you couldn't take this fear away with you, Miranda reflected, away from the performance. Then you could make a small fortune in extortion. They were all convinced you had this . . . *power.*

"I have a problem with tweezers; let me tell you about it and see if you have any ideas." Miranda outlined the history of the vanishing tweezers. She never understood why some comedians had therapy. It was like a bodyguard having a bodyguard.

The audience failed to come up with any suggestions. They stared at the floor. Mr. and Mrs. Sensible were obviously deeply ashamed at having failed this test.

"Okay," said Miranda. "I'm going to make you a deal. There's a very good American I've always wanted to see performing in the next tent. Tickets for his show cost two pounds more, but I can get you in. Anyone not happy with that?"

She led her audience out of the tent and round to the side of the other tent. Whipping out her penknife, she cut an entrance and entered to emerge doubled-up with her charges, from under a bank of seats. The American spotted them and was annoyed, doubtless, by their shuffling around and not paying, but he was in the middle of a long routine he was worried about and chose not to bring his humor down on them.

Mr. and Mrs. Sensible in particular were so overjoyed by this interloping that they hardly paid any attention to the set. Miranda could see that this escapade would be relived again and again by the shores of the Baltic. They were soaring in the very cockpit of comedy.

The American, as she had heard, was good. She had mixed feelings about it; she was glad she could cross him off her checklist of acts to see, but it was depressing that there was this continent with vast factories producing stand-ups and disseminating them all over the world. There was enough competition already.

Miranda was now annoyed with herself for not carrying on. But she was losing her taste for performance. She was getting better, but less determined. You come into this business with such high hopes. . . . She wasn't making it. She could feel her career slumping, getting as wobbly as a snake that had been dropped in a vat of lager.

She should have carried on; but she could pretend it was a daring twist to performance: gate-crashing humor, lamprey entertainment, metaperformance, and not just a cop-out. She could argue her way out of that one. But she should have carried on.

Even if it was all over, she mustn't give up.

$$\Sigma$$

Outside, she had never seen darkness like that before. It was reinforced darkness. Two nights' worth of darkness that had got jumbled together. On top of that, someone was standing on her shoulders. Someone large.

The omens were persuasive, and she took a taxi back to the hotel. The hotel was surprisingly cheap but a long way out. The facilities didn't extend much beyond handing over the key.

It was only nine-thirty, but she got straight into bed. She was glad there was no one around she knew so she'd have to pretend to be feisty. The day was a write-off. She went to bed tired and miserable, expecting her mind to deliver its own knock-out punch immediately. Instead her mind grew clearer and clearer, and the bedroom transformed from a living space into outer space. She found herself floating in a great void, infinity stuffed into her heart, a void which was both empty and full: empty of comfort and full of fear. Pure dread, uncut, imported from beyond the universe.

There was no use in trying to reason herself out of this terror. Stoking was the only solution. She re-dressed. Somewhere there was an after-hours club for the performers. The girl at reception didn't know where it was. Miranda had been sent the details, but she never kept pieces of paper. She found them aggressive; they always piled up on her and tried to wall her in.

Hoping to get picked up, she walked back into town. It was that time of night when single women were supposed to be preyed upon. She meandered around for an hour, asking after the club's whereabouts; annoyingly, everyone knew about it and that it wasn't far away, but no one had any precise or useful information. Her feet were getting sore, and it was thinning out—fewer people, fewer groups, far too many couples. Where were the bottom pinchers when you needed them?

A bevy of three lads stretched across the pavement in front of her. They were in their early twenties, but then she didn't want conversation. She positioned herself in their path and got ready to ask an inane tourist question to leave no doubt at all that she was a tourist in need of transitory pleasure. You couldn't rely on men to make the first move; there seemed to be only two models: the rippers who tried to tear your clothes off before they said hello, and the more numerous telepaths who tried chatting you up when they were safely around the corner and two blocks away.

One of them broke away unexpectedly, lunged at the pavement, and began dribbling his stomach contents over it.

"He's the lead singer with the biggest band in Dunfermline," said one of the others with pride and an absence of erotic curiosity that made a mockery of evolution.

Ten minutes farther on, Miranda found not one but two sterling prospects. First she saw a stocky man in a black bomber jacket and was delighted. This wasn't emergency rations; this was a lunch box to admire. She simpered up and asked for directions.

Out of nowhere, another rugged, handsome male suddenly materialized and offered to show her. In no time at all, the two of them were using their fists to get to know each other better. The police arrived with such alacrity that they must have been monitoring the whole drama and took both pugilists into custody. Miranda smiled invitingly at the police officers, but none of them took up the offer of escorting her back to her hotel.

Incontrovertibly, the end of the line, she called for a cab, thinking of the number of times she had been molested by minicab drivers when she really hadn't been interested. Ordeals on wheels.

The driver who arrived wasn't repulsive and had probably been considered attractive some years earlier by undemanding women. Now he was married with kids, so he had no need to beat back his gut, and he wore a terrible sweater that he wouldn't let his wife throw out because it represented his independence, his character, his territory, his very hisness. A steeple of hair leaned out of his left ear. Miranda wondered whether she could go through with this; but then sometimes pleasant surprises came in poor packaging. The sweater, though, was like a sworn statement that the bearer had no taste, no education, no aspirations, and never would have. She didn't have much time for those who didn't look around. But of course myopia had advantages. Why did the magazines say you had to admit you had a problem before you could do anything about it? Say you had a desire to be the Olympic hundred-meter champion, that this was the only thing you wanted to do in life; but you had a problem. You had all the qualities that guaranteed ineligibility. You had the wrong build, you never exercised, you were remarkably slow even for someone who never exercised, you smoked sixty cigarettes a day, you refused to take advice from anyone who knew anything about running, and you were so disorganized that even if you could run you wouldn't be capable of joining an athletics club or turning up at a meeting, and you had never run a race. Wouldn't it be better to believe the world had it in for you and that your talent had been obscured by jealousy and misfortune?

She handed over a fiver and asked: "You're looking a bit tired; why don't you come in and have a break for a while?"

"You must have a lot of diseases," he commented as he drove off.

Inside, the receptionist was still there. Miranda noticed a rickety camp bed in the room behind reception.

"Room nineteen, please. Do you stay up all night?"

"I try to put my head down for a few hours," she replied with a long-suffering smile.

"Look, I'm not making a sexual advance, but why don't you come up to my room for a bit?" The receptionist stared at her blankly. "Or if you prefer, I can make a sexual advance." Miranda couldn't face the night alone.

"Who do you think you are, talking like that to me?"

"I just want—"

"Unless you apologize, I'm not giving you your key."

Miranda considered spending the night in reception. It was lit, and someone else was there.

"I'm a comedienne. I find it hard to stop. I apologize unreservedly." Miranda then took the key and made grotesque lapping motions with her tongue. She really did find it hard to stop.

She went to her room, hoping all the roaming would have introduced some weariness into her veins. She sat in the armchair and waited to see what was going on inside her. Slowly she became aware of an awful happening in her chest; some atrocity was swelling up. She went back downstairs.

The receptionist waved a letter opener and hissed, "I bite."

Miranda managed to assure her she just wanted an all-night shop where she could buy some snacks. She was directed to a garage a stroll away. On entering, she found panacea in pants. On duty was a cheery boy in a jumpsuit who didn't pretend he wasn't staring at her breasts. He had dark curly hair, something that she rated highly. She purchased a packet of cigarettes and a bar of chocolate.

"So what time do you get off?"

He was surprised, but not that surprised. "Not till eight in the morning."

"Business is slow, isn't it? I don't usually do this sort of thing . . . oh hell, why don't you come back to my place? I'm just around the corner."

"First thing at eight."

"I need some company now."

"You can join me in the executive suite round back."

"Why don't you come back to my hotel?"

"You're gorgeous and I'd love to, but if I leave now I'll get fired."

This wasn't good enough for Miranda; recognition had to be given that she was more important than this McJob. He could tell.

"What's your name?"

"Miranda."

"Miranda—Declan. Miranda, I know this is a shit job. Believe me, I know that better than anyone, but I need it for a while."

Declan was saving up for a holiday in Bali. He had been on duty for nearly two days; the wages were risible, but he made some extra money selling cans of beer on the side to favored customers. He could disable the security camera, but his boss had a habit of turning up in the early hours unannounced. He reminded her of Owen, and she found herself liking him. One part of her thought about offering him the thirty pounds she had, to see if that would sway him, another part thought about sitting there for a few hours eating peanuts, but the stronger part said go. It was because she was desperate that she couldn't behave in such a desperate way. She bid Declan good night, thinking if she started walking to the station, by the time she got there a train would be running to London. Passing by the hotel she went in and set off the fire alarm, hoping that would flush out some good company. The results were disappointing: pensioners, a boy scout troop, and one chunky American who didn't understand he was being propositioned.

There was no escaping the walk to the station. Dread didn't work so well when you walked. She would stay in the wall of fire from now on.

Σ

"Would you mind not enjoying your food so much?"

"What?"

"You're enjoying your food too much."

Tony put down his cutlery. "This is outrageous."

"No. It's not. It's unfair that you're enjoying your food so much."

"And if I weren't enjoying what you cooked, then that would be the problem, wouldn't it?"

Miranda took a sip of water. "I'm not complaining about you enjoying your food. Don't you listen? I only asked you— nicely—not to enjoy it so much."

"What difference does it make to you?"

"Watching you chomping away so happily gives me a bigger appetite, and I don't want to eat too much."

"Miranda, I don't want to have to kill you . . ." Tony's breathing became frantic. Miranda wasn't afraid; Tony's fits rather bored her. He scurried around the room as if seeking a much-needed lavatory, changing direction every second step. Then he reached into the goldfish bowl, scooped out the goldfish, and threw it into the air. As it came down, he volleyed it with his right foot into the wall. The goldfish was Tony's. It hung on the wall momentarily before descending to the carpet. Tony slumped down next to the goldfish.

Nelson's Column had to be reevaluted. Despite all her efforts to prevent self-interest from infecting her action, she could now see the whole enterprise had only been sparked off by Tony's jibes. It hadn't come from inside her. It didn't count. Casting around her memory, she could detect only one act of pure generosity and selflessness—the beanpole passing her a chair months ago. The only noble moment in human history: a chair being passed a short distance across a comedy club.

"Don't you care how I look?" she asked.

Tony's only communication was a slight shaking.

"I only want to look good for you." She cut herself another mouthful of turkey breast. "What's the one thing you can't do in a dream?"

Tony was watching something in the air she couldn't see.

"You can do almost anything in a dream. Command an army. Run a bath. Fly by flapping your hands. Play poker with the dead. But there's one thing I think you can't do. Do you know what that is? Tony, I'm talking to you."

She took another mouthful.

"I'm surprised at you, Tony. You're always going on about the importance of communication."

Tony didn't take his eyes off his goldfish.

"The only thing you can't do in a dream is dream. If you're dreaming you're a faith healer, you can't have forty winks in your sleep and dream you're a world authority on humming birds. You can dream you're a faith healer and then become a humming birdist, but you can't dream you're a faith healer who dreams he's a humming birdist. That tells us something. And it's a good way of testing whether you're awake or not; if you can't dream, it's a dream."

"You need help, Miranda."

"Am I the one who goes round kicking goldfish? Your food's getting cold."

"Getting the enjoyment right would be too tough."

"Thinking about it, I'm wrong; there is something else you can't do in dreams."

"Yes?"

"You can't die."

The phone rang. Unanswered, the machine went into action. Viv started to leave a message.

"Aren't you going to pick it up?" asked Tony.

"No," said Miranda. "Do you realize that love is only saved-up pain?"

Σ

As she walked down to the tube, she heard shouts of "armed police," bangs, and then from around the corner a black man spilled onto the pavement in front of her, clutching the back of his right thigh with mild annoyance, as if he had cramp.

She stepped over him without thinking, as three policemen sprinted up to form a human cage around him, and carried on to the tube. Afterward it occurred to her it might have been dangerous, but she didn't care. Her thoughts had been elsewhere, and in Brixton you just have to step over whatever the High Street presents you with. You got into the Brixton shuffle. Shove, step, fuck off. Shove, step, fuck off, until you were clear.

She didn't know what it was about Brixton; it was over some fault and allowed a strange brew, a ghost beer, to snake out from the earth's entrails: screaming-food for screamers, more madness for the mad, more wildness for the wild, more murderousness for the murderers. Exotica from the most distant lands made a beeline for the High Street, the one place where no one could be out of place.

The television producer had been the first to disappear, then his French receptionist, now finally the office was gone.

Miranda looked into the empty office, nothing left but half a desk, a dented wastepaper bin, two phone books in a corner, and a few envelopes shoved under the door. The TO LET sign put paid to any misinterpretation. Now, she resolved she could give up the pursuit.

She heard someone coming up the steps and couldn't have been more surprised or disappointed to discover it was Ned, who gave her a nod of greeting, peered into the office, tried the door, and then let himself in and sat down on the phone books.

Miranda was astonished he didn't try a "quisquilious deblaterations" because the circumstances justified one, but then Ned probably sensed she wasn't a fan.

"Doesn't look like they're coming back, Ned."

Ned shrugged. "An old boat called Alf."

"You're not going to try out a new routine on me, are you, Ned?"

"Our old boats make life difficult."

"Old boats?"

"Yes. I don't want to make the mistake of using a word like *wish* or *want* or *desire*. The trouble with words like those is that they've been crushed by usage and contaminated heavily over the millennia, so that they're both meaningless and too meaning. In every era wishes, desires, ambitions, dreams are the qualities that have been seen as the centers of individuals; we all stand back in respect or awe at ambition or success, or even if you take the opposite view and reject worldly ambitions, then they still remain the targets of your attention. Whether you seek flesh or shun it, you think of it. By using those words you're enlisting in the age-old struggle, whereas *old boat* does a better job of conveying the truth. So what you would call a *desire* to get on television or a *hope* to be married with two children, a picket fence, and a dog, I call *old boats.*"

"Why *old boats*?" Miranda asked. She didn't have anything else to do.

"*Boat* conveys the transitory and fickle nature of our wishes, tossed about this way then that on the seas of contingency. It's also absurd."

"Yeah, you've got to get the absurdity in."

"And *old* emphasizes how our desiderata are creaky and worthless."

"And where does Alf come in?"

"Alf is the one commonly referred to as fame. I sometimes christen the old boats to make them even more ridiculous."

"And does the day pass better with Alf and the other old boats?"

"It's hard to tell."

"You staying?"

"I haven't got anything else to do."

Having had a stab at a career, Miranda left Ned and went to shop in the food section of Marks and Spencer's. She never bothered queue-guessing since she always ended up in the worst queue; the one with the dimwit assistant who got stuck on a particular item or the customer who paid in pennies sloth-fully withdrawn from several pockets. Admittedly, everyone believed they always got into the wrong queue, which couldn't be right. What was the explanation for that? That some people weren't very observant? That the people in the fast-moving queues weren't citizens but aliens from some other galaxy and were steadily getting the edge on humanity by spending less time queuing in supermarkets? Or that some shoppers lied about being in the wrong queue, in the way that billionaires fussed about the cost of living so that they might be mistaken for ordinary workers.

An Old Comptonite (number-one cut, midlength leather jacket) in front of her was revealed as the surprise enragement of her queue. Miranda watched him quizzically and sluggishly sift through the compartments and contents of his shoulder bag; this was maddening because as he was doing this he wasn't emptying his basket onto the belt. His delving was only going to add forty seconds or at most a minute to the proceedings, and Miranda acknowledged as she stared at the ingredients of bonbons that she was in no rush and that a minute extra wasn't going to adjust the quality of her life, but it rankled. She sought sanctuary in the ingredients. Pineapple comminute. Comminute?

He was a reporter; he had to report to a specific place at a specific time and do a specific job. His earring and tattoo were forty years too late to trumpet him as a mutineer, an outpost of self-government (after all, whose tax inspector didn't have pierced nipples?). His office probably pretended it wasn't an office; he'd work for a design company, a record company, or worst of all a public relations firm. But the money would come every week, and the voices that told him what to do came from outside his head.

While his items progressed past the cashier, the Old Comptonite stood by inactively. He made no effort to bag them and only began fumbling for his credit card once the total had been announced. What was exasperating was precisely that he wasn't being inconsiderate. He thought he was being considerate. He obviously worried about the government not doing more for poorer countries. He worried a lot about poverty across the nation. He certainly worried about animals and their treatment. And despite the packet of obscure cigarettes peeking out of his bag, he probably worried about the air and the polluting villainies practiced by multinationals. What he didn't worry about was the customers behind him.

This was the engine of the exasperation: that he didn't regard himself as uncaring. According to himself, he was a friend to the universe, compassion on tap twenty-four hours a day. If he had been trying to be annoying, it wouldn't have been; she could have had revenge by not getting hot under the collar. It was vexing because he was permanently stranded in a scenario of concern.

Miranda had some choice expletives ready; but it would only have bolstered his picture of himself as a besieged right-fighter, harried by hysterical selfishoids. Just as light could be both wave and a particle, so a person could be both right and wrong; a train and a kangaroo in one.

Why was there this aspiration to flee the ordinary so much? She had always had contempt for the reporters, but that was more because of their timidity, their lack of peril, rather than scorn for the dullness of their work. The Old Comptonite didn't want to be confused with a salaryman. He wanted to be stamped as one of tohu-bohu's representatives. An imaginator, maching around on the power of ideas, not someone who answered the phone. A flunky for the Great Monkey, one of those uncontrollable imaginators playing with colors, words, or beats, and not a fish gutter, sitting in a uniform, next to innumerable fish gutters, doing stinky drudgery that could never become interesting. Working for the Monkey might be lively, but it didn't make you any better. The Old Comptonite thought he could splash on art like an aftershave. Old boat. Old boat.

Her pursuit of fame was nevertheless the same thing from another angle. Why did she seek it? Surely an old boat if there ever was one? Was it that she really perceived something waiting for her after the finishing line? Did it really matter if the public noticed her or not? Was large applause going to make her life larger? And bearing in mind the undeniable bad taste of the public, was their applause worth it?

"So fame: good thing or bad?" she asked the man behind her.

"I'd say good . . . because it's pretty difficult to be famous without getting any money."

Worthy reply. Miranda started packing her purchases. The Old Comptonite was still there at the end of the counter taking up space, patting down his shoulder bag. He had put on a pair of death squad sunglasses, presumably to look hard. Even with the sunglasses, he exuded as much menace as a wet paper bag. Arguably, if you needed an accessory to get hard, then you weren't making it; the requirement was to be unflinching without the sunglasses. Or perhaps because everyone thought it was hard, it had reached the stage where hard nuts couldn't leave home without them because it was expected.

She couldn't remember whether Lee had ever worn sunglasses. Then, of course, Lee hadn't been hard. Small, prematurely balding, already in his early twenties into spare-tiring and well in contention for being the most boring man she had ever known, yes, but he had been the only hit man she had worked with.

She had met him when she had been waitressing at a bistro and Lee had been the sous-chef, which translated into him doing all the chips. While not being in the same league as the grunter of Oxford Street, Lee's repartee revolved around the word *yeah*, into which he could get three intonations: surprise, agreement, and aggression. Reading the newspaper once on a break, Miranda had become aware of Lee standing closer to her than was necessary for opening a packet of crinkle-cut. It was the sort of posture men adopted while getting ready to ask you out. But he limited himself to gazing wistfully at the uncooked chips. It had passed.

Months later, Miranda had been incredulous to discover that Lee had been arrested for the murder of two archery instructors gunned down having a cup of tea in a café in Ipswich. Going to court to verify that it was really that Lee, Miranda had watched

Lee yawningly receive two life sentences for killing two people he had never met before, two people who had never done him any harm or insulted him in any way, two people, to boot, who hadn't been the two people he had been paid to kill. Aside from wholesale incompetence, Lee had been stitched up by his employer phoning the police five minutes before Lee had rocked into action, to confess to hiring Lee to remove two of his neighbors with whom he was having a dispute over hedges, because he had changed his mind. Unsolicited confirmation of Ned's old boats.

The four thousand pounds Lee had been paid had been found unspent in his room.

Miranda had tried to get something comic out of this but had failed. Nor had she been able to work out exactly why.

Thirsty, she went into a pub on Brewer Street and ordered a lager. She never understood why people talked about drowning their sorrows. It must be a clever myth created by the booze industry because she didn't see how having several drinks could make her feel better about not having a crack at television or anything else. She didn't want drinks; she wanted a television slot. It was like wanting new shoes and someone saying to you have a baked hedgehog instead. She couldn't think of anyone who had been mended or even relieved by a drink. Drinkers like Phrank just kept on doing it because it was a commonly held belief that it made things better, just as a few thousand years ago people thought that drilling a hole in your head was the best thing or that strangling someone would be the best way to ensure a bumper harvest. Should she get a routine out of this, or just contact the Vintners' Association and threaten to blow the whistle on the whole con if they didn't cough up?

Across the pub, she saw a shriveled, elderly, blind woman white-sticking her way to the door. She considered getting up to help her, but there were plenty of people closer than her, and if they couldn't be bothered, who was she to save civilization? If she became blind, Miranda recognized she would never leave home, let alone attempt to navigate any part of central London.

The blind woman had just reached the door, when an enormous black guy strode in talking animatedly to two companions. He slammed straight into the woman. Physics seemed to be having a lunch break, because he ended up on the floor, while, unbelievably, the woman steadied herself, remained upright, and carried on out of the door as if she hadn't noticed a twenty-stone Colossus trampling her.

"You should watch where you're going," the Colossus snarled. No one said anything, not only because they were afraid of catching some of the Colossus's rage but because they were ashamed and sorry for him. It was beyond lack of manners, stupidity, callousness, or even aggression. It spoke of a far worse affliction than blindness. Miranda noted that the woman hadn't expected any explanation or apology for the collision.

This was what was so awful; not that every day was tough, coarse, unbetterable. If it were like that, there would be few problems. The terrible thing was it could so easily be easy, but it wasn't. Miranda could have come from a contract-waving producer, done her shopping in a trice, and had a drink that tasted of something while a smiling Colossus ushered the blind woman out to the street. But she hadn't.

There could be pats on the head and cake for everyone. A glut of pleases and thank-yous. A slovenly pupil, life getting a "could do better" on its report.

"I can't wait for the twenty-first century," she remarked to a neighboring drinker.

The Colossus was unaware of the awkwardness he had placed in everybody. He lived in a universe where he did everything brilliantly and was admired for it. He progressed to the bar with his support act, two brickwalls in clothes, but smaller than him. Dark, Turkish-looking, the support act probably had to go around together because one knew the way to the pub and the other knew the way back. Iron pumpers out for a pint.

Miranda knew from experience that they must have screaming insecurities and stringy penises (and if you had a pipette-dick, ironically the worst thing you could do was to make the rest of your body bigger). You didn't spend years of your life lifting bits of metal and then putting them down in the same spot unless something was profoundly wrong.

She went to the ladies' room with some bottles she picked up, and had to smash three on the basin before she was satisfied. She went to a phone and called for an ambulance. Then she counted off four minutes on her watch; the traffic in central London was . . . well, not really traffic. She thought of her routine on the greening of London. All motorists would be required to have a flower bed or a minilawn on the roofs of their cars, so there would be more oxygen in the city and petals and grass everywhere. Ergo, the traffic jams would look like meadows. The double-decker buses would look most splendid of all, draped with bougainvillea.

She went over femalely to the clump of muscles.

"You have big muscles," she said, stroking a bicep. "Hard."

"All the better to love you with, darling," chuckled the Colossus.

"You feel safe, don't you?"

"Safe as houses."

"I'm going to tell you two things you're never going to forget as long as you live. First, you're not safe." The glee in his eyes wavered, fearing that she might be some evangelist rather than a slapper who was going to suck him dry. "And there seems to be one part of you that . . . could be a little . . . harder."

"Where's that, darling?" The glee was out again.

"Here," Miranda said, beveling the broken bottle into his neck. Despite acting fierce, the Turks didn't handle the blood well. Miranda was glad she was wearing black.

As she walked out, the ambulance crew was dismounting. "Some bloke in there injured, love?" Miranda nodded. "We'd have been here sooner, but some clown on the Charing Cross Road called us because he needed some aspirin."

Σ

She packed the last two boxes simply by throwing in anything that was left: hairpins, spaghetti tongs, coasters, a flashlight with no batteries, some plugs, a canteen, one boxing glove, a pan and a brush that she realized were probably her oldest possessions (twelve years), a pouch full of lipsticks she was never going to use, two pitons, some soaps Tony had brought back for her from hotels he had stayed in that she had never used and probably never would, magazines, and a champagne glass she had stolen (it wasn't in her book) because it had a design of pi on it.

It was sobering to see her life boxed up. Five small boxes, two big boxes, two suitcases, two handbags. The sum of her twenty-seven years.

Her doing all the packing had surprised Tony. But he had gone along with it; he wasn't averse to a bit of laziness, and he had been busy at work. He had also started making ridiculous circular motions during intercourse, which he probably saw as the cause of her uncustomary compliance.

Nothing else had gone missing, apart from the tweezers. Eight or nine pairs, she hadn't been counting. To the current pair she had tied a big green card, which had so far prevented disappearance.

The flat was bare. She had shaken every book, every item of clothing, every shoe, every object. Now vast and stark, the flat had nowhere for the tweezers to hide. Under the furniture, inside the chairs, under the bed, inside the fins of the radiators, she had tried them all. She had peeled up the carpet, checked behind the fridge.

Tony's stuff was in a separate mound of boxes. She had diligently worked through his pockets, his golf clubs, everything.

She gave the flat a final inspection. It was time to give up. She had lost this one.

Tony had been told she had wanted to move because she had had her bag snatched and she was sick of the area. That was untrue. Their landlord had indicated to Miranda that he would pay them three thousand pounds if they moved out before the lease was up, because he wanted to sell off the building.

This was the best way to say good-bye. The word *good-bye* had always seemed adequate to her. It did the job. And it could carry stacks of regret if you wanted. But most people liked ritual. Simply bolting had been a course of action she had pondered, but that would have been too much mystery for Tony. He might have imagined her murdered. He would certainly have made efforts to track her down. Doing a runner would have left a need for elucidation.

The minicab drew up. "I'll put my stuff in this one," she said. She turned and shook Tony's hand. "I didn't tell you, the place I've sorted out isn't for us, it's only for me. You're better off without me for all sorts of reasons. This is good-bye. Not see you."

Tony stood there as if struggling with a complicated railway timetable.

"I know I'm a comedienne, but when I put my finger in my ear, I'm not joking."

She put her finger in her ear.

By the time the minicab turned the corner, Tony was a thousand miles and ten years away. He had been wounded. But it had been pride, distress at loss of thrusting rights, and heart in that order.

Was there any good in the world? Miranda speculated. Evil there was aplenty, but it was always assumed its foil—however sickly, however ineffective, however disorientated, however mislaid its diary—good, was out there.

The enemy was approaching; that was fine by her.